# DON'T
# LOOK BACK

*Also by S.B. Hayes*

POISON HEART

# DON'T LOOK BACK

## S.B. HAYES

Quercus

First published in Great Britain in 2013 by Quercus

55 Baker Street
7th Floor, South Block
London W1U 8EW

A CIP catalogue reference for this book is available
from the British Library

ISBN 978 0 85738 681 6

1 3 5 7 9 10 8 6 4 2

Printed and bound in Great Britain by Clays Ltd, St Ives plc.

*For Karen Bond –*

*there could never have been enough time with you*

# Prologue

'One, two, three, four . . . come on, Sinead, I'm not far away.'

'But I can't see you, Patrick.'

'Five, six, seven, eight . . . follow my footsteps, it isn't difficult.'

The wind is whispering through the treetops like hundreds of voices telling me their secrets. I arch my neck and see night clouds creeping in. The trees are tall and tightly spaced, which makes me confused and dizzy. 'Patrick, it's getting dark and I'm frightened. I don't want to play this game any more –'

'Don't be a scaredy-cat. You're almost there . . . Just a few more steps.'

The wind whips my hair into my eyes and blinds me. Clumsily I shuffle forward, trying to follow his voice, but it's eaten up by the roar of panic in my ears. The ground is soft and muddy. It imprisons my foot and sends me tumbling into the undergrowth. Solid ground ends and I'm sliding down a sheer bank of wild grass, shrubs and stones. Somehow I manage to dig in my heels and slow my descent. I grasp a tree growing at an angle to the steep verge. It shakes and dips, its branches vibrating with the weight of my terror. My heart beats so loudly and so fast that I can't catch my breath. I look down and see absolutely nothing; the blackness is densely terrifying. I want to reach out and tear at its fabric to find a crack of light. My foot slips and the slender tree bends even more. I hear a snapping sound and I scream for my brother to help. He's taller and stronger than me, as sure-footed as a mountain goat. And he's so brave, completely without fear. He reaches me in seconds. I clasp my arms around his neck and he drags me back to safety. Blood is trickling from my head, and my arms and legs are covered in scratches, but I barely notice.

'Your stupid clues, Patrick,' I scold. 'I almost fell to the bottom, and I can't see how deep it is.'

'It's fathomless,' he tells me.

'What does that mean?'

'It means it doesn't end and you'd keep falling forever.'

I want to peer over the edge again but I can't in case the blackness swallows me up. 'What's down there?'

'Can't you guess?'

I shake my head.

His lips curve at the corners. 'Remember the story Mum told us about the pit? It's where you go when your soul is black and you never, ever get to come out.'

I can feel butterflies everywhere, even in my throat. 'Thank you for saving me,' I choke out.

Patrick bends down to kiss away my tears and his voice is full of a strange joy that I've never heard before. 'I'll always be here for you, Sinead, you know that, but you must never stop trying to find me.'

'Why? Where are you going?'

Patrick grasps my hand in his. 'When we play our game together, silly. You'll always follow my footsteps, won't you?'

'Suppose.'

His grip on me tightens and his nails dig into my cut palm, which makes my eyes water. 'This is important, Sinead. You have to promise.'

I nod gravely. 'I promise, Patrick.'

He takes hold of one of my fingers and draws two lines across my chest. His eyes are vibrantly blue, just like the sky before it thunders. When I look into them they make me feel as if I'm falling all over again.

'Now swear, Sinead, swear a solemn oath.'

'I won't go back on my promise, Patrick,' I answer obediently. 'Cross my heart and hope to die.'

# One

We were in the middle of a July heatwave, the atmosphere fizzing and crackling, charged like it is before a storm. I could tell something was wrong as soon as I stepped through my front door. My mother's eyes were red-rimmed, the whites webbed with tiny red capillaries. It looked as if she'd been crying all day.

'Patrick still hasn't been in touch. It's over two weeks.'

My bag thudded on to the wooden floor. 'He's done this before,' I pointed out. 'Why are you so worried this time?'

She clamped one hand across her heart. 'Something's wrong, Sinead. I feel it here.'

'I'm sure he'll be OK, Mum.'

My complacency seemed to infuriate her. 'You of all people understand his . . . *condition*, how vulnerable he is.'

I chewed my lip in frustration. I'd been expected to look after Patrick since I could walk, even though he was three years older than me. It had always been this way. Patrick's problems were my problems. And the 'condition' my mother coyly referred to was a toxic mix of addiction, depression and frequent threats to self-harm. I was used to picking up the pieces of his shattered life.

My mother squeezed out more tears, her hands fluttering around her throat like a dazed bird. 'I really think you should go to his flat.'

There was no point suggesting she should go herself. As usual it was down to me. Resentfully I looked at my watch. 'But I don't have time now. I've arranged to meet Harry.'

'Don't have time, Sinead? How often have I heard that excuse from you? You need to get a grip on your irrational *obsession* and think about your brother's welfare.'

*It isn't irrational. Time is so precious. Am I the only one who can feel it slipping away from me? Every heartbeat is another second passing, and it's like a drum beating, recording every moment in your life . . . especially the wasted ones.*

I faced her squarely. 'You know why I'm like this. It's not something I can help.'

She cut the air with one hand, her voice mockingly sing-song. 'You had an asthma attack when you were a child and thought you were dying.' She shook her head at me. 'Must you bring everything back to yourself? Patrick is my main concern. Now, will you go to his flat?'

My mother seemed to bring out the worst in me and

sometimes I took a perverse pleasure in frustrating her. 'I'll go tomorrow.'

She paused and tried another tactic, her tone now softly wheedling. 'You're so strong, Sinead. Patrick isn't like you. He needs me so much more, and I must do everything I can to protect him. The bond between a mother and a child is sacred.'

*What about our bond? And you've never given me the chance to need you. Patrick has always consumed all your love and attention. Since Dad left, I'm invisible.*

To escape the intensity of my mother's gaze my eyes took in the new decor. The room had recently been repainted, a subtle shade of primrose, and a new beige carpet fitted, but it still felt cold and unlived-in.

'Patrick is highly sensitive and intelligent,' my mother went on. 'He lives on a knife edge.' I still didn't reply and she played her winning card. 'You promised to always look out for him, Sinead.'

I nodded reluctantly in agreement. My mother knew how to make me feel guilty, and deep down I *was* worried about Patrick. I quickly changed into sweats and grabbed my bike, taking the quickest route, which was through the town, trying to avoid buses belching black smoke, the outsize wing mirrors of white vans and drivers in high-performance cars who thought they owned the road. It was late afternoon, the humidity still increasing, and the city felt ready to erupt. Soon I was short of breath and my chest felt tight, a leftover from my childhood asthma. It always got worse around Patrick, as if his very presence suffocated me. By the time I reached his flat, my clothes and hair were wet and stuck to my skin, rank with the smell of traffic fumes.

Patrick didn't buzz me in when I repeatedly rang his bell, although someone had noticed I was here because a pair of green striped curtains in a ground-floor window twitched. There was a single entry code for all the occupants, which wasn't exactly the greatest security device, but at least it deterred people from walking in off the street. I punched it in and rested my bike against the half-panelled wall in the hallway before walking up a winding flight of wooden stairs. The building used to be some sort of chapel, and it still had one of the tallest spires around and a musty smell of yellowing prayer books, polished floors and candle wax.

Patrick's flat was at the top of the building and included the bell and clock tower, but the landlord was insistent that they were both off limits. When I reached the top stair I remembered our last conversation. Patrick had told me that the sound of ringing seemed to reverberate in his head, although the bells had been silent for years. He hadn't mentioned the clock, but I knew the hands had been stuck on six for ages. If I lived here I would have found a way to get it working again, glad to hear it chime every fifteen minutes to remind me how quickly time was passing.

I thumped on his door with both fists, painfully aware that I was thinking the worst. A feeling in my stomach told me that something was badly amiss and that this time Patrick might have carried out one of his dark promises.

*'You'll all be sorry one day. Sorry you didn't listen to me, that you didn't understand me or love me more . . . I won't be around much longer. That will teach everyone a lesson . . . especially you, Sinead.'*

The door was made of sturdy oak with a Gothic arch mellowed with age, the grain prominent in blackish whorls and knots. My ear rested against the warm wood for at least five minutes, trying to pluck up the courage to enter. I wasn't naive. My father was a doctor and had never protected me from the realities of his profession, which seemed like a curse just now. But there was no going back. With trembling hands I inserted the spare key into the lock. One small turn, a twist of the door handle and I hesitantly entered, clumsily moving forward, all my senses working overtime. There were no strange smells or unusual sounds; in fact the silence was eerie. I couldn't even hear any street noise floating upward. My eyes quickly scanned the living room as I moved into the bedroom, lifting the duvet with the toe of my trainer in case anything was lurking underneath.

No matter how hard I tried to block it out, my mind conjured up the horrors I was expecting to see – a red tinge stained my vision as if I'd recently peered at the sun. Terror, apprehension, guilt – whatever Patrick had done this time, some of the blame had to be mine. I'd heard my mother say so often that we'd failed him, all of us. I approached the bathroom; time stood still and my heart thumped like crazy. Inch by inch, I moved to look around the door as if limiting my vision would somehow shield me from whatever was there. But the reality was simply plain white tiles with an electric blue border. The shower cubicle was completely dry, not a droplet of condensation remaining, which told me it hadn't been used recently. The kitchen was the same except for one tantalizingly slow drip from the mixer tap.

With a huge sigh of relief I sat on the sofa and tried to swallow, my lips so dry that they stuck together. Now I could get angry.

*You are completely selfish, Patrick, without a thought for anyone but yourself. Everything revolves around you. I feel like your prisoner. You make me so furious I just want to explode.*

I took a moment to cool down and calm my pounding heart, unable to stop myself from reflecting how different things might have been without the spectre of Patrick hanging over us. My parents might still be together instead of torn apart by years of arguing over their wayward son's behaviour. I didn't blame Dad for leaving. Whenever he'd suggested getting tough with Patrick, Mum had stopped him. Patrick needed love, she would insist, nothing else. Four years ago, when I was twelve, Dad had accepted a medical posting overseas, working for an aid organization, and since then I didn't get to see him often. Patrick had robbed me of so much, but there was no use feeling sorry for myself. I'd always looked out for him, and as long as he needed me I couldn't abandon him.

I stood and rotated my neck, trying to release some of the tension. It was then I noticed what was weird about the room, so weird that I stood up and turned three hundred and sixty degrees to absorb every detail. It only took a minute for me to realize that I had to tell someone. Now.

# Two

'Slow down,' Harry said, 'take deep breaths and tell me what's happened.'

I blew out noisily, trying not to pant. 'Patrick hasn't been in contact for over two weeks. I went to his flat and found it's been totally cleaned. It's freakishly spotless.'

Harry shrugged. 'So he's turned over a new leaf and decided not to live like a slob any more.'

I shook my head doubtfully. 'You know Patrick – his space reflects his personality: chaotic and out of control. I think something's very wrong, and so does Mum.'

Harry pursed his lips. 'Why didn't your mum go herself? It wasn't fair to send you alone.'

My eyes widened. 'You don't understand, Harry. It's what I'm expected to do, what I need to do.'

I'd asked Harry to meet me at our local police station and he pulled me on to the wall outside. I looked affectionately at his shaggy hair, scruffy T-shirt and ripped jeans; Harry never gave his appearance a thought. He was

11

my best friend, but I'd always tried to spare him the mess that was Patrick's life. I smoothed the creases from my forehead with my fingers, my eyes squinting in the low sun.

'You've never really explained this thing between you two, Sinead. Why this huge sense of duty?'

'He's my brother, Harry . . . Isn't that enough?'

Harry's silence spoke volumes. He always knew when I was holding out on him. I stared into his soft blue eyes wondering why someone as easy-going and well adjusted as him would bother with someone like me. We were both science nuts, only one school year separating us, and he'd made it more than plain he would have liked me to be his girlfriend, but I didn't feel that way about him. I never seemed to have the time to think about relationships.

'OK, there is something else,' I said, sighing. 'Patrick used to play this game with me when we were younger; "Following Patrick's Footsteps", he called it. He made me promise that whenever he went, I'd always come looking for him.'

Harry looked grave. 'I worry about you, Sinead. You're so manic and . . . angry. Don't you ever feel it's time to let go of Patrick, and stop running from everyone?'

I ignored the last part. 'Of course I'd like to be free of Patrick . . . and not be so constantly wound up . . . but family stuff's complicated.'

'Help me to understand,' Harry urged.

I stared into the distance at a group of children having fun spraying each other with water and shrieking with laughter. 'The thing is . . . I feel responsible in a way. Everything changed when I was born. Patrick's jealousy got out of hand.'

'Sibling rivalry is . . . kind of normal.'

'Not like this,' I came back fiercely. 'Patrick was so jealous it wasn't safe to leave us alone together. Mum really feared for my safety until . . . she devised a way to pacify him.'

'What was it?'

I swallowed with difficulty because I'd never told this to anyone before, but I had a compulsion to finally make Harry understand what it had been like living with Patrick.

'I had to stay completely covered with a blanket. If no one saw me or paid me any attention, then he didn't mind. I'm not sure how long it went on for, but Mum told me when I was older as if it was funny or endearing.'

Harry grimaced. 'That's bizarre.'

I raked my fingers through my short hair. 'I don't know why Mum had another child – she's spent the last sixteen years trying to make up to Patrick for it.'

Harry put a hand over mine, his voice suddenly gentle. 'You should have told me more before. I knew things weren't good at home . . .' He trailed off and then kind of shook himself. 'I'll help you find Patrick. This could be his wake-up call . . . and a chance for you to escape and get your life back.'

*It's too late*, I wanted to say. *The damage was done a long time ago and I can't ever go back. I can't even remember my life before Patrick's problems consumed me.*

I stood, flexing my hands. Before we set foot in the police station Harry gave me his usual pep talk.

'Don't lose your temper, Sinead. It will only backfire.'

I smiled at him. He was always trying to keep me in check, although he wasn't often successful. The automatic doors opened and I went in first. The police officer behind the glass screen was obviously practised in intimidation. He listened to my story about Patrick with a dead-eye stare that was crushing and antagonistic at the same time.

'So, let me get this straight,' he said. 'You want to report your brother missing because his flat has been mysteriously tidied?'

'No, of course not,' I answered. 'That's just one of the strange things. It's the fact he's been missing for over two weeks that concerns me the most –'

'No beer cans or wine bottles around,' Harry interrupted. 'Now that's *really* weird.'

The police officer pulled a resigned heard-it-all-before face. I gave Harry a furious sideways glance. From when Patrick had first began to go off the rails I'd been schooled in covering up his drinking, and this was so ingrained that I grew hot at the nakedness of Harry's words. In an instant he had stripped away all the years of pretending and keeping up appearances. I coughed affectedly, but now it was in the open I felt I should elaborate.

'You don't understand. My brother has an . . . um . . . addiction problem and is quite . . . vulnerable.'

'Does he have a social worker?'

'No . . . he has a therapist . . . a private therapist.'

That didn't go down well. It smacked of elitism and snobbery. The police officer didn't reply but a deep V-shape appeared between his eyebrows. Something told me I was losing his interest.

'I really think you need to investigate,' I persisted. 'The entire flat isn't right. Someone's gone to a lot of trouble to erase . . . something.'

'Are his possessions still there?' the bored voice continued.

'Yes, his clothes are still in the wardrobe, but I couldn't find his wallet.'

'Are you eighteen?' the policeman demanded.

I shook my head.

'Your parents should have come themselves.'

I winced. 'They would, but my mother is really . . . distressed and my father is abroad, working for an overseas aid organization . . . he's a doctor.'

The police officer held one hand against the screen as a colleague appeared and they put their heads together, deep in conversation. This was obviously his you'll-have-to-wait-don't-bother-me-any-more gesture. Someone sighed very close behind me and the hairs on the back of my neck stood up in anger. I hated anyone invading my personal space, and this person was doing just that. Their arrogance made me instinctively assume that whoever it was was male, and I slowly turned my head, pleased to be right.

He was a few inches taller than me. His hair was sun-bleached and his skin tanned. The colour told me it wasn't from a couple of weeks frying on a package holiday. The white vest, denim cut-offs and sandals made him look like he'd just come from the beach. I could almost smell salt and sun cream. He was muscular, although not in a pumped-up way, and he flashed me a cocky smile. I disliked him intensely at first sight.

Unconsciously I threw back my shoulders and raised my head to look him in the eye. My stance was confrontational – arms folded, face set hard.

'Sorry? Can I help you?'

He took a step back. 'My phone's been stolen. I'm waiting to report it.'

He had an accent that sounded Australian. 'Your phone's been stolen,' I repeated with as much contempt as if he'd said that someone had pinched his lollipop. 'My *brother* is missing, and all you can do is breathe on me.'

'Sinead!' Harry said warningly.

I thrust out my chin but tried to simmer down. 'Any-way . . . a little space would be nice.'

The beach boy weighed up Harry, which took me by surprise. Harry used to be so geeky, but he'd undergone a transformation these past few months, shot up in height and got broader shoulders. Even his face had lost its roundness. It was my turn next. I could feel a pair of hazel eyes moving from the top of my black spiky hair, down to my nose stud and long legs. I was skinny and sometimes I'd been mistaken for a boy from behind. Harry's nickname for me was Big Bird. Only he could get away with that.

'You must be the rudest girl I've ever met.'

Despite Harry's disapproval I was glad to have needled the stranger. 'You obviously don't get out much,' I said, and indicated the benches running either side of the room. 'That's the waiting area.'

Something about this tickled him because he gave a cynical smirk. 'Life's just one big waiting room,' he drawled, and lazily flopped on to a bench, arms clasped behind his head and legs outstretched.

I was strangely incensed at his words. 'Thanks for the philosophy lesson,' I shouted across. 'But my time's precious.'

He leaned forward, his face serious, and ran one hand through his tousled hair. 'So is mine . . . it's always later than you think.'

# Three

'Uppity, arrogant, opinionated, macho . . .' My tirade ended only when I ran out of insults.

Harry shook his head at me in amazement. 'He's in a strange country, Sinead, he doesn't know the system and you bawl him out just for standing behind you.'

'He was too close for comfort and I didn't like his attitude.' Reluctantly I grinned, noticing Harry's stunned expression. I had a terrible attitude problem and I knew it. I swiped his arm with the tips of my fingers. 'He mentioned time. You know how much that gets to me.'

'I know,' Harry soothed. 'Your obsession it's a bit . . . unusual.'

'I almost died when I was little, remember? Maybe I'm still running from the grim reaper.'

'You're so completely weird,' Harry said. 'That's what I love about you.'

I looked away, uncomfortable. 'It's always later than you think,' I mocked, still livid at the stranger. 'As if I needed reminding. That guy was like a weird messenger of doom.'

Harry's eyebrows peaked. 'Most people don't constantly measure time as if it's their last day on earth.'

'Well, they should. We spent thirty-three minutes in that police station, in a pointless exercise in going nowhere.'

'You need a shrink, Sinead.'

I pulled a face. 'Patrick has the shrink . . . my mother didn't think I was important enough to get one.'

We reached Patrick's flat and I impatiently keyed in the entry code and ran up the stairs three at a time. I flung open the door and absorbed the whiteness of the walls and the pristine space, not a thing out of place.

'Look, Harry, I wasn't exaggerating. This could be a monk's cell, and the bed is made like in a hospital, so tightly tucked it's impossible to get into.'

'It *is* pretty dazzling,' he agreed.

'Isn't it?'

Harry twisted his curly hair absent-mindedly. 'I don't know what to suggest.'

'Something weird's happened here,' I insisted.

'What about Patrick's friends? We should ask them before we do anything else.'

I rolled my eyes. 'He doesn't really have any. He's so unpredictable . . . one minute the life and soul, the next aggressive and then morose and depressed. Not many people will put up with that.'

Harry reached to brush my fringe from my eyes and

I instinctively drew away. 'If the police aren't going to do anything, then . . . we should search the place and look for evidence.'

'They said we could file a missing persons report.'

'Yeah, yeah . . . I'll put it to Mum, but she won't be impressed. She'll expect the entire country to be on high alert and a giant manhunt underway . . . at the very least. Now come on and help.'

Harry set to work with all the enthusiasm of a deranged detective, opening drawers and cupboards and closing them again, his forehead creased with concentration. I decided he was just acting out what he thought he should do without really having a clue. There were a few letters on the mat and a bank statement that I tore open. Patrick got through roughly the same amount of cash each day, most of which he spent in the pub or off-licence, but the last transaction had been fifteen days ago. I knew before I opened the fridge that it would be empty. On the bedside table I recognized a children's Bible, bound in red leather. I used to have a matching one, but I didn't have a clue where mine had gone.

'Sinead!'

Harry's urgent tone made me look up quickly, banging my head on an overhanging cabinet. He was holding some sort of notebook in one hand. I went over and took it from him. There was a heavy iron key resting between the blank pages; it had a distinctive fleur-de-lis design. I weighed it with one hand, trying to imagine the sort of door that would need something so heavy and ornate. A quick glance around told me that none of the doors in the flat had a keyhole.

I scratched my head, a suspicion beginning to slowly filter through. All those years that Patrick had left me a trail to follow. Was he still playing our game? But surely we were too old now. Even so, the blank notebook was classic Patrick and I had an idea what to do. I picked it up, making sure to keep it open at the same page, and took it to the quatrefoil leaded window in full glare of the late afternoon sun. The pages began to scorch, revealing two words of spidery writing: *Tempus Fugit*.

'What the . . . ?' Harry looked at the sky in awe as if a thunderbolt had struck him.

I gave him a playful shove. 'You're a scientist, Harry! Lemon juice turns brown when heated.'

He cleared his throat. 'Sorry . . . I just wasn't expecting it. It's the building – all old and strangely . . . hallowed. It gives me the creeps.'

'It's just a building.'

'When we came in you lowered your voice,' Harry said. 'Didn't you notice?'

'You're right,' I said. 'It does have an atmosphere. Maybe . . . chapels have memories and all those years of praying and singing hymns have kind of seeped into the walls.'

'Suppose.'

A shaft of light burst through one of the panes and

illuminated a circle on the floor. I stared at the pattern of swirling dust motes. 'Mum thought it would protect Patrick. We looked at loads of places but she insisted on this one even though it was more expensive. She thought he might be saved – probably expected him to have an epiphany at the very least.'

Harry looked vacant. 'Epiphany is like a . . . revelation,' I said, 'a blinding flash of self-awareness.'

'Oh,' he said vaguely.

I sat down heavily on the smooth white bed sheet, studying the letters on the page, deep in thought. 'I think this is part of Patrick's game, leaving me clues to decipher to make me follow his trail. It's definitely his hand-writing.'

Harry peered over my shoulder. 'Latin?'

'Yeah,' I muttered. 'Patrick went to a posh school where they studied dead languages.'

Harry looked at me questioningly. 'Do you know what it means?'

'Time flies,' I answered, 'or time flees. It comes from a poem by Virgil.' I decided to enlighten him further whether he wanted me to or not. 'The saying is sometimes used on clocks and sundials. It was very popular with the Victorians because they liked to remind people how short life is and how you can never get back the time you've lost.'

'You didn't study Latin, Sinead.'

'No, but it's about *time*, Harry,' I said pointedly. 'I know the full quotation by heart.'

'What's the point of putting it there, except to wind you up?'

My stomach lurched and my hands flew to my face. I should have seen it immediately. The clue was so obvious; Patrick had to be directing me towards the clock tower. My frightened eyes were drawn to a tiny door tucked away in one corner of the flat. A bookcase had been butted against the jamb and almost concealed it. I stood up slowly, my heart thudding, and silently pointed to the door. Harry caught my drift and immediately jumped in front of me, offering to go first. I shook my head. Patrick was my brother and I couldn't run away from this.

The door was tight-fitting or had swelled with the heat and I had to yank it open with both hands. I could immediately smell fresh air and feel a slight breeze. There was a scratching noise that made me freeze, but a reassuring coo let me know it was only pigeons. Patrick had mentioned that they'd taken to nesting on the ledge outside the clock face. Anyone else would have complained, but he said he liked to listen to them because they sounded so content and free.

Harry was right behind me, his palm in the small of my back. I felt as if I was being taken to the gallows. I noticed that there were footprints in the dust on each stair tread: someone had been up here recently. The feeling of dread coiled deep inside me. At the top we found ourselves in a small round space, empty except for general dust and grit, a few feathers and bits of chipped wood from a broken stool. I was so relieved that my legs momentarily turned to jelly and I clutched the wall for support. There were openings in the bricks, little more than slits completely exposed to the elements, and some of the wooden floorboards looked blackened with age. Harry pointed upward to the set of even narrower steps leading to the belfry, but there was nowhere for anyone to hide; only the bells were up there, screened from view by a fretwork panel.

'Thank goodness the tower is empty,' I said, the gnawing pain in my stomach subsiding slightly.

Harry nodded in agreement.

'Why doesn't anyone try to fix the clock?' I said. 'The movement doesn't look very complicated. I don't know anything about clock workings, but it's not exactly Big Ben.'

Harry gazed out over the town with one hand above his eyes as if he was a tourist. 'It's a great view. Patrick's so lucky. But you said he didn't really want to leave home?'

'It was one of Dad's conditions. If he was going to continue to support Patrick financially then he had to stand on his own two feet in other ways.' Distractedly I wrote my name in the dust. 'Dad wanted to get him away from Mum. She loves him too much.'

Harry turned baleful eyes on me. 'I didn't think it was possible to love someone too much.'

I was annoyed with myself because I'd meant to say, 'She dotes on him too much,' but the truth had slipped out.

'Sometimes love isn't that healthy,' was the only explanation I could offer.

I felt an incredible wave of sadness remembering something Patrick had once told me: that he'd found a place to make the buzzing inside his head go away. I was certain he'd meant up here. It was easy to imagine him at night, watching the stars and pondering on all the things that got him down, which was just about everything. He must have felt like the loneliest person on earth.

Harry squeezed my shoulder. 'Come on, let's go. You can make me a coffee.'

I took one last lingering look at the inside of the redundant clock, wishing I could stop time as easily, when a flash of white caught my eye. I could already hear Harry's feet on the stairs and resisted the urge to call him back. The clock face was transparent and I was staring at a mirror image of the numbers, but there was a piece of paper attached to the axis between the hands. I had spotted it only because we'd startled the group of pigeons and the movement of their wings had caused the paper to flutter. But now that I'd seen it, it was impossible to ignore.

There was a gap of at least a metre between the wooden balustrade and the clock face. A platform must once have existed to allow access, but now there was a sheer drop. Peering down gave me instant vertigo. The paper wasn't faded and so had to have been put there recently – could it have been left by Patrick? I leaned across the gap, holding on to a hook in the wall for extra support. The wooden rail dug into my hip as I tested its strength. There was a slight creak, but I was strong and had finally found an advantage to having long arms. I was tantalizingly close; another couple of millimetres would do it. The wood creaked again, slightly more ominously, but it held under my weight and I grew more confident and made a lunge for the paper.

The floor dropped away beneath my feet as I overbalanced, my hands flailing in the air as I desperately sought to grip something solid. I dangled, clutching the lowest rung of the rail, my fingers numb and my arms torn from their sockets. Time slowed down. My mind detached itself and all kinds of unconnected things invaded my consciousness, circling in my head like planets in the solar system. Someone small and supple might have been able to swing their legs back up to the walkway, but I was too gangly to be good at gym. I couldn't scream because a strange paralysis had set in, and I knew the effort would sap what little strength I had left.

Who would miss me? I mean *really* miss me? Now that school had finished for the summer even my friend Sara had cooled off. I wasn't even sure why; after years of being close tension had recently grown between us that I didn't understand. It was such a shame that I didn't have any romantic feelings for Harry; I knew he should be with someone who liked him in the same way. My mother might finally realize that she had a daughter who needed her, but it would be too late. I'd never find out my exam results, fall in love, get a tattoo, climb to the top of the Empire

State Building, see the Great Wall of China. The beach boy from the police station flashed through my mind. Perhaps he had been a messenger warning me that this was *the* day, the day I'd been running from. I shouldn't have been so hard on him. A boy with sun-kissed hair and a handsome face had tried to warn me that I was about to die in a few hours' time, and I'd chewed him out. *It's always later than you think*.

There was a moment of intense clarity as I anticipated the drop and was able to predict my injuries – broken legs, shattered pelvis, internal injuries, skull fracture – my chances were negligible. My ears were suddenly ringing with the music of a thousand bells. I didn't even hear Harry until he was standing above me, his face weirdly contorted and his mouth opening and closing. It was like watching TV with the sound turned down and I almost laughed, but it was too painful.

Harry tried to clasp my wrists. For a moment his eyes locked with mine and I saw despair reflected in them. There was no way he could support my weight, and time was running out; my arms were so dead they had ceased to feel connected to the rest of me. He disappeared from my vision and my eyes closed as I floated out of my body. It would be over in seconds. Harry must have returned because there was a voice close by, but a strange feeling of inner calm washed over me. My fingers, blistered and split as the wood gnawed into them, loosened their hold and I slipped further.

Finally, with one last breath, I fell backwards into the vacuum, waiting for the falling sensation. But it never came. Instead I found myself moving upward, a pair of strong arms supporting my torso, almost crushing me, and there was a heartbeat as loud as my own pressed against my chest. It didn't seem possible, but I was dragged on to solid ground, a dead weight, incapable of doing anything to help. My body eventually lay curled in the foetal position, unable to move, my bloodied hands cupped to my face. Harry's laboured breathing was somewhere close by but I couldn't orientate myself and the world was still spinning. A haunting echo of the past resounded in my head: *I won't go back on my promise, Patrick. Cross my heart and hope to die.*

# Four

Harry tried to smile, but he looked badly shaken and the corners of his mouth could barely turn up. 'It's a good thing you're so skinny.'

I didn't reply, but I did reach out one hand for him to hold. My eyes gradually focused, astonished by what I was seeing. Harry had one end of a rope attached to his belt and the other end to the hook in the wall.

He tilted his head in the direction of the church bells. 'One of the ropes must have frayed. Talk about lucky.'

'You just saved my life,' I croaked.

'I know,' he said, 'but don't try to thank me.'

Harry was still able to joke, knowing I wasn't very good at being grateful. I concentrated on regulating my breathing, overwhelmed with the knowledge that I was still alive. After another few minutes he hoisted me to my feet and helped me down the stairs, stopping to pick up the folded piece of lined paper that I'd managed to dislodge and which had gracefully glided down to earth like a paper plane. My hands were trembling with shock and exertion. I washed them carefully under the tap in the kitchen sink, astonished that I still had the capacity to feel like a complete moron. Then I went to join Harry in the living room and sat cross-legged on Patrick's rug, picking splinters from my palms with a desperate need to concentrate on something.

'You need bandaging up,' Harry said with concern.

'It's OK, Harry.'

'It's not OK – your hands look sore, and you should drink sweet tea for shock.'

He was being so considerate, but I waved aside his concerns. There was only one thing on my mind. 'Can I see the note?'

Harry ruefully handed it over and with fumbling fingers I opened it. There were four lines of Latin text written in an elaborately curved hand.

'You risked your life for that?' he said incredulously, peering over my shoulder. 'More Latin!'

I nodded grimly. 'I'm sure it's Patrick leaving me another message, this time in his best handwriting.'

'Why go to all that trouble?'

I shrugged and jumped up, my ears still buzzing. It was probably the adrenalin rush of the shock of nearly dying, or just the blood pumping crazily round my body, but I felt totally wired. I roamed around the flat, my mind bursting. Patrick's disappearance, the sparkling flat, the secret writing in the notebook, the key, and now this piece of paper attached to the clock face . . .

'Patrick has a brilliant mind,' I said, more to myself than to Harry, 'despite his attempts to destroy his brain cells, and he always got a kick out of setting me puzzles, but he's never done anything as elaborate as this.'

'What do you think . . . *really*?' Harry asked.

'I think this is Patrick still playing his mind games, trying to get me to follow him, but . . . it feels like there's something more. I think he might really be in trouble.'

'What kind of trouble?'

I tried to swallow, recalling the details of Patrick's psychological reports that I'd heard my parents discussing over the years. They'd confirmed how messed-up he was. Harry watched me pacing backwards and forwards across the room.

'He might have had some kind of breakdown,' I said eventually.

'And the weird notes or clues are a kind of cry for help? For *you* to help, Sinead?'

'Maybe.'

I went into the kitchen to make us both a coffee. Harry followed me and tried to take over, but I needed to keep busy. In one of the cupboards was a tiny jar of own-brand coffee with just enough granules for two small cups. I switched on the kettle, scraped out the jar and filled two stained cups with boiling water. I was suddenly overcome with a sense of absolute conviction about what I needed to do.

My voice was resolute. 'I need to find Patrick, whatever it takes.'

Harry glared. 'Remember what I said, Sinead. You need to shake him off and think about yourself for once.'

'After I find Patrick, then I'll be able to move on.' I gave him a look. 'You said you'd help.'

Harry's expression was weary but resigned. 'So how do we start?'

'Solve his *clues* . . . wherever they lead me. They were meant for me.'

Harry placed one hand on his chest. 'You know you can rely on me, Sinead.'

He was always there for me, though I didn't treat him as well as he deserved. I hated myself for being this way. There was something warped inside me that made me lash out at the people who cared. But that was all going to change. I studied Harry now. He did himself no favours, with his bed-head hair and the air of someone who never looked in a mirror. He didn't stand out in a crowd, but once you knew him it was impossible not to like him. I smiled at him warmly and went back into the living room to study Patrick's message.

Harry joined me on the rug, eagerly expectant, his untamed curls framing his face. It was only when the temperature had reached the seventies that he'd finally taken off his woolly hat. My stomach gave a loud grumble.

'Hungry?' he asked.

I just murmured, my eyes still studying the paper. Two of the Latin words had caught my eye. Years of church attendance meant I was able to translate them: *domus dei* – house of God.

'I'll go and fetch you something to eat,' Harry insisted, jumping to attention and making for the door. 'Stay here and rest.'

I shook my head. 'I can't rest yet. There's somewhere I have to go.'

Saint Peter's church was less than five hundred metres from Patrick's flat and I made my way there, dodging the after-work revellers lining the pavements. I wrinkled my nose. Simmering concrete gave off an ugly smell and the drains weren't that fragrant either. We were so starved of sun for most of the year that the first glimmer made everyone think they were abroad. The outside areas of the pubs and restaurants were littered with tables and chairs occupied by people eating, drinking and languidly smoking under huge umbrellas. The temperature had risen even higher in the last hour, but there were grey clouds moving in and the first stirrings of a breeze. Some plastic glasses moved ominously and I gazed up at the sky, certain there was a storm brewing.

There was a short cut through the nearby park but my path was littered with sunbathers, picnickers and entwined couples gazing adoringly into each other's eyes. The air was filled with the heavy scent of wild flowers and newly mown grass. A girl lying on her back adjusted her sunglasses and squinted at me. Her brief scornful glance reminded me why I had more guys as friends than girls. I was compelled to look again and found myself almost blinded by her glow. Her skin was the colour of dripping honeycomb and she was so petite in her micro sundress and strappy sandals. I saw myself through her eyes in my sweats and shapeless T-shirt. I couldn't even carry off the sporty look that was everywhere, all toned and perspiring with a bottle of spring water glued to my lips.

I limped on, my body still curiously weightless, certain that when tomorrow came I wouldn't be able to lift my arms. As I turned the corner into the square the sound of singing reached me and I slowed my pace and hovered outside the church. I was surprised to hear a service going on at this time of night until a notice advertising evensong made sense of it. There was something about church choirs that made my spine tingle, a reaction to the pure voices soaring into the vaulted ceiling like beautiful songbirds nesting in the topmost branches. Tonight they seemed doubly poignant.

People began to file out, and I waited impatiently until I thought that everyone had left. With a deep breath, and for no obvious reason given that the doorway was over two metres high, I ducked to enter. There was only one solitary figure left in the church, wearing a black cassock buttoned all the way from the neck to the floor. He looked like he was in his early fifties, slightly plump with thick greying hair and a ruddy complexion. It wasn't hard to work out who he was.

I said the first thing that came into my head. 'Sorry, you're trying to close.'

He digested this for a moment with a wry smile. 'It's a church. The opening hours are flexible. Would you like a moment to yourself?'

This was embarrassing; the priest thought I was in need of spiritual solace when all I wanted was to pick his brains. 'Erm, no, not really. Thing is . . . I need help translating something. It's in Latin and . . . this was the only place I could think of to come.'

His eyes definitely twinkled. 'Well, you might be fortunate. I did study Latin. Hopefully I might be qualified for the task.'

'More than qualified,' I responded, feeling a certain triumph. Patrick had meant for me to come here. I was definitely in the right place.

The priest took a pair of reading glasses from his pocket and propped them on the bridge of his nose. 'May I ask what this relates to?'

I shifted awkwardly from one foot to the other and caught a glimpse of my T-shirt; it was filthy and bloody. I couldn't imagine how I must look.

'Sorry . . . Father . . . I've been cleaning my brother's flat and . . . had a slight accident. There wasn't time to change.'

'Does this belong to him?'

'Kind of . . .'

The priest took the note from me and sat down in one of the pews. It seemed impolite not to join him and I walked down the centre aisle, instinctively dropping one knee in front of the altar. Feeling distinctly uncomfortable I slid into the wooden bench beside him. I glanced around. The church was a riot of shimmering gilt-edged mosaics and different-coloured marble and coloured friezes. The onion dome with suspended lantern hinted at some kind of eastern influence. I had a sudden memory of long, boring Masses every Sunday, when Patrick would pinch me and make me cry. My mother would throw me desperate looks, wanting everyone to think we were the perfect family. I felt empty inside.

The priest took off his glasses and stared at me. 'It's a very impressive piece of writing,' he said, appearing strangely moved.

'Is it?' I answered in surprise. 'Latin wasn't Patrick – my brother's – favourite subject at school.'

'This isn't schoolboy Latin,' the priest said. 'Nor is it classical. I would call it more . . . ecclesiastical – a style used in the liturgies and documents of the Church. It's unpretentious but still very elegant and correct.'

'Wow,' I gushed, hoping to sound impressed. 'And what does it say?'

'Well . . . it's quite abstract but . . . it talks about a place, a place where time will have no meaning . . . one second will seem like an eternity, as those . . . beneath the earth cry out for release . . .' He paused and gave me a sharp glance. I nodded to spur him on. 'Torments will precede the joy of release,' he continued, 'and the fire will heal. A church is mentioned – the first church – a gateway to a place of penance where the dead will weep and the lake run red.'

'Torments, fire, the dead weeping . . .' I repeated, chills running through me. This message was seriously creepy and seemed to ooze pain, death and suffering. Why would Patrick write about the afterlife? Unless he'd been thinking of doing something stupid. My stomach lurched horribly.

'Would you like me to write it down for you?' the priest asked.

I nodded. 'Yes, please.' He produced a pen from somewhere and began to scribble on Patrick's note. I found it hard to sit still and the movement of the second hand of my watch was distracting me.

'Could it be taken from the Bible?' I asked.

'I think not,' he replied quickly, as if I was doubting his knowledge of the holy book.

He handed the note back to me, the black ink still glistening.

'Patrick has probably copied it from somewhere. Sorry to have bothered you . . . Father.'

'It was no bother,' he assured me. 'It must have a special significance for him.'

'Do you think he's describing hell?' I asked edgily. 'I noticed the word *infernus* in the text, which reminded me of infernal hellfire?'

The priest listened patiently, a curve of amusement on his lips. '*Infernus* can mean hell, but it can also mean subterranean or underground. In this context I've translated it as *beneath the earth*. Is. . . is your brother spiritual?'

It was impossible to keep the sarcasm out of my voice. 'Well, he doesn't speak in tongues or have visions —'

'And what about you?'

'That's easy,' I answered immediately. 'I'm beyond redemption.' He looked so shocked that I babbled, 'I mean, my mum always said I was . . . in a jokey way, but it kind of stuck.'

The priest shook his head in disagreement but I refused to meet his gaze. 'You're very angry,' he said. 'I wonder what or who could have made you so angry.'

My teeth clenched, thinking about Patrick. 'You really wouldn't want to know.'

He spread his arms. 'Try me, I'm a good listener . . . it goes with the job.'

Damn. I could feel tears pricking behind my eyes because he was being so kind and sympathetic. It must have been delayed shock from the accident because I rarely cried and didn't want to now.

'Sorry, Father, but I don't have enough time.'

'I guessed that. You've consulted your wristwatch at least ten times.'

Now I felt as if I had been plain rude and I was filled with an overwhelming need to explain. 'It's not just tonight – I don't have enough time in general. I mean, that text could have been written for me . . . *a place where time will have no meaning . . . one second will seem like an eternity.*'

'I don't understand.' The priest smiled, his bushy eyebrows arched.

I didn't want to be here like this, pouring my heart out to a complete stranger, but he was drawing me in and I was too tired to fight it. 'When I was little I almost died, and I have this kind of obsession, all to do with . . . time running out.'

He pursed his lips. 'Why would that worry someone of such a tender age as you?'

'Well . . . I've got so much I want to do and I'm not sure I'll be able fit it all in.'

'Before what?'

*Before I die, of course.* But I didn't say this, just sat fidgeting on the hard bench and tapping my watch face.

'Do you want my advice?'

I didn't, but I nodded anyway. I could sense a sermon coming. 'Try to accept that there is *never* enough time . . . for any of us . . . so make the most of what you have. We're all living on borrowed time . . . borrowed from the man Himself.'

'Borrowed time,' I repeated woodenly.

'Because this life we're living now isn't the main feature . . . it's only the trailer.'

The priest scrutinized my face with a concentration

that made me squirm. 'Has your brother ever visited this church?' he asked unexpectedly.

'I don't know, Father. Why?'

He frowned. 'There was a young man studying our statue of Saint Peter recently; he seemed quite rapt by it.'

'But . . . what makes you think it was Patrick?'

'It only occurred to me now but . . . your features are strikingly similar.'

The hairs on the back of my neck bristled. Patrick had been here. I was still following his footsteps – the flat, the clock tower and now this church.

'Did you speak to him?' I asked.

The priest shook his head. 'I didn't approach him because I thought he wanted some contemplative time alone.'

I got up from the pew and walked over to the statue, my footsteps echoing in the cavernous space. I wanted to stand in the same spot as Patrick had, and I stared at Saint Peter, waiting for inspiration.

The priest followed me. 'Is your brother in some kind of trouble?'

I gave a hollow laugh, wishing I knew the answer. 'This could all be just a stupid game. Patrick's missing. He left me some clues to follow, and a key that doesn't seem to fit any lock.'

The priest smiled again. 'Then let us hope it has the same purpose as the keys given to Saint Peter himself in the gospel . . . the keys to the kingdom of heaven.'

My returning smile was a definite cringe. I'd been trying for so long to escape my mother's diet of force-fed religion and this felt like I was being drawn back in again. Plus the idea of me being allowed into heaven was just too embarrassing for words. I muttered a tepid thank-you and he offered his hand for me to shake, but I just brushed the tips of his fingers as though there was something nasty on them. This had all got too close for comfort. I made for the door.

'Goodbye, Catherine.'

His voice made me stop in my tracks. I turned, my trainers making a squeaky noise on the woodblock floor. 'How do you know?'

He gestured to his throat. I wore a gold chain around my neck from which dangled a letter C, a present from Dad. It was usually hidden but must have slipped outside my T-shirt.

'No one calls me that,' I said. 'I use my middle name – Sinead. And how did you guess it was Catherine?'

He smiled. 'It was an inspired guess. I was already confident that your mother would have given you a saint's name. You made a sign of the cross when you came into church, and genuflected before the altar.'

'That's just habit –'

As I struggled with the heavy door I could detect a slight smugness when he called out, 'All the same, Catherine. Welcome back.'

# Five

The weather finally broke. I'd walked no more than fifty metres when the heavens opened. Rain splattered down in huge droplets that fell with such force they stung my skin. Within thirty seconds I was so thoroughly drenched that there was little point in seeking shelter. I tried not to laugh at the sight of the same people I'd seen on the way to the church now frantically grabbing their possessions and running for cover. In another few minutes the road was starting to flood because the drains were either blocked or couldn't cope with the volume of rainfall. I had to wade through a pool of water just to get back to the park, my tracksuit bottoms weighing me down and my trainers waterlogged. The wind had picked up and staff from the restaurants and bars struggled to get the chairs and parasols inside before they were blown away. After the endless mugginess it felt exhilarating. I gazed upwards to feel the full power of the rain on my face as lightning forked and a clap of thunder shook the charcoal sky. It was beautiful to watch.

When I finally arrived at the flat, soaked to the skin, Harry looked anxious. 'Where did you go?' he asked.

'Let me change,' I said. 'I'm dripping all over the floor.'

I ran into the bathroom to peel off my clothes and towel-dry my hair, which hung in rats' tails around my ears. My skin was red and tingling. I emerged wearing one of Patrick's old shirts and his jeans held up with a tie.

'Eat while it's hot, Sinead.'

I was famished, so hungry that I felt light-headed. I could smell Chinese takeaway and saw that Harry had completely covered Patrick's low coffee table in foil-topped containers. It looked as though he'd bought a banquet to feed a family of six. He began to peel back the tops.

'I've never known anyone eat so much and stay so slim,' he teased, while I scooped the different dishes on to a plate without caring about the jumbled flavours. 'Aren't you going to tell me?'

'What?'

'Where you went? After you nearly killed yourself, that is.'

I licked the saltiness from my lips, my head still buzzing. 'I recognized two of the words in Patrick's note – *domus dei* – house of God.'

'And?'

'So I went to the local church of Saint Peter and a priest translated the rest for me.' I thrust the note at Harry and gave him a minute to read it. 'Fire, torments and dead people – it's totally freaked me out. What could Patrick be thinking of?'

Harry was still reading, his forehead creased in concentration.

'And that bit about a place where time will have no meaning and one second will seem like an eternity is really sinister.'

'That's almost provoking you,' Harry said, his concerned eyes searching mine.

I dropped my gaze, my stomach fluttering at the notion of such a place; somewhere I could breathe easily without being compelled to race through life frantically, counting the minutes. I took a deep breath and faced Harry again.

'That's not all . . . the priest thought he might have seen Patrick recently – in his church, staring at the statue of Saint Peter.' My voice rose. 'See? I followed him again like I was supposed to . . . if only I knew why.'

I could tell from the line of Harry's mouth that he was uneasy. 'What do you make of the ending, Sinead – *a gateway where the dead will weep and the lake run red*?'

I scrunched my face. 'I haven't a clue. There's something about it that sounds familiar, but my mind's whirring so crazily I can't grasp it.' I picked at the skin around my blistered fingers as if I somehow needed to feel Patrick's pain. 'I'm more worried than ever, Harry. The words in that message are so bizarre. Patrick could have seriously lost it.'

'Not with all those time references,' Harry insisted.

'They're calculated.' He lowered his voice as if someone was listening. 'You know how screwed up your brother is. Think about yourself for once, and stop this . . . right now.'

I shook my head. 'I owe it to Mum; she'd be heartbroken if anything happened to Patrick. You know I'd feel responsible.'

'What if you get hurt searching for him?'

'Nothing will happen to me,' I insisted.

'But how would I ever survive if it did, Sinead?'

His seriousness made me wriggle with embarrassment. I knew Harry found it hard to hide his feelings, and I loved him to pieces, but only as a friend. He must have noticed my discomfort and quickly changed the subject.

'So what does it all mean then? Where is he?'

I shrugged, annoyed because I knew something was staring me in the face but I couldn't see it. Each time I thought I had a connection it escaped from me like a balloon in the wind. I had warmed up again though, and the food was making me more relaxed. The pelting rain had subsided, the thunder now only a distant rumble. Harry and I continued talking but my mind couldn't fully concentrate on our conversation. The words of Patrick's note were on a constant loop playing over and over in my head, separating phrases and joining them with others like crossword clues.

I suddenly sat bolt upright. '*Lake run red* – I remember now. There is an actual Red Lake in Ireland. Mum told us about it when we were little. It always fascinated Patrick.'

'Go on,' Harry said encouragingly.

My hands flew up to my face in horror. In all the commotion I'd forgotten about calling Mum. She'd be frantic with worry. I grabbed my phone from my handbag and groaned at the number of messages and missed calls. I'd switched it to silent in the police station. With a sinking heart, I pressed the number for home.

My mother berated me for at least five minutes and I didn't say a word in my defence. It was pointless once she was this worked up, and I was used to being the fall guy. She stopped abruptly, exhausted and overwrought. I tried to reassure her that Patrick would return soon and that I would stay over at his flat and ring her immediately when there was news. It seemed to do the trick. I hung up, sighing with relief. Harry smiled with mute sympathy. I rolled my eyes and threw my phone on to the rug. The massive dinner had made me sleepy and my eyes were beginning to water. I stifled a yawn and stretched, wincing with pain. The muscles in my arms were tightly knotted and welts had erupted all over my raw hands.

'Red Lake?' Harry prompted, but his voice sounded far away and I had to jerk myself back to reality.

I leaned back against a battered armchair to make myself comfortable. 'When Mum married my dad she moved from Ireland to the north of England, but she's always liked to tell us Irish legends. I remember the story about the Red Lake so well because Patrick used to frighten me with it.'

'What's so scary about a lake?'

'Because this one surrounds Station Island . . . a mystical place – barren, rocky, misty and –' I paused – 'long held to be a gateway to the next world.'

'OK,' said Harry carefully.

'It's to do with Saint Patrick – you know, the patron saint of Ireland?'

'The snake guy?'

I gave him a mock stern glance. 'Yes, the guy who chased all the snakes from Ireland.'

'And what did he do on this island?'

'Erm . . . Saint Patrick was busy converting the Irish to Christianity and some kind of cave or pit was revealed to him where he was supposed to have been shown the afterlife. Then it became a place where pilgrims visited. Some of them reported awful visions and if they survived the ordeal it meant they were saved from the punishment of –'

'Hell?' Harry interrupted.

I frowned. 'Some people believe there's another place, kind of halfway between heaven and hell.'

'And that's what frightened you?'

I looked skyward. 'No . . . I was terrified of the pit. Patrick used to tell me it was fathomless and I'd never get out again. I can't believe I was so gullible as to believe him.'

'But . . . why would he want you to remember the Red Lake and this island?'

'Search me. Maybe there'll be another clue.' I twisted my head to one side. 'You know, it feels like I've been doing this for most of my life.'

'Then don't do it, Sinead. Throw away the stupid clues, go back home and refuse to play Patrick's stupid games.'

I cupped my hands around my mouth and blew out. 'I can't. I know he's moved out and I should be free of him, but I can't stop myself . . .'

'He's brainwashed you for so long,' Harry said. 'That's why you can't stop.'

I sighed, pulling small loops of wool out of Patrick's rug. 'I don't know how not to follow him and . . . deep down . . . he needs me.'

Harry's expression was gloomy but he didn't push it. I was so tired that I climbed on to the sofa and nestled my head against a cushion. The light was fading and the sunset beautiful after the storm – shades of pink, yellow and turquoise all blended together as if someone had thrown a whole palette of paint colours on to a canvas. The temperature was still warm but the high ceilings in Patrick's flat made the space echo, something that wasn't noticeable in the daylight, and there were draughts from between cracks in the floorboards. I shivered. Patrick hadn't got around to hanging any curtains and I wondered what time the sun rose, debating whether to hang a sheet over the windows.

Harry twitched nervously and pulled at his curls. 'Maybe . . . you shouldn't . . . I mean it might be creepy here alone . . . I could sleep in the chair?'

I stifled another yawn. 'I'll be OK . . . Patrick might turn up in the middle of the night and that would be awkward.'

This was an excuse and we both knew it, but Harry nodded understandingly. This crisis with Patrick had made me feel closer to him, but I didn't want to hurt him by giving him false hope. Sometimes though, I couldn't see a way not to. I must have dozed and didn't realize he was still there. His lips brushed my cheek and a blanket was gently laid across me. My eyes flickered but I purposely didn't open them.

'I know you don't feel the same about me, Sinead, and I'm willing to wait . . . just not forever.'

'I wouldn't ask you to, Harry,' I whispered as the door closed behind him.

# Six

I woke with a start, disorientated as laser rays of sun hit my eyes. I wondered what time it was and groped for my phone. It was after nine. Amazingly I'd slept ten hours. My mind went over the events of yesterday, running through all the clues again and racking my brains trying to work out exactly where Patrick could be leading me. I drew a blank and was fearful I'd hit a brick wall. I swung my legs off the sofa and winced, realizing how tightly bunched my muscles were. My body felt even stiffer than yesterday. I hobbled into the bedroom and slid my phone back on the cabinet and my fingers touched Patrick's Bible. I traced the gilt lettering on the cover. I hadn't given it much thought yesterday, but it struck me now that the flat was so bare and yet this had been left out. And the priest had quoted from the Gospel, something about Saint Peter and the keys to heaven.

I picked up the Bible slowly and held it in the palm of one hand. The book immediately fell open at Saint Matthew's

Gospel as if it had been opened there many times, the thin pages fluttering to release the same fragrantly musty scent as a church. I stared down at the text. The words *Love thy neighbour* had been overwritten in red ink. This could be another clue. My pulse galloped and I closed my eyes for a moment, overwhelmed by a sense of relief. The trail hadn't gone cold. It was almost as if Patrick was watching my progress, nudging me whenever I stalled. He couldn't be in danger; he was enjoying this too much. I could almost hear his voice inside my head: *You'll always follow my footsteps, won't you?*

I had to tell Harry. I called him and explained in a torrent what I'd found in the Bible and that I planned to talk to Patrick's neighbours later that morning. I could tell from his voice that I'd woken him.

'Great idea,' he said, and I heard the muffled sound of a yawn. 'I'll come over now.'

I smiled to myself, suspecting he would have agreed to whatever insane scheme I suggested. 'I probably should go alone, Harry. People might respond better to a girl by herself.'

'I'll still come by, Sinead. Anything you need?'

I looked down at Patrick's cast-off clothes. 'Would you fetch me some more sweats and a clean T-shirt from home? I'll text Mum and tell her to pick something out for me, but don't breathe a word about what's happening here. She will question you, and it won't be pleasant, but just don't say anything useful.'

Harry laughed nervously. 'How about some food? You know how grumpy you are when you don't eat.'

'Some bagels and jam would be nice.'

'Anything else?'

I could picture Harry's long-suffering smile. 'My laptop. And Harry?'

'Yes?'

'Try not to be long. Time is of the essence.'

When Harry arrived I'd showered and was unsuccessfully trying to style my hair without a hairdryer. He placed all the things that I'd asked for on the bed.

'She's suspicious,' he announced, looking a bit shell-shocked after his encounter with my mother. 'She gave me the full interrogation but I didn't crack. I pretended not to know anything.'

'Well done,' I said, and he grinned. 'I'll have to face her sooner or later, but I couldn't stomach it yet.'

'She's checked with all the hospitals and with Patrick's landlord, but he hasn't heard anything and he knows nothing about the flat being given a spring clean.'

'That was a good idea,' I said with amazement. I'd have expected her to just pace about wringing her hands and doing nothing constructive. I went into the bedroom to change. It was amazing the difference some fresh clothes made to my mood. Despite having a bare face and floppy hair, I felt almost human again.

Harry peered at me with renewed interest. 'You look different somehow.'

I touched my cheek self-consciously. 'I don't have my make-up.'

'It suits you . . . makes you look softer . . . I mean, prettier.'

He looked away, but it was obvious what he meant; I looked less forbidding without my scary eye make-up, which would be a bonus if I was attempting to butter up Patrick's neighbours. I looked in the mirror and hardly recognized myself. I studied my features critically – wide mouth, deep-set greyish-blue eyes, high jutting cheekbones. Harry often told me that my smile transformed my whole face but I didn't smile often enough. I glanced at my watch. The time was now a respectable 11 a.m., and it was Saturday so there was a decent chance of catching people at home. I gave Harry a feeble wave and stepped outside. There were five flats in all and it seemed sensible to begin at the one closest to Patrick's.

I walked down a small corridor and through a fire door, threw back my shoulders and rapped decisively on the door. It flew open almost instantly, which caught me off my guard. A suspicious face stared back at me. 'Yes?'

I tried to smile, but my mouth distorted as if I was in pain.

'I'm . . . looking for Patrick, who lives in the next flat . . . I wondered . . . have you seen him lately?'

This guy was fairly young with gold-rimmed spectacles

and an annoying goatee beard. I could smell bacon wafting into the corridor.

'Hmm,' he considered, stroking his facial hair. Something about his expression told me he wasn't going to be helpful. 'I saw him a few weeks ago when he borrowed twenty pounds off me for a family emergency. I haven't seen him since. I think he's been avoiding me.'

'Oh,' I mumbled.

'Are you a relative?'

'Just a . . . friend. I'll be sure to remind him about the money when he turns up.'

'Do,' he snapped, and slammed the door in my face.

OK, bad call, I reflected, but they couldn't all be like that. I was ashamed that Patrick had borrowed money and failed to pay it back and disgusted with myself for not admitting we were related. The shame wasn't anything new; Patrick had mortified me by his behaviour so many times that I should have been immune, but I'd never denied him as a brother before and it wasn't a nice feeling.

I trudged downstairs starting to think that this exercise would produce nothing worthwhile. There was no reply from the second flat. By the time I reached the third, my knock was softer as if I was determined no one should hear. I was about to leave when a figure appeared in the doorway with the astonished look of someone who never has anyone knock on her door. I took a breath and choked on a wave of heavy, cloying perfume. This lady was middle-aged with orange skin and Barbie hair, dressed in a flowery garden-party style two-piece. She glided past me, surprisingly light on her feet for someone so plump. She peered into the hallway, saw that it was empty except for me, and seemed disappointed. I launched into the same patter as before, and again lied about my relationship with Patrick. Despite the guilt, it tripped easily off my tongue.

'I work all day – I don't have time to socialize,' she said petulantly.

'Well, it's not really socializing I had in mind . . . Patrick is kind of . . . missing, and his family are worried about him.'

'That is most disconcerting,' she said, appearing anything but. 'Have you asked his employer?'

'He doesn't work,' I muttered, physically edging away from the questions and her perfume.

'His college perhaps?'

'He doesn't . . . I mean . . . yes, I'll do that. Thanks for the advice.'

Her gracious smile didn't fool me for a second. I tried to stop anger from engulfing me and felt sorry for Patrick, having to live next door to these people. They didn't have to tell me what they thought of him; I could see it in their eyes, and I'd already used up twelve minutes on this fruitless exercise.

I almost lost the nerve to knock on the last door. The TV was turned up loudly and there was scuffling and movement inside, but it was a couple of minutes before an elderly woman cautiously popped her head outside. She was the first resident to appear friendly and I relaxed slightly. I'd only just mentioned Patrick's name and that I was a friend when she interrupted.

'You have his mouth.'

I stopped because she'd rumbled me. 'He's my brother,' I admitted.

She gave a little nod of recognition. 'Would you like to come in?'

The door opened wide and I stepped over the threshold. Inside was as different from Patrick's minimalist flat as it was possible to be, crammed with heavy, old-fashioned furniture and opulent upholstery. I counted two sofas, three armchairs, a leather chair next to a writing desk and a chaise longue in a green striped fabric. There was barely a hint of wall space to be seen because of the abundance of paintings, all different sizes and themes. This flat was larger than Patrick's but felt more cramped and much darker. The lady motioned for me to sit on the uncomfortable-looking chaise longue. It had carved animal legs that looked so real I almost expected them to nip my ankles. She perched on the smaller sofa with both hands resting in her lap and turned to me with interest.

'My brother hasn't been in contact for about two weeks,' I began, 'and we're all quite worried.'

'Such a polite boy,' she said. 'I often see him passing my window of a morning and sometimes we meet in the hallway. He's always very kind and picks up my letters. And so very good-looking.'

'But . . . do you remember seeing him recently?'

She studied the ceiling for inspiration. Ten seconds passed, then twenty and my right leg began to twitch uncontrollably.

'I might have,' she answered finally. I held my breath and eventually she continued. 'I often find . . . that if I need an answer to something . . . it helps to banish it from my mind before the answer comes to me.'

Every sinew in my body began to tighten with frustration and I found it impossible to sit still. *Patience is a virtue, patience is a virtue*, I chanted to myself and nearly jumped into the air as a grandfather clock boomed the quarter-hour.

'I'd love to live on the top floor,' her voice chattered, 'but my legs would never stand the strain. It's hard to believe but I was a dancer in my youth. Arthritis has crippled me now but . . . listen to me . . . I shouldn't depress you about getting older.'

'It doesn't depress me,' I said, trying not to look at her blue-veined lumpy legs.

This was going nowhere. I stood up and managed to reach the door, but she wedged herself between the umbrella stand and the hall table, blocking my exit. Now that I was leaving her memory suddenly returned.

'I did see Patrick . . . a week, maybe two weeks ago. I can't be certain but I do remember he was excited because he had a new job. He was in too much of a hurry for me to ask him any details.'

Patrick had a job. Patrick was rushing somewhere to work. This was completely unexpected, but it might explain his unusual behaviour. He'd been distant and even cagier than normal. Maybe he hadn't wanted to tell Mum and me because he was worried that he wouldn't be able to hack it. I thanked the old lady and made my way back to the flat. I'd been gone for twenty-three minutes, but at least I had some information.

Harry was looking flushed and pleased with himself, brandishing a screwdriver in the air as if it was a weapon. As a surprise he was fixing a security chain to the door so I'd feel safer inside. I was a bit worried about not consulting the landlord first, but I said how great it was, pretending not to notice the huge plaster on his thumb. He was also eager to tell me that he'd checked all of the Latin references in Patrick's message on my laptop and the only hits were millions of religious texts.

'It was pretty dismal talking to the neighbours,' I said. 'An old lady remembers seeing Patrick some time recently. Apparently he boasted about having a job, but she doesn't have a clue where he was working.'

Harry looked unimpressed. 'That's not much to go on.'

'Well . . . it isn't, but . . . we could narrow the search. Patrick isn't the model employee so the job would have to be casual – flexible hours, few references required . . .'

'You always said he could talk his way out of any-thing . . . Maybe he's got work as a salesman? There're always vacancies for them.'

'That's a possibility,' I said, and grabbed my bag. 'Let's check out the job centre and local paper. Patrick won't have gone far – I'm sure of that.'

He groaned. 'Do we have to go straight away?'

I fixed him with reproachful eyes. '*Tempus fugit*, Harry. *Tempus fugit*.'

# Seven

We sat in a coffee shop and I flicked through the local newspaper to the jobs pages. The advantage of Patrick's flat was that it was in the city centre, with everything close by and buzzing. I'd never gone in for that whole people-watching thing before, but I couldn't help but stare when an Italian-looking guy wearing city shorts and carrying a briefcase strode past the window. Even the fashion victims with their spray-on tans and glow-white jeans fascinated me, and I noticed that every second girl was wearing a maxi dress with gladiator sandals and holiday hair. I put the paper down.

*Maybe I could change. I could become one of those people who wander about aimlessly with a serene smile, soaking up the atmosphere and watching the grass grow. I could lie in the park and pick the petals off flowers, instead of frantically blowing any dandelion clocks that I happen to pass. Sara and I could do all the girly stuff I avoided.*

Harry brought me back down to earth. 'This seems

like such a long shot,' he said, and it was obvious he was wondering exactly what we were doing there. 'Patrick's job advert will have been withdrawn.'

I screwed up my face. 'I know but . . . something might jump out at me, a job that Patrick would be perfect for. I need to think like him to solve these clues.'

Harry went back to the counter to buy a toasted sandwich and I grumbled to myself. *If Patrick hadn't sold his computer I could access his files, see if he'd registered with any employment agencies.*

A male voice broke into my thoughts. 'Have you finished with that newspaper?'

I didn't even look up, intent on studying the vintage soft top parked outside with the engine still running, a tiny blonde girl in the passenger seat. She looked a bit full of herself in her diaphanous sea-green dress, smoothing her hair in the wing mirror.

'It belongs to me,' I barked, placing my hand across the headlines.

There was a small snort of satisfaction. 'So you *are* rude to everyone.'

I looked up quickly to find the beach boy holding a takeaway cup in each hand. Only this time he was groomed to within an inch of his life – crisp white shirt, midnight-blue skinny tie, pale grey trousers and expensive aftershave. His hair had been slicked back, which made him look even more handsome. He flashed me a smile, but this time it wasn't as cocky; there was warmth to it, lighting up the entire place as if a giant sunbeam had burst through the window. Something flipped inside me, and it hurt.

'I'm not,' I managed to reply. 'It's only you who has this effect on me.'

He smiled. 'You didn't know it was me.'

'I recognized your accent,' I lied, annoyed that I hadn't. The Australian twang conjured up golden beaches, miles of electric-blue sea topped by frothy white foam and a beach boy running along the sand with a surfboard and bare chest.

'I'm sure they run anger-management classes in this part of town,' he said, but there was a playful look in his eye.

There was something so irrepressibly good-humoured about his expression that I began to smile. He was right – I'd been unspeakably rude and here was a chance to make amends. Normally I didn't do apologies, but he was worth making an exception for. It was nothing, just two small words. He was waiting, and the challenge in his gorgeous hazel eyes set my heart fluttering. Guys didn't generally flirt with me, yet his body language was undeniable. But the mood was suddenly broken and his attention distracted. He began to mouth and gesture to someone outside, and when I looked the sea goddess was half standing in her seat pointing to her watch. They were a couple – of course they were – and the car must be his.

'Don't keep the lady waiting,' I urged. He picked up the cups from where he'd placed them on the table, and regarded me intently, but now it made me feel like an insect under a microscope. 'Hope we don't meet again,' I added.

'You're still the rudest girl I've ever met,' he said.

'And you still must have led a really sheltered life,' I quipped, but this time almost wistfully.

He walked towards the exit without giving me another glance, but he had the nerve to check out a pretty girl sitting in the corner. A stern female traffic warden was just about to put a ticket on his car when he breezed through the glass door. Unbelievably, he blew her a kiss, raised a cup as if to say cheers and she put away her machine and waved him on his way. He even honked his horn in appreciation. Harry returned with a giant sandwich and I tried to hide the overwhelming feeling of misery that had descended as quickly as fog. The beach boy and his girlfriend looked so happy, without a care in the world, and I felt ten years older and weighed down by burdens I couldn't even express. I sipped my tepid coffee and tried to console myself with the thought that a passing lorry might shower his girlfriend with loose chippings and grit.

I couldn't get him out of my head. My first assumption had been totally wrong; he didn't look like a backpacker today, more a public schoolboy with his own expense account. I was usually so good at putting people into categories, but he seemed to elude me. And he'd been so outspoken about my rudeness. This wasn't the first time, but his words hurt like never before.

I fidgeted in my seat, already knowing the answer to my question. 'Harry? Do I have an anger problem?'

'If I say yes, will you punch me?' he joked.

'So I do?'

'Sometimes you're on a short fuse. You know that,' he answered diplomatically.

I nibbled my fingernails. 'Give me an example.'

Harry sat up straight and folded his arms stoically. 'OK. You get angry at wasps, men with beards, people who don't queue . . . people who do queue . . . anyone who sneezes next to you . . .' He took a breath. 'Women over forty who wear skinny jeans or Lycra, ring-pull cans, cartons of milk, pips in oranges, traffic cones –'

I held up both hands to stop him. 'OK, I *am* the most intolerant person in the world.' I took a minute to reflect on this, astonished to find that it really bothered me. In an instant it felt as if someone had held up a mirror and I'd seen myself in all my ugliness. When had I turned into the kind of person that I despised? The realization floored me and I was overtaken by an unnatural urge to spill my guts to Harry. There was even a wobble in my voice.

'Do you remember the fairy tale about the Snow Queen?'

Harry smiled weakly.

'It's about a magic mirror that magnified and distorted everything and everyone so they looked horrible and repulsive. The mirror broke into millions of pieces and some people got splinters of glass in their eyes and only saw the ugly things in life, and some people got a shard in their heart, which turned into a lump of ice –'

'And you think that's what happened to you?' he asked softly.

I let a breath go. 'Sometimes I imagine I don't even have a heart. There's a hole in my chest where it should be and my . . . mission is to rush through life frantically, trying to fill the void.'

'That's so daft, Sinead. Being a bit impatient and snappy doesn't make you a bad person . . . and it's understandable, after what you've had to cope with. You spend your life worrying about your mum and Patrick . . . more than they deserve. Repeat after me,' he said sternly, '"My heart's in good working order."'

I spaced out momentarily. *You know your heart's beating. You felt something when you looked at that boy – you felt your heart sing, and that's scared the life out of you.*

'Sinead . . . ? What's brought this on?' Harry was asking.

'Don't know,' I said morosely, already regretting the confession. First the priest and now Harry; since Patrick disappeared I'd become an emotional wreck. I had to stop feeling sorry for myself and remain focused on finding him. I clenched my hands under the table. 'It's been twenty-four hours and I've got no more leads, Harry. I'll have to break the news to my mum. It'll be awful . . . no, worse than awful . . . She'll fall apart completely.'

'Has she filled in the missing persons report?'

I pulled a face. 'I put it to her, but she isn't keen. Patrick's had a few minor run-ins with the police and she thinks they're not sympathetic to him. She wants this to stay in the family.'

Harry picked at his worn sleeve, seemingly at a loss for what to say. Eventually we decided to leave. We tried the local job centre but our computer search there flagged up nothing useful, and then we spent a hot and sticky afternoon mooching about, trying to come up with more leads. Harry wanted to find a shady tree to sit under and relax but I couldn't. The lack of direction had made me more wired than ever.

He tried to calm me down. 'Patrick couldn't be sure how long it would take you to find his clues. Just because you haven't found another one doesn't mean it's not there . . . somewhere.'

I considered his words, remembering the Bible. 'You're right. I'm going back to Patrick's flat. There might be something else I've overlooked.'

Harry offered to keep me company but I let him down gently. 'I need some time alone to think.' I looked at him and sighed. 'Maybe this is part of Patrick's game.'

'What do you mean?'

'Taunting me. He knows how impatient I am. Waiting for anything tortures me.'

We reached the flat and Harry left me at the door. His parting smile looked sad, beaten. 'One day, Sinead, you might find something . . . or *someone* worth waiting for.'

# Eight

My eyes flew open and I clutched at my throat, gasping for breath. For a moment I was a little girl again, back at home in my bedroom, feeling the night thicken around me and the darkness smother me. I actually pummelled the air with my fists before I remembered where I was. I was in Patrick's flat. I was safe. It was 3 a.m. and still dark. I strained to listen. For a moment I thought I heard a noise outside the door, but it was probably just my nightmare still weighing heavy. It had never felt so vivid before – the sensation of not being able to breathe stronger and more terrifying than ever. I padded into the kitchen and filled a glass with water. Feeling restless, I walked over to the window. Under the lamp post there was a figure looking up at the flat, which made me draw back into the shadows. There was something familiar about it and in my sleepy state I was convinced it had to be Patrick.

Without thinking I ran out of the door, down the stairs and on to the pavement, calling his name, but the street was now empty. I crossed over to the lamp post and stared at the glowing butt lying on the pavement. Whoever it was had been smoking a cigarette. I would have extinguished it but my feet were bare.

It took me another minute to realize how dangerous it was, out in the middle of the city in the early hours of the morning. Suddenly there were shadows everywhere, in doorways, behind cars and in alleys, a million places where someone could hide. I must have been sleepwalking to have come out here like this. I wrapped my arms around myself and tiptoed back across the road to the flat, thankful the door hadn't closed, because it locked automatically and my keys were inside. Tiny bits of gravel were embedded in the soles of my feet. Apart from a few creaking timbers and the sound of water filtering through the pipes, everywhere was as quiet as a grave. I climbed back into Patrick's bed, but I knew that sleep would elude me; I was in a strange room, feeling horribly uneasy, and worries always seemed magnified in the small hours. My mind took me back to the clock tower, reliving what I had feared would be my last moments. *It's always later than you think.*

It wasn't until dawn began to break that I dozed off again; this time my head was full of crazy dreams all involving me in pursuit of Patrick. The most vivid and memorable one came closest to waking; I was climbing a steep hill, chasing a purposeful figure that refused to slow down or turn around, but I knew it was Patrick. I began screaming at him, punching the air with my fists and bawling, when he stopped abruptly and launched himself downward as skilfully as a bird of prey swooping for the kill. I wanted to follow but the drop was immense; I was teetering on the edge of a precipice. And when I looked into the depths they resembled the inside of a volcano, billowing smoke and ash scorching my face and my hair. And Patrick was swallowed up inside. Then the cries began, so awful that I had to cover my ears.

My phone alarm beeped and buzzed, a loud, intrusive sound that shocked me into instant consciousness. As I tried to switch it off I knocked the phone from the cabinet and heard it skitter across the wooden floor. I tumbled out of bed, still woozy, and crawled on my knees until I grabbed it with both hands and cut the beeps. I stood, stretching, my sleepy eyes trying to focus. The door was open and I blinked at the strange sight that greeted me, and then blinked again to make sure I wasn't still dreaming. Dazed, I lurched into the living room and ran one shaky hand across the startling image that now covered at least a square metre of the white wall.

There was a church, identifiable by a large cross on the apex of its roof. It was positioned on a sheer rock face that rose out of some kind of chasm filled with layer upon layer of bodies, a writhing, seething mass, their arms held out in supplication, their faces stricken. Misshapen trees jutted out of the rock. Some of the tormented figures had branches woven like vines around them, some had hair made of serpents that imprisoned them in the same way.

Most of the image was drawn in black, but the chasm was surrounded by a lake, the ripples stained a startling blood red. This was unreal. Panic flooded through me, my legs gave way and I dropped to the floor again. With shaking hands I texted Harry just five words. *Urgent. Get over here NOW.*

Harry must have been so worried by my text. Even in shock I noticed that his shirt was inside out and he was wearing odd socks. As I brought him inside and showed him the wall his face blanched.

'Is it ink or paint?' he asked, copying my first instinct and running his hand over the surface.

'Who cares about the technique?' I said. 'This has to be Patrick showing me the Red Lake and the pit on Station Island.'

'It's very fine,' he went on. 'Some kind of line drawing?'

'Harry! You're missing the point.' This was mean of me because until he arrived I had been perched on the end of Patrick's bed too frightened to move. 'I was here all night . . . sleeping. How was it done? When was it done?'

Harry still looked too stunned to speak. He jumped up to examine the door in a strangely male way. He was completely impractical and wouldn't have been able to tell if the lock had been tampered with, but his concern was touching.

'It doesn't look as if the door's been forced, but you can't stay here any longer, Sinead.'

I narrowed my eyes. 'Patrick is behind this.'

'I don't know how,' Harry said.

Gingerly I lifted my foot, a memory slowly filtering through. There were still tiny scratches on the sole where the gravel had pitted the skin. It hadn't been a dream.

I coughed, squirmed and steeled myself for the confession. 'Thing is . . . I ran outside in the middle of the night, when I noticed someone under the street light . . . and I left the flat door open.'

'Sinead!' Harry said my name with disbelief. 'Anyone could have walked in.'

I looked sheepish, knowing it had been an insane thing to do. 'Well, whoever it is, they don't mean me any harm,' I tried to joke. 'I mean, everything was normal at three o'clock, and if someone slipped inside when I left the door open, they only wanted to decorate the wall.'

'We're going back to the police,' he said firmly.

I rubbed my nose, still annoyed with myself. 'We can't. Strange art appearing on the walls would go down even worse than the flat-tidying story. There hasn't been a break-in and nothing's been taken. They'd accuse me of wasting police time.'

'So what'll we do?'

'Sit tight, I guess.'

'Did you go straight back to sleep?'

'Yes,' I fibbed, choosing not to mention my strange dream. He might think I really did need a shrink.

I went into the kitchen to get some coffee. The full glare of the morning sun bathed everywhere in a golden light that bounced off the walls, the floor and worktops. It was a high-spec design – solid wood cabinets, granite worktops and a slate floor. Mum always spoiled Patrick. Harry appeared at my shoulder.

'I don't mean to depress you, Sinead,' he began, taking a mug from one of the open shelves. I took the hint and filled it with coffee, certain that he *was* going to depress me. 'I did some research last night, and apparently thousands of people go missing every year in Britain.'

'That's impossible,' I said. 'How could so many people disappear from such a small island?'

He gave a meaningful shrug. 'Some of them want to disappear; they engineer it.' He took a sip from his mug and winced, probably because there was no milk. He stirred the coffee anyway. 'Some just need a break and then find it hard to return . . . some start a new life or escape from a bad situation . . . only a small percentage are genuinely unexplained.'

'Patrick wouldn't run away deliberately,' I said with complete conviction.

'How can you be so sure?'

'Because he can't survive without an audience. All this he's doing now . . . this is for my benefit. If he was completely alone, cut off and no one cared what he did . . . I think he'd just . . . fade away into nothingness.'

Harry studied the pattern on his mug as though it was

the most interesting thing in the room. 'So what do we do now?'

'We should have a look round before we leave. The mad wall artist could be holed up somewhere.'

But there was nothing to suggest that anyone apart from us had been in the flat. I was still certain that Patrick was responsible and that he was somewhere close by.

'Patrick could have set up a diversion for me last night,' I said, 'then sneaked into the flat and waited until I was asleep to make the image . . . but . . . it's so detailed, way beyond his capabilities.'

'Maybe it's a giant transfer,' Harry suggested. 'You moisten the back and the image is transposed on to a surface – that wouldn't need any skill.'

I tugged my hair in frustration. What was I missing? I clutched my head and did my impersonation of *The Scream* painting. It usually made Harry smile, but not today. His tongue rested against his top lip as if he was brooding on something.

When he spoke his tone was subdued. 'I think I noticed some letters in the bottom right-hand corner of the mural . . . they might be a signature.'

'Why didn't you tell me before?' I asked crossly, sloshing my coffee over the worktop.

I went back to the living room, asking Harry to grab a pen and some paper. But every time I bent down to study the wall, he did the same and I had to point out that he was blocking the light and we should take it in turns. It took us both over ten minutes to decipher all the letters, and even then we were unsure if they were correct because some were indistinct and others written back to front.

'It's too long to be a name,' I said. 'It could be another maxim, like *Tempus fugit.*'

Harry's fingers busily keyed in words on the Internet, his brow furrowed with concentration.

'Any match?'

'Bingo.' He turned my laptop towards me and grinned. '*Sic transit gloria mundi* – So passes away earthly glory.'

Passes away . . . time passing . . . earthly glory . . . reminding us of our mortality.

*OK, Patrick. I'm starting to get the picture, but what's this all about?*

Harry read from the screen. 'It was the motto of a mission house that used to be based in Brick Lane. Now it's the Treatment Centre, a charity for recovering addicts.'

I clutched Harry's sleeve, my heart lifting. 'Patrick used to check in there sometimes. He might be there now, just waiting to be brought home. Will you come with me?' I begged, heading for the door and checking the time.

Harry gave me a hard stare. 'I want you to stop looking for Patrick.'

'What? Why?'

'I don't have a good feeling about all this, Sinead. He's leading you into danger, knowing you can't resist. You're worried about him being in trouble, but what about *you*?'

I was itching to leave. I wedged the door half open, my

foot already edging outside. 'I can look after myself. Really I can.'

'No, you can't,' Harry said, unusually fierce. 'You think you're somehow responsible for Patrick's problems – you even feel stupidly guilty about being born. Nothing about Patrick is your fault and you shouldn't be following him. I know I said I'd help you but that was before this got too heavy. You should walk away . . . now, Sinead.'

'I can walk away any time,' I insisted. 'And I have to do this.'

Harry turned his baby blue eyes to me. 'Part of your *quest*? Still following his footsteps?'

My eyes narrowed. 'Maybe. I have this weird feeling that if I find him . . . I'll be free of him for good.'

He nodded slowly, with a crooked half-smile. 'OK then, Sinead. Let's go.'

# Nine

'There's no point taking my car,' Harry said, following me down the steep chapel stairs. 'The one-way system will take us miles around, and there won't be any parking spaces.'

'We could walk it in fifteen minutes,' I suggested, matching his broad stride. 'Cut up Victoria Street, then down by the Cross Keys, shortcut through the university, bypass the multistorey and we're there.'

'Speed up,' Harry mocked as my breathing grew more laboured as we walked uphill.

'Keep pace, Harry,' I retaliated, and broke into a run. He had no choice but to follow suit.

We arrived in Brick Lane panting and clutching our sides. I had to sit on a wall to get my breath back. Harry's face was beetroot-coloured and his hair damp with perspiration. I used my fingers to comb my own hair and composed myself while Harry tried to cool down. I glanced around at the old buildings, the bricks blackened and honeycombed with age. There were three skips in the lane, all full of building materials, and I remembered the area was undergoing some regeneration. There was a sign advertising flats to rent, a newly opened bistro, an antiques shop with a few chairs outside and some kind of specialist art shop. The Treatment Centre was a single-storey building. It was set apart with its own courtyard, but there were metal bars on the windows.

'Will you go first?' I whispered nervously.

Harry seemed surprised. 'Haven't you been here before?'

I shook my head. 'This kind of place makes me feel a bit weird and . . . not that comfortable.'

Harry's eyebrows shot up. 'Shall I go alone then, Sinead, in case it's too *uncomfortable* in there for you?'

I didn't reply, feeling ashamed and knowing that I deserved this jibe. I threw back my shoulders and reached for Harry's hand. Together we edged through the double doors. They opened straight into a hall with two long refectory tables running side by side and a counter serving food. The walls were lined with posters offering advice on everything from housing and welfare to drug and alcohol rehabilitation. Every seat was taken. It smelled like school dinners mixed with sweat and unwashed clothes. There was little ventilation and I immediately felt nauseous.

I made for the first person wearing an identity badge. She was young with short brown hair, dressed casually in faded jeans and a checked shirt.

'I'm looking for my brother . . . he hasn't contacted his

family for over two weeks.' I got out my phone and showed her a photograph of Patrick.

She didn't seem at all surprised and I could only imagine how many relatives came here looking for family who had fallen off the radar. This made me feel flustered and even more anxious.

'How long has he used our services?' she asked.

I felt as if I had to whisper. 'He isn't . . . I mean . . . he doesn't come here that often.'

'He does look familiar,' she said reservedly, 'but we have so many comings and goings. You'd probably be better off talking to the regulars.'

'Talking to –'

She must have seen my reluctance. Her pale eyes stared at me while I visibly wilted. I examined the floor and by the time I had the courage to look up she'd walked away.

Harry had heard every word and he sounded puzzled. 'I thought you used to help out in a hospital?'

I groaned. 'Yes, but only with the medical side of it. I'm not a social worker.'

'I'll help,' he offered.

I licked my dry lips and took one step forward, catching the eye of a woman staring into space. Her face was hollow, her eyes sunken into the back of her head. Her arms were a pockmarked mess of collapsed veins and her bare legs angry with weeping sores. Something about her made me stop dead, and it only took a few seconds to realize why – it was like looking at hell on earth. I couldn't do this.

'Don't feel well,' I muttered.

I stumbled outside into the baking sun and clung on to the gatepost. I knew I was being unfair. These people weren't Patrick and I had no idea what circumstances had made their lives turn out this way, but I couldn't disconnect from my unspent fury at my brother and what he'd done to our family. Harry didn't say a word and his silence stung more than his previous criticism.

I shuddered. 'Sorry, I'm not very good at sympathy . . . It was all exhausted on Patrick.'

'They don't need your sympathy, Sinead; just treat them like they're human.'

'It just . . . overwhelms me,' I tried to explain.

'Most of them are shunned by everyone . . . but I never expected it of you.'

I glanced at the people strolling by enjoying the sunshine and wished I was anywhere but here. Feebly I attempted to defend myself. 'When I see them, all I can think of is Patrick and all the times he said it would be different, all the promises he broke and how he hurt us all . . . I see *him* in ten or twenty years' time, and it's frightening.'

'Come back inside with me,' Harry said, his tone a little softer. He pulled at my T-shirt and managed to drag me into the building without further protest.

Harry approached another staff member, taking my phone from me and showing her Patrick's photo.

She didn't even have to think. 'I do recognize him. Let

me check our register but . . . you must realize, people don't always give their real names.'

She took us to a small office. I gave her Patrick's full name, told her that he was my brother and watched her flick through some kind of ledger. 'Here he is . . . Patrick Mullen. He left us eighteen days ago.'

I smiled gratefully. 'I wonder . . . Did you notice anything . . . *strange* about him?'

Her expression was rueful. 'We treat people at their lowest ebb, often people who have nowhere else to turn. Everyone here acts a little strange.'

'I don't suppose you'd remember where he slept?' I asked, convinced that Patrick must have left something for me.

She looked back at the ledger. 'The room he stayed in is currently occupied. And every room is cleaned before the next guest arrives.'

'Even so, could we take a quick look?' I persisted. 'My brother's disappeared and we're looking for anything that might help us find him.'

After a moment's hesitation the woman nodded. We followed her down a shiny, antiseptic-smelling corridor that reminded me of a hospital. She opened one of the many doors and ushered us into a spartan room that had only one tiny window. She stayed in the doorway watching us as we looked around. The current occupant had very few possessions for us to disturb. My eyes immediately scanned the walls for writing and I peered underneath the iron bedstead. I rummaged in the bin, already knowing it would have been emptied. Harry checked out the chest of drawers, which was the only other furniture in the room. He shook his head.

The woman came inside and stood in front of the window, her eyes skyward. 'Your brother's very observant. If you crane your head you can see a line of starlings sitting on a nearby roof. Like soldiers on parade, he said. I'd never noticed them before, but now I enjoy watching them.'

'Patrick likes birds,' I answered dully.

I grimaced at Harry. There was nothing here, and I'd already sussed that the door didn't have a keyhole. I was about to leave when something pulled me back. It was unthinkable that Patrick would lead me this far and send me away empty-handed. There must be something I'd missed. I stuck my hand inside the pillowcases and threw aside the bedcovers. Then I patted the hollow mattress all over and towards the foot of the bed heard the faint scrunch of paper. My blood tingled. I reached my hand underneath, felt around and drew out a rolled-up newspaper. I checked the date. Eighteen days ago. I unrolled it carefully. The paper had been folded at the employment section and there was a job advert circled – LIFE-CHANGING OPPORTUNITY AT BENEDICT HOUSE. Harry was watching me intently, but I didn't move. My skin was prickling. At that moment Patrick felt so close, like when we played our game as children and he was just around the corner, waiting for me to find him. It was the strangest sensation. I collected myself and showed Harry.

'The advert stands out, doesn't it?' he said, frowning.

I looked to the ceiling for inspiration. 'I don't even know what or where Benedict House is. There isn't a contact phone number or even a job description.'

'It's a private house,' the woman piped up, 'possibly the oldest in the area. I'm surprised you haven't heard of it.'

'We're not that interested in ruins,' I said.

Harry shot me one of his looks. 'What can you tell us about it?' he asked politely.

She shook her head. 'Very little. I believe it used to be a manor house, but I thought it was derelict now.'

I scowled. 'Obviously not, if they're putting adverts in the paper.'

I tucked the newspaper under my arm and thanked her for her help. Harry and I walked back to the flat, the sun's afternoon rays burning our necks.

'We've come a long way,' I said. 'We now know where Patrick's working . . . all we have to do is go there and find him.'

'You're not going to just turn up at this . . . manor house?'

'Why not? Patrick's probably passed out somewhere and needs to recover. Maybe his employers don't realize he has family who'll be worried.'

Harry gave a poorly concealed sigh. 'Let's hope the trail ends there, Sinead.'

As we were walking he Googled Benedict House on his phone. 'There isn't much about it on the Internet. It dates from the eleventh century, and the Benedict family are mentioned in the Domesday Book. There's a bit here about the architecture. It's a jumble of different styles and later additions: Tudor, Elizabethan, Jacobean . . .'

I checked my phone messages. There was one from my mum insisting I come home to give her a progress report. I groaned. 'It's time to face the music.'

# Ten

Harry offered me a lift home and reluctantly I agreed. I slid into the front seat of his car, glum at the prospect of seeing my mother again. Harry tried to cheer me up but I wasn't in the mood for conversation. Every now and then he flicked a glance my way.

'Why do you keep rubbing your throat?' he asked.

I wasn't conscious of doing this, but as soon as he pointed it out I realized why. 'I had that nightmare again, the one where I'm choking and it feels like I'm dying. It was so real, worse than it's ever been.'

'It's all this stress over Patrick,' he said. 'Is there any point me telling you again to just stop?'

My reply was to burrow further into the seat. Harry didn't nag me. He'd made his feelings perfectly plain, but then so had I; my search wouldn't end until I found my brother. When we reached my house I heaved a sigh and flung open the passenger door. I walked up my front drive trying to dodge the cracks in the flags, the way I used to do. *If I don't step on a crack, Patrick will be happy and Mum and Dad might stop arguing. Maybe Mum will learn to love me.* Before I had time to insert my key the front door opened. My mother was standing on the doorstep bristling with expectation, her eyes slicing into me.

I held up both hands as if to deflect a blow. 'I've made progress, but it might take a bit more time.'

My mother stayed silent as I stepped inside, which I always found worse than being roared at. I walked into the living room and sat down in a chair, inhaling the scent of lemon polish. The room was spotless as usual, hardly homely, the wood sparkling like glass. I joined my hands in my lap, feeling like I was five again, in trouble for something. My mother remained standing, waiting for me to speak.

'I know how worried you are about Patrick and . . . I didn't want to tell you until I was sure but . . . I think he's playing our game, Mum, the one where I follow his footsteps.'

Her face immediately brightened. 'I remember how much you loved that game. Patrick was always so clever like that. And how close are you to reaching him?'

I was momentarily stunned. Mum was reacting as if all this was totally normal. I searched her face, but she only seemed interested in my answer. 'Well . . . Harry's been helping me and we know from one of Patrick's neighbours that he's been working, but she didn't know where. We think he might have been taken on at a place called Benedict House.'

'Benedict House?' she repeated.

'You know it?'

She pursed her lips and nodded slowly. 'The Benedicts were one of the oldest Catholic families in Britain.'

'Were?'

'I'm not sure they're resident any more. I heard the family broke up or even died out. They have some arrangement with the Church to take care of the estate.'

'What could Patrick be doing there?'

'I really don't know. The house is overgrown and crumbling . . . like the house that time forgot.'

I grimaced at this awful cliché, wondering if she was trying to annoy me, but she seemed strangely distracted. I wondered how we could be so different. I was tall and skinny with dark hair and olive skin; she was much shorter and quite stocky, with fair flyaway hair that seemed to frizz when she was angry. She always seemed to be angry when I was around, and today was no exception. I should have been used to it, but it still hurt.

Her mouth crimped. 'You'll go there and bring him home, Sinead.'

This wasn't a request but an order. Remembering my recent conversations with Harry I had a compulsion to put the record straight. But it wasn't easy. I'd never stood up to my mother over Patrick, and my heart was thudding violently. I cleared my throat and managed to hold her gaze without flinching, but my eyes widened nervously.

'This is the last time I'm . . . going to do this, Mum. I think Patrick needs to stand on his own two feet more and I need to . . . kind of . . . find my own life.'

'Find your own life?' she echoed with contempt. 'Life is about looking after family. If the situations were reversed, Patrick wouldn't abandon you.'

*But the situations aren't reversed, and Patrick is draining my life blood.*

'I'm not *abandoning* him,' I said, 'just trying to make him take more responsibility for himself.'

My mother switched to sweetness, her voice falsely cloying. 'You and Patrick were so close when you were children – everyone would comment on it. He loved you so much, Sinead, and he still does. I know he has his . . . *issues,* but remember how things used to be. Remember your golden childhood.'

I tried to recall this golden childhood. When Patrick was in a good mood everywhere appeared sunny and bright, full of dancing rainbow colours, but whenever his dark mood descended the world would instantly turn black. Seeing his features turn ugly and brooding always made me want to crawl under a stone and hide.

My mother sniffed. 'What's brought on this change of heart?'

'I'm feeling ill,' I answered. 'I think my asthma's come back.'

I don't know what made me say this because I rarely managed to get any sympathy for myself. My mother did a spectacular eye roll. 'It's all in your head, Sinead.' She muttered under her breath, 'Maybe it always was.'

I looked at her indignantly. She knew how deeply my breathing problems had affected me, but now she was making out it was all in my mind. *What's going on?* I was still wary of challenging her, but Harry had made me feel stronger and more determined to take control. I took a breath. 'What did you mean, Mum, *maybe it always was?*'

I saw a shadow of fear cloud her features. 'Nothing. It was just a slip of the tongue.'

I couldn't let this drop. Something wasn't right, but it felt as if I was wading through quicksand. I straightened my back. 'If my asthma was so trivial, then why did I always wake up choking? I still have nightmares about it.'

She pressed one hand against her brow. 'You're being as dramatic now as you were when you were little, making a crisis out of nothing.'

'It wasn't nothing to me, Mum. I remember slowly blacking out . . . my throat gurgling as I struggled to breathe . . . I knew what was happening; I knew I was dying.'

'Rubbish!' she snapped. 'You were too young to know anything of the sort.'

'Dad took me seriously,' I said quietly.

My mother's eyes fluttered violently and she swayed a little as if she felt faint. She usually tried this if she wasn't getting her own way, blaming it on her nerves, the heat or a sudden headache. Astonished that for once I'd out-manipulated her I stood and guided her into a chair, pretending concern. I even went into the kitchen to get her an aspirin and a glass of water.

She looked at me wanly. 'You've made me so out of sorts, Sinead, coming home and dredging up things from the past.'

I didn't bother pointing out that she had summoned me home. I still refused to let her off the hook. 'My asthma attacks?' I prompted.

She gave a small shudder and sipped the water suspiciously as if it had been poisoned. 'I barely remember . . . you were an incredibly wilful child. You could hold your breath until you turned blue.'

This was news to me. I glared at her, a deep frown scoring my forehead. 'But it can't have been deliberate, and I can't have been holding my breath. I was always asleep when it happened.'

She rubbed her thumbs on her temples, her expression pained. 'Whatever you think *might* have happened, you must remember that in childhood nothing is real. Every shadow and sound in your room becomes a monster trying to hurt you.'

My voice grew shriller. 'I don't *think* anything. I don't remember. I want you to tell me – you must know.'

'I know how it feels to be a mother,' she replied, her tone injured. 'I know about difficult choices and how you have to trust your instincts to protect your child. You'll be a mother yourself some day, Sinead, and then you might understand.'

*I'll never become a mother. I can't even imagine myself properly grown up, no matter how hard I try. I can't conjure any future for myself at all; I never have been able to.*

The doorbell rang and relief crossed my mother's face. I went to answer it. I was so shocked to see Sara that I gawped at her and couldn't say a word.

'Aren't you going to invite me in?' she asked.

I took Sara into the kitchen and motioned to her to sit at the table. I boiled the kettle and groaned inwardly, already sensing an atmosphere. I was no good at this suppressed-tension/walking-on-eggshells thing that other girls seemed to do so well. Boys just came right out and said why they were pissed off with you. I placed a cup of coffee on the kitchen table, making sure to use a coaster and wipe the drips from the spoon to stop my mother going ballistic. I noticed that Sara was dressed up. She was wearing a fitted floral dress that suited her curvy figure, and cork sandals with wedge heels. Her face was made up as well, smoky grey eyes and shiny lips.

'You look really great. I love that dress,' I said, hoping that compliments would cover the fact that our friendship seemed to have waned. 'Are you going out tonight?'

'I'm meeting some of the girls from school; I thought you might join us.'

I wrinkled my nose with regret. 'It isn't a good time right now. There's stuff going on at home . . . Mum's upset –'

I waited for Sara to ask why but she didn't. She looked at me closely. 'No one's seen you for weeks, Sinead. It's like you've cut yourself off.'

I gave a tight smile. 'I've just been busy, you know me, so much to do and never enough hours in a day.'

'So you're not avoiding us? Some of the girls think you're being really . . . standoffish.'

Her tone had a definite edge and my face grew hot. 'I am not standoffish. I've a lot on at the moment, stuff I can't get out of.' Her sceptical glance made me defensive. 'Besides, it's not as if I won't see everyone again. Most people are staying on at school.'

Sara carefully put down her cup. 'Not everyone.'

Our kitchen was stifling and I picked up a place mat and fanned myself. 'Why? Who's leaving?'

She looked at me so strangely that I cringed inside. She seemed angry, let down and sad, all at the same time. 'Me, Sinead – I'm not coming back to school.'

'Don't be daft,' I answered, now confused.

'I'm going to college to do a vocational course in social care.'

'But . . . why didn't you tell me?'

Sara began counting on her fingers in a really sarcastic way. 'Well, I texted you six times and called you five times, but you were always too busy, always desperately rushing somewhere.'

'If you'd just explained why –'

'I wanted to tell you face to face.'

Something stuck in my throat; Sara was so angry with me and school wouldn't be the same without her. And now I had to confront my fear that this really was the end of the road for our friendship.

'I'm really happy for you,' I muttered. 'I just didn't see it coming.'

Sara shook her head at me in a way that implied I was beyond hope. 'You never see what's under your nose, Sinead; you're just too busy steamrolling your way through life, trampling everyone in your path to save time . . . but you don't know what for.'

I tried to laugh this off but it was difficult because she sounded so final. 'Surely I'm not that bad?'

Her voice was dangerously low. 'What about the way you treat Harry?'

Guilty feelings stirred inside me but I chose to ignore them. 'What about Harry?'

Sara rummaged in her bag. I think she was inventing an excuse not to look at me. 'Everyone knows how he feels about you . . . and how you just string him along.'

'He's a big boy now, Sara, and makes his own decisions. Anyway . . . he's a good friend and I really care about him.'

'Not the way he cares about you,' she answered pointedly. 'You should let him go, Sinead, so he can find someone who –'

She stopped abruptly and my eyes went wide as the

penny dropped. Finally I understood the tension that was always present when Sara was around Harry and me. She resented my relationship with him because she wanted him for herself, but why did she wait until now to let me know? Until she was ready to dump me?

'Is that what this is about, Sara? You like Harry?'

Her face momentarily lit up but she quickly put her head down. 'I just don't like to see him used –'

Guilty feelings rose inside me. 'I've never encouraged him . . . and . . . I'm sorry if you're jealous.'

'I'm not jealous,' she answered, taking out her compact and rubbing more lip gloss expertly on her lips. 'I actually feel . . . sorry for you. You're going to end up isolated and really lonely.'

I didn't want her to see how much she was getting to me. 'I'm sorry I let you down,' I said sarcastically. 'Sorry I'm not a better friend, sorry I have the emotional range of an android, but I've been busy with Patrick . . . He isn't the easiest person . . . and now he's –'

'There you go again.' Sara got up, slinging her bag over one shoulder in a way that told me she wanted to end the conversation and was determined to have the last word. 'Patrick is always your excuse.'

'Excuse for what?' I asked angrily.

'Excuse not to live.' She gave me one last crushing glance before she walked out of my house and left me staring at the wall.

# Eleven

Harry picked me up just before midday to take me to Benedict House. As he drove I studied his profile, Sara's words still in the back of my mind. The weird thing was he seemed especially attractive today and I feared this might be because I knew Sara wanted him. The decent thing would be to tell him once and for all not to waste his time hoping for romance between us, but something prevented me from being honest. Only five miles from the city were fields filled with corn as tall as a child, jaunty scarecrows and Lilliput houses with doorways that would barely come up to my chin. I even saw a sign for an old forge and a museum of farm vehicles, which couldn't have been the most exciting attraction in the world.

'What do you know about manor houses?' I asked Harry.

'Er . . . not much. Only that the rich landowner or squire would live in the big house and the peasants in his cottages.'

'And he owned them . . . body and soul.'

'Guess so. In the case of the lord of the manor, he owned the whole village.'

'Don't you think it's bizarre these places have still survived?'

He shrugged. 'Thought you said it belonged to the Church now?'

'According to my mother.' I chewed my lip. 'I can't see any sign of it.'

'Does it even exist?' Harry asked in a spooky voice.

'It's here somewhere,' I replied. 'The village has only one road. They can't hide a giant crumbling ruin.'

Harry made a sudden noise, did a sharp U-turn and abruptly stopped the car.

'They can,' he said, staring ahead in amazement. 'They can hide it behind these.'

The wooden gates were at least three metres high. They were joined together by a thick chain threaded through circular metal handles and fastened with an impressive padlock. On either side was an irregular stone wall extending as far as the eye could see. It must have encompassed the whole estate. Trees and foliage of every description covered the perimeter, their branches hanging down to the pavement, in some places causing the wall to bulge.

'Wow,' he breathed. 'And what are those freaky stone things on top of the gateposts? They look like an eagle's head with a lion's body.'

'They're griffins,' I muttered. 'Mythical creatures

renowned for guarding priceless treasures or . . . protecting from evil.'

'Fascinating,' Harry said, with an oblique glance in my direction. 'There's no bell or intercom. What'll we do?'

I got out of the car feeling daunted by the formidable entrance. Annoyed, I yanked the chain and my hand was immediately stained with thick yellow rust. I looked back at Harry, who shrugged and pulled a face as if to say *don't ask me*. Cautiously I pulled one of the gates towards me and had my first glimpse of the grounds. Immediately inside the entrance was a tiny gatehouse with semicircular clay roof tiles, which reminded me of the gingerbread house in 'Hansel and Gretel'. The chain was long and there was a gap, large enough for me to squeeze through. Harry wound down his window and I went back to the car.

'I'm going in,' I said.

'You can't just wander in there, Sinead.'

'I'll be fine,' I said, too brightly.

Harry shook his head emphatically. 'I'll find somewhere to park and come with you.'

'It's OK, really. I'll just go and ask about Patrick. I won't be long.'

Harry thought about this for a few seconds, still undecided. He took out his mobile and laid it on the dashboard. 'Keep your phone on. Call me if you need me.'

Quickly I wedged my legs and feet through the gap followed by my shoulders and head, for once glad I was so skinny. I stiffened, expecting alarm bells to sound or an irate gatekeeper to appear, but the place was so quiet it was unearthly. *The house that time forgot.* I was acting more confident than I felt. The moment my feet began to walk along the path, a chill ran through me and I rubbed my arms as goosebumps appeared. I didn't dare turn around in case I lost my nerve, so I concentrated on putting one foot in front of the other and listening for the sound of guard dogs.

The path was in shade from the wildly overgrown trees, but shafts of sunlight would intermittently burst through, making me blink as though someone was flashing a torch into my eyes. I jumped as something registered in my peripheral vision. There was a face staring at me, pale and ethereal, but it was only a statue of a woman dressed in classical robes. She was sculpted in a pose of distress, one hand on her forehead, the other held out in a plea to someone. I smiled at myself for being frightened by a lump of stone.

The path weaved and I crossed a cattle grid, but there was still no sign of life. I could barely differentiate between a prize rose and a dying weed but everywhere was in full bloom and the fragrance heady and musky, so strong it almost choked me. But then the air seemed to grow danker and there were clouds of hovering midges that were impossible to avoid. I shuddered as they stuck to my face and caught in my hair.

As I walked I couldn't stop thinking about what I'd say to Patrick if he was here. The fact that he was still playing his game made me so angry I almost didn't want to find him. I was also worried about what to ask his employers. I didn't want to get him in trouble, but he had to realize how much he'd scared Mum and me. I trudged on, feeling as if I'd already covered half a mile. As I rounded a blind corner Benedict House materialized, still a way in the distance but visible in all its glory. It took my breath away.

The house was perfectly proportioned and symmetrical, the old red bricks warmed by the sun. There were at least twelve chimneys reaching to the sky, as straight as arrows. My pace quickened. Close up the house was even more impressive, the entrance jutting out like a castle keep and the long elegant windows made up of leaded panes. Two of them had a small Juliet balcony. I was so busy staring at the facade that I didn't notice the stooped, dark-robed figure that seemed to have appeared from nowhere. My hand flew up to my mouth and I lost my footing, stumbling backwards. As if the black habit and extra-wide wimple weren't scary enough, looking into her face was like peering into a skull. I'd never seen anyone so cadaverous; her eye sockets were little more than black holes, her flesh shrivelled. The thick dark material of her habit reached the ground, which gave her a strange impression of weightlessness.

'I'm sorry to bother you,' I blurted. 'I'm looking for my brother Patrick. I think he might be working at Benedict House.'

She seemed reluctant to speak and stared at me with strange black eyes that looked overlaid by an opaque centre.

I was just reaching into my pocket to show her the photo of Patrick when something on the ground caught my attention. I bent down and picked up a silver Saint Christopher medal, running my thumb across the engraved image. It was Patrick's, I was certain. My mother had given it to him to keep him safe on any journey, and he always wore it. My spine tingled. I hadn't expected to find him so soon.

'My brother Patrick?' I repeated. 'He replied to your job advert.'

She might have knitted her brow, although the pattern of deep furrows made it difficult to tell. 'I don't know what you mean,' she replied stiffly. 'We never advertise.'

Liar, I thought. 'But you've taken on new staff?'

'We have had no new workers here. You should go. Leave by the path that brought you here – the grounds are not safe for strangers.'

I stared at her mutinously, furious at being dismissed like this. I made a decision to ignore her. I began to head towards the house, but her voice stopped me in my tracks.

'How did you get in without an invitation?'

*What did she mean by an invitation?*

'The gate was . . . sort of open,' I lied, and then lied some more. 'I . . . erm . . . knocked at the gatehouse, but no one answered.'

'You shouldn't have come, it must be a mistake –'

She suddenly froze and put one hand across her heart, her breathing alarmingly shallow. I wondered what could have affected her so badly. She moved closer, and I had to stop myself from flinching. One of her bony hands touched me, but it was in a strange patting gesture, as if she was checking I was actually flesh and blood. She muttered something to herself, which I strained to hear. 'If the house has chosen you to stay, then it's out of my hands. But why now, after all this time?'

My stomach curdled and I wondered if Patrick had had the same reception. What had he got himself into this time? This place was so remote that anything could be going on. I decided to tackle her again, making sure my voice sounded confident.

'I know my brother came here. This is his Saint Christopher medal. He told his neighbours he'd recently started a job and I'm sure he answered your advert in the local paper.'

'Is that all?' she asked.

I couldn't help myself. I put my hands on my hips, half wishing Harry was here to restrain me. 'No, it isn't all. He left me . . . messages, some in Latin, but everything led me here. There's no mistake. This is where Patrick meant me to come.'

Her withered fingers interlaced. 'Then I believe you. The answers you're seeking must lie here.'

*'The answers you're seeking must lie here.' Why did she speak in riddles?* I narrowed my eyes. 'So where is my brother?'

'Only you can find him,' she answered, 'if you truly wish it.'

'Of course I want to find him, but where is he?'

'We can take you on for a trial period of fourteen days.'

I looked at her in horror. 'You expect me to work here?'

'For fourteen days,' she repeated, 'and then you'll have your answers.'

I made a noise of disbelief. 'You really think I'd agree to something like that? Give me one good reason why I should?'

'I recognize the hunger in your eyes,' she answered. 'You can't let this opportunity go. You'll do exactly what I ask of you – we both know it.'

This was so bizarre that I was rendered speechless, my mind racing with wild thoughts. I could phone Mum and tell her to call the police but it would be my word against that of a nun, albeit a seriously creepy nun. I opened my mouth to protest again but closed it, realizing I'd been backed into a corner. What other options did I have? If I refused, I'd have no other way to follow Patrick. She was right; I was hungry to find him and I couldn't let this go. But she wouldn't get the better of me. I'd agree to work here, but only to get my foot in the door so I could search for Patrick. I wasn't going to actually graft in some dusty old heap, and definitely not for fourteen days.

Although seething inside I tried to keep my face unemotional. 'OK . . . I agree to your terms.'

I waited for her to continue, but she didn't enlighten me further.

'What will I do here?'

'You will work for the good of the house.'

'And when—'

'Tomorrow, at ten,' she interjected before I could finish. 'You can call me Sister Catherine.'

'I'm Sinead.'

She scrutinized me for a moment. 'Remember you came of your own free will, Sinead.'

And then she walked away. I shivered involuntarily. Sister Catherine, my namesake, was a ghoulish nun who looked as if she'd been dead for several centuries. There was a sense of nightmarish unreality about all this, but how could I give up my search for Patrick when I was so close? Sister Catherine had promised me answers, and nuns didn't lie, did they? I twisted my nose stud, pondering the awfulness of my situation and cursing my brother.

I took a minute to look around. There didn't appear to be anyone else in the immediate vicinity, nor any vehicles. I was conscious of how long it had taken me to reach the house and how worried Harry would be. I tried to send him a text, but I had no signal. It seemed even more of a slog on the way back, and when I reached the first bend the path forked. There was a choice between the winding, undulating one I'd come by, or a route which looked more direct. It must have been well trampled to stop the shrubs from encroaching.

The path was a normal width at the start, but within minutes it narrowed considerably and I had to consciously draw in my arms and make myself smaller. The plants and bushes had grown so tall that I couldn't see what was in front of me and my feet were tangled in greenery. I stubbed my toe on a stone and swore with pain, then picked up a stick and began to beat back the foliage which was scraping my face. I pushed my hair back from my sticky forehead and had to peel my vest top away from my skin. This felt like wading through a steamy jungle. It didn't make sense – the other path had been cold and dank, but this one seemed almost tropical. My vision began to swim. Water. There must be some special kind of pond, a type I'd never come across before, because there was steam rising and a gurgling noise like water echoing down a plughole.

I'd been completely obstinate in disregarding Sister Catherine's instruction to leave by the way I had come, but it was time to admit my mistake and retreat. I'd only wasted ten minutes or so. Soon I'd be in Harry's car, telling him the whole story. I pivoted and came face to face with a sea of giant triffids blocking my way. What had been a clear path minutes ago was now a wall of greenery. And it was so much denser and pricklier than what was in front of me; each stem, stalk and branch seemed to be interwoven and crossed with another, like a tangled mass of barbed wire. Panic sent pins and needles all over my body. There was no going back. I had to keep moving forward, realizing how stupid I'd been. I could be heading in any direction. I tried to call Harry but again failed to get a signal.

I lurched on, aware of a strange feeling behind, a sensation of something bearing down on me. A nervous glance over my shoulder revealed nothing but the same impenetrable jungle. I began to run, a frantic clumsy run that got me nowhere fast; it wasn't just leaves scratching my face, it was branches clawing my hair, stabbing my face, and brambles pulling and ripping my clothes. I fell and rolled, my hands instinctively protecting my head. I tried to scramble to my feet but thorns embedded themselves in my head, my hands, even my feet, tearing my flesh.

'Sinead! You're like a great clumsy giraffe crashing about in there. Come out now.'

There was hazy blue sky. The gates rose in front of me but I had no idea how I had got there. I managed to crawl through the gap and lay on the concrete staring up at the griffins. Harry's face loomed somewhere above me, but his features were rippling as if he was underwater. My throat was making a horrible gasping sound. Momentarily I was back in my bedroom, staring at my pink lampshade and wondering why I couldn't get my breath. Harry's hand held mine and there was a pulling sensation on my arm as he dragged me to a sitting position.

'They came alive,' I mumbled. 'Everything came alive.'

My vision began to clear, and Harry gave me an exasperated look. I stared at my hands and feet and then touched my head. There was no blood, no abrasions or any wounds that I could feel.

'Is my head all right? I mean, is it bleeding or . . . scratched?'

He looked puzzled. 'There isn't a mark on you.'

I examined my clothes. There weren't any rips in them, yet I could still feel both my flesh and my clothes being torn apart. I pulled up my T-shirt. The skin was perfectly smooth and unbroken.

'What made you turn back?' Harry asked.

My breath was still ragged and my chest heaving. A sob welled deep inside and I tried to swallow it.

'I didn't turn back, Harry. I reached the house . . . sorry I was so long. It took ages.'

He shook his head at me in bemusement. 'You really are weird, Sinead. You've only been gone for ten minutes. I barely had time to realize you weren't there.'

# Twelve

I clutched my head. What was happening to me? It was one thing to mistakenly see a figure outside Patrick's flat in the middle of the night, quite another to imagine being attacked and ripped apart by brambles. And what about the time issue? I was sure I had been gone for over an hour yet Harry claimed it was only ten minutes. A glance at my watch told me he was right. How could it be?

'Are you all right?' Harry asked with concern. 'You look a bit shaken.'

'I just . . . fell over a branch or something,' I muttered.

'What's it like in there? Have they seen Patrick?'

I self-consciously pulled at my earring. 'I didn't get a straight reply, but he's definitely been there.'

'How can you know?'

I wormed my hand into my pocket and took out the medal. 'I found this in the grounds. It's Patrick's Saint Christopher medal; I'd recognize it anywhere.'

Harry rubbed the three-day growth on his chin. 'Well, who did you speak to?'

I gave a nervous cough. 'The place is deserted and I only saw one person – a decrepit nun who was tight-lipped about giving up any information.'

'If you're so sure Patrick's been there, Sinead, we definitely should tell the police. Remember your time obsession? It's almost three weeks since he disappeared.'

This was the second time he'd suggested this. 'Go to the police and tell them what? How threatening does this sound – an elderly nun is holding my six-foot-two, nineteen-year-old brother prisoner?'

Harry ran one hand through his tangled hair. 'You're right. If he's there, it has to be willingly.'

His words suddenly made me remember something. 'That nun – Sister Catherine – muttered this weird stuff about me not having been invited to the house, and then she said, "Remember you came of your own free will, Sinead."'

'Why would she say that?'

I braced myself, already anticipating Harry's reaction. 'I don't know, but she said I could find the answers I wanted at Benedict House, if I . . . erm . . . worked there for fourteen days.'

Harry's eyes flared and he stared at me in total disbelief. 'Tell me you're joking?'

I threw my hands in the air. 'What other choice do I have? I thought you understood Patrick's game. His Saint

Christopher medal is obviously the next clue. Benedict House is where I have to be.'

Harry massaged his forehead. 'You're not safe out alone,' he complained.

I winced. 'You're right.'

'That probably explains the nun's comment. She doesn't want to be accused of exploiting you. It'll be slave labour for crap money.'

'It's the only way to find Patrick,' I said. 'I owe him this.'

Harry's voice rose in frustration. 'He wouldn't put himself in danger for you. His only brush with danger is falling down the stairs when he's wasted.'

My head was still throbbing and there was a catch in my voice. 'Patrick has chosen me to do this . . . and I wouldn't be able to live with myself if I didn't at least try.'

Harry tucked a stray strand of my hair behind my ear. 'You were never the saintly type, Sinead. Maybe staying in a converted chapel has got to you.'

I didn't pull away and his hand lingered on my cheek. 'Maybe it has,' I said absently. I took one last look at the massive gateway with its griffins.

Harry's eyes followed mine. 'When you were gone I found another website – the Ancient Houses of Britain. It says centuries ago the black sheep of the Benedict family went missing in mysterious circumstances. The story was . . . he promised his soul to the Devil after his death.'

'Of course he did,' I said dismissively.

'But the Devil tricked him and took him to hell early, Sinead. Thereafter the house lures people in and acts as judge, jury and executioner. The moans of the damned can still be heard today.'

'An urban legend,' I scoffed. 'Is that the best you can do?' I remained deliberately unimpressed. 'It'll take more than that to stop me going back.'

His mouth suddenly hardened. 'You don't know anything about these people.'

I waved aside his concerns. 'Mum said the house had been given over to the Church. Finding a nun in charge is quite normal. She's a bit snappy, but I'm sure she'll come round.' Harry still wasn't happy, but I was too tired to argue with him further. 'Can you take me back?' I asked. 'I'm desperate for a shower.'

I wanted to be alone, but after Harry had left I felt unsettled and mooched about the flat. A quick search on Google had done nothing to improve my mood. Hallucinations could be attributed to a whole host of conditions – bipolar disorder, schizophrenia, psychosis, seizures or a brain tumour, all of which I really didn't want to have. Something else was haunting me – Sara's final words to me. Did I use Patrick as an excuse not to do the things I wanted, an excuse not to live? I raced, dashed and hurtled through life, desperately trying to save every second without any idea why I was hoarding time. It wasn't a quirky habit any longer; it was more like an illness. I needed to be normal, to realize that I had many more tomorrows to look forward to.

The day had left me feeling so wiped out that I decided to rest on the sofa for five minutes. The last thing I expected was to doze. I woke with a start, unsure where I was and whether it was morning or evening. A glance at the clock told me it was almost five. I'd been out for almost three hours and had wasted so much of the day. Then I remembered my resolution. It wasn't wasted time; it was relaxing time, something that regular people did. I stretched and, for a second, had another sense of Patrick. I shouldn't be so worried that he was lost; he was somewhere near, trying to show me where to find him. If only I knew how.

*What are you trying to tell me, Patrick?*

On a balmy summer's evening like this, it would have been nice to climb the clock tower and look out over the city, but I couldn't face it alone. I moved towards the light. The view from the windows was still impressive. My eyes swam at the sea of colours, shapes and movement. Things were heightened in a city; the crush, the rush and volume increased tenfold. It was as if everyone had to wring every last minute from the day, make the most of each last drop of sun before it dimmed, in case it didn't rise again the next morning.

From this perspective the people ceased to exist; they were just pinpricks moving down below, but their lives seemed to clog my throat and my senses. I felt an ache somewhere deep inside for everyone I didn't know and would never meet and it was as though I could feel their emotions. My own life seemed inconsequential and transient, filled with hopes and dreams that would never be fulfilled. Then I realized that this was how Patrick had suffered, by feeling too much and seeing the beauty and the ugliness of the world, the hope and the despair.

A feeling of complete sadness swept over me and I held on to the window for support. I'd seen heaven and hell through Patrick's eyes and the sensation had left me reeling. I grabbed my bag, letting the door close behind me, and tumbled downstairs on to the street. Heat didn't dissipate in the city; it was retained by all the glass, concrete, brick and steel. It hit me like a wave. My feet pounded the pavement as I thought how easy it was to be invisible here; sometimes I found this comforting, but not tonight. Everyone seemed to know where they were going, but I was directionless.

I sat at a table by the window of the first cafe I found, ordered a glass of iced water and tried to remember who I was: my life had again taken on the semblance of a dream. Maybe the stuff that had happened at Benedict House was real and I was dreaming now. Patrick had studied philosophy and often rambled on about alternate realities. I always figured that his head was so messed up he saw things that weren't there, but maybe he saw things the rest of us missed.

I left the cafe and walked past an Italian restaurant,

still weighed down by my own sadness. I stopped dead outside. The beach boy was eating spaghetti with a girl – a different girl – and they were sharing the same strand and meeting in the middle. He wasn't just handsome, he was completely beautiful, and I didn't know how it had escaped me before. He took my breath away and made my aching loneliness worse. It seemed as if everyone had someone, and at that moment I was sure that someone was better than no one. It was easy to banish Sara's words from my mind. There was one person who understood me and liked me, warts and all. I don't know what he thought of my message, but he came, as I knew he would.

'I don't want to be alone tonight,' I told him.

Harry stepped inside and closed the door behind him.

# Thirteen

It was a perfect midsummer morning, with fat fluffy white clouds and a turquoise sky, the heat just beginning to rise. I set out in plenty of time, unsure how long it would take to cycle to Benedict House, but certain that Sister Catherine wouldn't appreciate me being late. It felt great to zip along winding country lanes, although the speed of some passing cars meant that I almost ended up in a hedgerow more than once. It was hard not to dwell on last night. Thinking about Harry brought a lump to my throat that simply wouldn't budge.

How could I have used him like that, and where would we go from here? We'd done nothing but kiss, which had been sweet and safe, but it hadn't exactly set my pulse racing. I'd slept more soundly than usual, although Harry had teased me about talking in my sleep and kicking him in the night. Waking enfolded in his arms had been nice, but now he thought that we were in a relationship. Meanwhile, my only distraction today was the prospect of being ordered about by an ancient nun who probably thought a woman's place was in the kitchen. But I had to find Patrick. I had to concentrate on this and nothing else.

The gates had been left unlocked, but they were difficult to open. They seemed top heavy, as if I was pushing against a resistant force. Either that or they were reluctant to admit me. Maybe this was part of the fourteen-day trial and I'd already failed. But if Sister Catherine thought I'd give up so easily she was mistaken. I used a shoulder-barge tactic and managed to create a space large enough for my bike to pass through. I was barely back in the saddle when the gates closed behind me as if the hinges were spring-loaded. I peered at the gingerbread house looking for an explanation, almost expecting to see a witch appear to lure me in with promises of candy.

*Get a grip, Sinead.*

The griffins appeared aloof today, as if they wouldn't even deign to look at me. I childishly blew them a raspberry and began to pedal. The path was rocky and every now and then a bump or a hole would jolt my bike and throw me forward, but I became used to weaving around them. I looked nervously for signs of movement but there wasn't a leaf stirring. The marble lady appeared to have turned her head slightly because I could see more of the smooth curve of her cheek, but I figured I was imagining it.

Sister Catherine was waiting by the entrance. She stared straight ahead, but didn't react until I got nearer and my tyres skidded on the loose stones.

'You're two minutes late,' she said coldly.

I dismounted and thrust out my chin, determined not to be intimidated.

'I'll show you your duties, Sinead.'

Sister Catherine's manner was irritatingly high-handed and I was tempted to rudely bob a curtsy, but I was dying to see inside the house. I followed her up the steps and over the threshold, the set of keys on her waistband jangling and her black robes billowing behind her like the sail of a pirate ship. It was the proportions of the interior that first struck me; the hallway was gigantic, with plaster columns reaching to the lofty ceiling and a sweeping staircase complete with threadbare red carpet and polished oak banister. Patrick would love it, was my first thought. It was very romantic, faded but opulent, and would have appealed to his love of decadence.

'Do the rest of your order live here?' I asked.

Sister Catherine held herself rigid. It was obvious she didn't like being questioned. 'I'm the guardian of the house,' she said. 'There are no others.'

I drew a circle with my hand. 'You live here all alone?'

Her lips thinned. 'Mrs Benedict, the last incumbent of the Benedict family, is still resident, and Squire James.'

So there was a squire. I had a sudden vision of a fifty-year-old man with mutton chop whiskers and florid cheeks, dressed in baggy breeches and a tweed waistcoat.

I frowned. 'But . . . doesn't the house belong to the Church now?'

'The house has always belonged to God,' she answered abruptly.

'And will I meet Mrs Benedict and Squire James?'

Her cloudy black eyes glinted. 'Mrs Benedict is infirm and does not receive visitors, but you will be able to meet the squire. He is home for good, I'm pleased to say.'

'He's been away?'

'In the wilderness,' she answered, with a pained expression. 'But he is in his rightful place now and the house will be prepared.'

I fidgeted with annoyance. Her words were completely obscure, as if she enjoyed baffling me. 'It'll be a manor house again?'

Her jaw was taut with tension. 'A foundation stone was blessed in the fifth century and in the twenty-first century we still embrace the Word and dedicate ourselves to the lost souls.'

*Well, that made perfect sense.* 'And what are my duties?'

'You'll be tasked to clean the house, Sinead, to restore it to its former glory.'

I grunted something unintelligible.

She paused and gave me a critical glance. 'Can you work with diligence, modesty and obedience?'

It was on the tip of my tongue to say that I didn't want to join a convent, and how immodest did she imagine I'd be, cleaning some filthy old mausoleum. Maybe I'd got this all wrong and she was confusing me with someone else.

Maybe she hadn't understood how serious this was, that Patrick was missing.

'My brother came to the house, Sister Catherine, didn't he?'

She pressed her lips together demurely. 'If he was invited.'

'Did you give him a trial too?'

'Every trial is different, Sinead.'

I clenched my teeth and tried again. 'What happened? When did he leave?'

'I have already told you that the answers are here for you.'

My frustration bubbled over. 'Patrick's missing,' I almost yelled, 'and he could be in trouble. Will you give me a straight answer?'

Nothing rattled Sister Catherine. She fingered the set of rosary beads threaded through her hands and bowed her head. 'In fourteen days you will know.'

I pushed my fingers into my hair. She was truly insane. I wasn't prepared to wait fourteen days for her to give me answers. I'd look for them myself. All I had to do was to give her the slip and I'd begin my search. I glared at her as she beckoned me to follow her through the magnificent hallway, down a long corridor and into a small room resembling a scullery. It was filled with a big enamel sink, various cleaning tools, a granite-topped washstand and an overhead clothes pulley. There was even an ancient mangle for wringing out clothes. To my right I could see a large kitchen with a worn quarry-tiled floor and scrubbed pine table. This had a definite feel of being the servants' quarters. I had a sudden vision of a cook, complete with mob cap and frilly white apron, kneading pastry to make a game pie for lots of fat lords and their pampered wives. Sister Catherine was so superior about everything that it was impossible to resist the urge to needle her again.

'You said the squire is home to stay. Is there a Mrs Squire?'

Sister Catherine didn't answer. She filled my arms with some of the cleaning materials and then beckoned me to follow her again. She led me to a vast room, open to the rafters, with a galleried landing and a hearth as big as most people's kitchens. The walls were half-panelled, painted in a soft green, the upper half papered in a leaf pattern in warm autumn colours. A long trestle table had seats for twelve people, the chairs upholstered in red velvet. The rest of the dark wood pieces could have been heirlooms or just from a junk shop; there was no way of knowing. The floor seemed to be made of dusty stone flags under a large moth-eaten rug. I examined the things I'd been given – carbolic soap, white vinegar, beeswax polish, squares of material, a wooden-handled broom and what appeared to be a real feather duster. There was already a ladder propped against the wall and I wondered if Sister Catherine had even heard of health and safety. I stifled a loud yawn and received a disapproving glance.

'So . . . where shall I start?'

She nodded. 'The windows. It's been a long time; you could let in some light.'

The windows were long and narrow but there were eight of them and sections of the leaded panes were concave and would have to be washed extra carefully. There was nothing to do but grit my teeth and begin. Sister Catherine watched me for a few seconds and then glided off. A minute later I saw her disappearing into the grounds. The ladder was light and strong with two reassuring safety catches, but I was instantly distracted by all the cobwebs, some as thick and opaque as a pair of stockings. The irony of all this hadn't escaped me. I had the staying power of a butterfly and the idea of engaging in dirty, laborious, time-consuming and mind-numbingly boring physical work was laughable to anyone who knew me. I once told Mum, who was a perfectionist and liked everything in our house just so, that cleaning was soul-destroying and I never intended to do any. In fact, thinking about it, this was one of the worst jobs anyone could have devised for me.

I decided to use the time to consider my plan of action. I'd done well in tracking Patrick so far; it shouldn't take long to discover what he was trying to show me next. I had the ornate key from the flat safely tucked away in my bag. Patrick had to have left it for a reason. It was a substantial key that I could see belonging in an imposing house like this – maybe there was something here that I was meant to discover.

I managed to wash four of the windows before Sister Catherine came to check up on me. My arms were already aching and my face was streaked with dirt and perspiration. I pretended not to notice her and pressed on, wondering if she'd have the manners to speak or just survey me like she was spying on some kind of skivvy. I blinked and she was gone, but every time I thought about exploring she seemed to reappear. A feeling of unreality swept over me again. I couldn't really be taking orders from a weird over-controlling nun, with nothing more than her word that after two weeks' slave labour she would tell me about Patrick.

I wiped my face on the bottom of my old T-shirt. My stomach was growling and I was parched. There was a small jug on a side table with two glasses beside it. I poured myself a drink. I gulped thirstily, but my tingling tongue immediately told me something wasn't right and I spat it back in the glass. There was no mistaking the taste – vinegar. I marched into the scullery, the glass in my hand, and turned on the dull limestone-mottled tap. It was stiff and heavy and the water took ages to run through the pipes as if it hadn't been used for a while. I let it flow for a few seconds, checked it was cold, and then sipped it. The taste was exactly the same. I was hot, bothered and now fuming. What was wrong with this stupid place?

When Sister Catherine appeared again I confronted her. 'There's something wrong with the water. It's rancid.'

She didn't respond but took hold of the spare glass and filled it to the top. She drank in one continuous stream while I looked on, feeling as if I was going mad. Was she part of Patrick's weird mind game? Maybe they were in this together. She shielded her eyes to assess my work so far and managed a tiny nod, which was probably her idea of praise. I went outside and took a minute to check my phone messages. There was a soppy one from Harry hoping I was OK and saying that he'd come round tonight because he missed me already. I felt guilty all over again.

I suddenly noticed the time and stared in disbelief. It was just before eleven, which meant I'd only been working for fifty minutes. With my phone nestled in the palm of my hand I began slowly counting, staring intently at the numbers in front of me. I reached sixty and took a deep breath, certain that nothing would happen, but the minute moved on. I repeated this again.

*What did you expect? It's impossible for time to slow down; it defies the laws of physics.*

It was only my perception of time that had altered. Even five-year-olds knew that time dragged when you were doing something boring. Interminable tasks made the day . . . well . . . interminable. Thankfully I'd brought a sandwich and sat on a bench in the sun, eating it greedily before scrunching up the wrapper to put in my pocket. Back inside the hallway I heard an odd noise and stopped in my tracks. It sounded like the softest voice, coming from somewhere close by. I strained to listen. It could have been a *shhh* sound or even someone sighing, but it was so faint I decided I had imagined it.

I was desperate to start my search, but Sister Catherine kept her vigil over me and made it impossible. I finished the windows and then opened the rusty tin of beeswax and scooped some on to a clean cloth. I rubbed it into the table in a circular movement. The wood was so dry that it took half the tin just to polish the table top, and the chairs had so much fancy fretwork that I was soon ready to scream. I worked for what seemed like an eternity, my mood growing uglier as my mind contemplated the enormity of the task ahead. There was the panelling to be washed down, the flagstone floor to be scrubbed using only soap flakes grated from the bar. The rug would have to be cleaned without the benefit of something normal like a vacuum cleaner and I'd probably be expected to climb the chimney to check for birds' nests.

The afternoon dragged in a way I never thought possible. My tongue stuck to the roof of my mouth as the heat increased. This was when I realized the truth of the situation – I'd never survive fourteen hours let alone fourteen days. Why allow myself to be tortured like this? Patrick had already made me suffer and stolen enough from me – especially my time. No matter how much I wanted to find him, I simply wasn't up to this. I'd thank Sister Catherine but say that the work wasn't for me. As if on cue, a black figure moved through the hallway, her voice a gravelly whisper.

'Squire James would like to meet you now, Sinead.'

# Fourteen

We stared at each other for what seemed like forever as my mind tried to make sense of what was in front of me. The beach boy. He was a vision, a beautiful strutting peacock versus my imitation of a scraggy crow. I self-consciously rearranged my spiky black hair, trying not to contemplate how awful I looked. Sister Catherine must have detected a certain tension in the air.

'Is everything all right, Master James?'

A firm hand gripped my arm and I was too stunned to shake it off.

'We'll just take a walk in the garden, Sister, straighten a few things out.'

He was so attractive it was criminal, and everything about him, from his slight swagger to the arrogant tilt of his chin, told me that he knew. He was wearing ordinary blue jeans and a V-necked white T-shirt, plus a pair of grey canvas laced pumps. Casual but still smart, yet I'd always prefer him as the beach boy.

He rounded on me, his gorgeous eyes blazing. 'Are you following me?'

'Me? You have to be joking. I've done everything to get as far away from you as possible, but here you are . . . popping up again.'

He stood back to survey me at arm's length. 'Was it you outside the restaurant last night?'

Damn. He *had* clocked me. 'Yes, I happened to be passing on my way home to cook dinner for my *boyfriend*.'

He jammed his tongue to the side of his mouth. 'Oh yeah, I remember. Shaggy?'

I winced for effect. 'His name is Harry, and he just isn't vain like you. Conceited guys are such a turn-off.'

He had the nerve to smirk.

'What are you doing here?' I asked coolly. 'Sister Catherine made me think you had some posh title.'

He seemed surprised. 'Benedict House is my family home. I was brought up here.' He smirked again. 'Don't worry about the title . . . just call me James.'

My mouth dropped open. He was actually revelling in being master of this ancient pile. Questions about Patrick were bubbling up in me, but I had to turn away, annoyed with myself for letting him get to me.

Out of the corner of my eye I saw him shake his head. 'How's it possible for anyone to exist with so much hate and anger inside?'

'It's surprisingly easy,' I answered with acid calm.

'I really want to understand you,' he went on. 'Fate

seems to have brought us together and I haven't got long . . . so . . . humour me.'

I was exhausted, emotionally and physically, a dangerous combination coupled with my incredibly short fuse. 'We can't all sail through life without a care in the world . . .'

My words wiped the smile off his face; he momentarily closed his eyes as if in pain. After a minute or so he looked at me again, his expression anguished. 'You're sure you know things about me . . . but it's not what you think.'

I looked at him with contempt. 'You own a classic sports car, date a different girl every week, like to be called Master – or sometimes Squire James – and the villagers probably bow and scrape to you.'

He took a step closer. 'The car is on hire and how many girls I date is my own business.'

I made a small noise of scorn. He moved closer still.

'No one bows and scrapes, and only Sister Catherine uses those stupid titles.' He pointed a finger to emphasize his words, but managed to jab my arm.

I froze. 'Did you just prod me?'

James shrugged, which made me even angrier. In retaliation I used the flat of my hand to give his shoulder a small push, but I must have caught him off balance. He went down like a house of cards and lay sprawled on the grass.

'Sorry,' I mumbled, moving to help him.

James studied something on the ground as he tried to

get his breath back. For the first time I noticed that he looked wan beneath the tan and there were dark circles beneath his eyes. Too much partying, I figured, remembering the stunning, high-maintenance girls he hung around with.

He scrambled to his feet and dusted himself off, trying to appear nonchalant. Eventually we had to look at each other. I nibbled my top lip and shifted from one foot to the other, waiting for him to start arguing again. Our eyes locked for what seemed like ages. I couldn't have looked away if my life depended on it. He began to smile ruefully and then to laugh. Despite my attempts to remain straight-faced, I had to join in.

'You're some sort of demon sent to make my life hell,' he said, looking me up and down in a way that made me shiver.

'Angel, you mean,' I corrected.

'With a mean right hook.'

'You should see me on a good day.'

'I'd like that.'

I had to turn away again because he was having such an effect on me. *Stop ogling him, Sinead. He flirts with every girl he meets. Ask him about weird Sister Catherine. For goodness sake ask him about Patrick – that's why you're here.*

'Thanks for not ratting on me to Sister Catherine,' I said. 'I . . . need this job . . . Have you seen any other new workers around?'

'I've barely had time to unpack and visit my gran,' he

replied. He saw my look of puzzlement. 'I don't live here any more. I'm visiting from Australia . . . only arrived this morning.'

'Hold on . . . I saw you three days ago, at the police station.'

'I've been staying in a city hostel with a friend who's backpacking for a year. It might be the last chance I'll get to see him . . . for a while . . . so I delayed coming to Benedict House.'

'And . . . when did you leave?' I asked.

'Mum and I emigrated when I was ten. I haven't been back since.'

I sighed, and blew my fringe into the air, inexplicably frustrated. James had only just returned after years of being away, but he still must know things about the set-up here. 'Do you know Sister Catherine well? Has she been here long?'

James shrugged. 'Gran thinks Sister Catherine's always been around, but she wasn't here when I was a kid.'

'She describes herself as some kind of guardian,' I said. 'More like a weird sentry.'

'She does seem a little *eccentric*,' James said tactfully. 'I've already noticed her endlessly circling the grounds.'

I didn't want to arouse suspicion by firing too many questions at him so I tried to soften my tone and almost managed to fluff my hair. 'I've heard the house belongs to the Church.'

James nodded. 'Benedict House has always had some

kind of codicil, which means control reverts to the Church when . . . I mean, if the Benedict line dies.'

'You're a Benedict,' I pointed out.

His eyes looked sorrowful again. 'But I'm not staying –'

I tried to hide my disappointment. 'Sister Catherine said you were home for good.'

He shrugged. 'She must be confused. Gran wrote and invited me to visit, but I'm only here for another fortnight.'

'So this is just a holiday?'

James's face settled into tired creases that made him look older. 'Kind of. There're things I need to do while I'm here, important things, but . . . my return flight's booked.'

There was a terrible ache somewhere deep inside me at the thought of James getting on a plane. I had a mental picture of him, rucksack slung across one shoulder, walking across the hot runway with the sun on his face, then up the steps without a backward glance, leaving me to watch the plane soar into the summer sky and away to the other side of the world.

'Fourteen days,' I said suddenly. 'That makes sense.'

'Why?'

I sighed. 'I'm on a fourteen-day trial to clean the house. It's probably for you.'

He scowled. 'Hope it's not some awful leaving party.'

It could have been the exertions of the day or the fierce sun or the thought of James leaving, but a terrible weakness seemed to wash over me and wavy lines swam before my eyes. I murmured that I didn't feel well and lurched over towards my bike, which was still propped against the side wall where I'd left it. My hands rested against the bricks but my body involuntarily slid down until I was sitting on the gravel. The sun didn't reach here and I welcomed the shade. I blinked to restore my vision but my eyes were dry and gritty.

'What's Sister Catherine done to you?' James called over. 'You're absolutely destroyed.'

He must have followed me, because in another few seconds he was standing before me, an indistinct blur. He offered something to me and my parched lips closed with relief around a bottle of water.

After I had drunk deeply I said, 'There's something wrong with the water supply here. It tastes horrible.'

'Really?' he answered, frowning.

*Was I the only one who could taste vinegar in the water? That didn't make sense, but then nothing here did.*

My legs were inelegantly splayed on the ground and I closed them, suddenly conscious of my tomboyish behaviour. James held out one hand and hauled me to my feet. 'Come on. I'll run you home.'

'Thanks,' I said grudgingly. 'I'll pick up my bike tomorrow.'

I would have to come back after all, but that didn't seem so bad now. The red sports car was parked around the back of the house, which was new territory to me. As I looked into the distance at the continuing line of woodland I gained some idea of how vast the estate was.

'Does that wall run right the way around?' I asked.

'Yeah . . . the locals call it the wooded wall.'

'And it keeps the peasants out.' I pressed my lips together to conceal a smile.

The door of the car was opened for me and I tried to slide gracefully inside but being tall couldn't manage this at all. I ducked, but still managed to bang my head, and my legs were jammed inside, my knees almost reaching my chest. The horrible image popped into my mind of Patrick, who used to capture daddy-long-legs and squash them into matchboxes. James must have realized my problem because he rolled the soft top down, but I felt so exposed that I shrank into myself, like a snail looking for its shell. I'd never been in a sports car before, let alone one this old, and the sensation was strange. We were so low down that the undercarriage seemed to be trailing on the ground. James reached the monstrous gates and jumped out to open them. He made sure to lock them again. As we turned on to the village road, he pointed to a fountain of ivy cascading down the ancient bricks.

'There's a hidden door beneath there,' he said. 'Sister Catherine likes to keep the main gates closed, but it's easy to find. Just keep walking until you see the first sign for the public footpath.'

I nodded and closed my eyes. It was impossible to talk above the roar of the engine until we reached the city and the volume of traffic slowed us down. My head felt as if it had been through a spin dryer. I took a minute to compose myself and then tried to pump James for more information.

'Has the house changed since you went away?'

He nodded, slamming on his brakes at the last minute, inches from a blue van. 'It's much more run-down and shabby, but there're structural problems too. The west wing's almost fallen down and is off limits.'

'A website said the house has been around since the eleventh century.'

He nodded. 'That's true, but the estate's been enclosed since the fifth century. The house was first a church . . . well, not the whole house obviously.'

My pulse began to race. *The house was first a church.* Just like Patrick's note; *The first church – gateway to a place of penance.* This must have been why Sister Catherine insisted the house had always belonged to God. I gave James a sidelong glance. He had grown up at Benedict House. Should I tell him about Patrick's disappearance and the strange deal I'd been forced to make with Sister Catherine? But I didn't know him enough to trust him and could only imagine how crazy I'd sound.

There was a moment's silence and James said defensively, 'This Master James thing . . . I was never a spoilt brat when I lived at Benedict House – ask anyone in the village – and I never wanted to be the squire like my dad.'

'I never imagined you to be a spoilt brat.'

'It's written all over your face.'

I grinned. 'I didn't realize I was so expressive . . . By the way, where is your dad?'

James took a sudden interest in wrestling with an ancient radio and didn't answer. I reclined in my seat and gazed longingly at the plush 4x4 next to us with enormous tyres and elevated seats. The driver was staring back at me and it struck me that everyone gawped at a classic sports car. But I didn't have the hair, face or attitude to fit the image. No wonder James usually dated small blondes.

'It's just here,' I said as the chapel came into view.

James looked at the building and then at me. The raised eyebrows conveyed an unmistakable message – I was hardly starving in a garret somewhere.

'Thanks for the lift.' My voice was nonchalant.

I tried to open the car door but it refused to budge and I wondered if it was locked. James reached across me to tug at the handle and I immediately stiffened. I suspected he might be deliberately taking his time, but I stared impassively straight ahead, my skin buzzing with the heat from him. My heart was beating so loudly I was sure he must be able to hear it. The door opened with a loud *clunk* but he still didn't move and neither did I. Time stopped again, but in a way I'd always dreamed about. I could hear the gentle rush of his breath, and feel his arm brushing against mine, making me tremble. He had only to turn his head fractionally and we would be face to face. My body didn't seem to belong to me any more; I couldn't stop myself inching forward, when I suddenly pictured

Harry's face with his crooked smile. I uncurled my long legs from the uncomfortable crouched position, breaking the moment. James shot back into his seat.

'Maybe I'll see you tomorrow, Sinead.'

I touched my hot cheek. 'Not if Sister Catherine has her way. She doesn't give me a free minute.'

'Time's short,' he said, and there was the sadness again.

I swallowed with difficulty, wondering if I'd finally met someone who understood. I slammed the car door and his right indicator blinked on and off as he tried to pull away into two lanes of traffic. I kept staring like a complete idiot until another car flashed him to go. His tyres squealed as he left the kerb.

# Fifteen

It had never taken me this long to get ready before, even for a party. I'd spent over an hour studying my reflection and choosing my clothes with extra care, knowing it was a waste of time. They would only get covered in dust and grime again. The hardest thing was not to appear to have gone to any effort at all, especially as Harry would be calling in a moment and might notice. I turned my cheek first one way and then the other to examine my face. Despite the exertions of yesterday and my even worse than usual sleep, I was amazingly bright-eyed. James was a strange mixture, I mused, peeling off one T-shirt to replace it with another just a little more fitted, even though I wasn't exactly curvy. Occasionally there was a kind of world-weariness about him that didn't match his carefree attitude. He'd been evasive about his dad as well, and made his trip sound like some kind of ordeal. What had he really come home for?

I looked at myself in the mirror. I wouldn't flirt with James any more, and he'd soon be gone from my life.

My only mission was to solve the mystery of Patrick's disappearance. James had unknowingly helped by telling me that Benedict House used to be a church. Today I'd make sure I found an opportunity to explore and try out the key. I wouldn't get sidetracked. But . . . I didn't want to look back once James had returned to Australia and wonder what it would have been like to kiss the beach boy with the easy smile and golden skin. I glanced out of the window and rapped my fingers on the sill. There was still no sign of Harry. He was usually on time.

The sound of the flat's bell made me jump. I pressed the door-release button and it was only seconds before Harry's footsteps echoed on the stairs. I'd barely unlocked the door clasp when he burst in, even more untidy than usual; his T-shirt was covered in oil and the bottoms of his jeans were black and torn where they trailed on the floor. I guessed he'd had car trouble.

'Have you broken down?' I asked, terrified that I wasn't going to be able to get to Benedict House.

'I had a problem getting started, but don't panic, my car's on a meter.' His face was unusually grave. 'You might not need it after you hear what I have to say.'

I opened my mouth to object, but Harry actually raised his voice at me. 'For once I want you to sit down and listen.'

I perched on Patrick's sofa with my hands between my knees. Harry obviously needed to sound off about something and he deserved some of my time, but my eyes were continually drawn to my watch.

He paced back and forth across the rug. 'Things are different now, Sinead . . . I have more of a right to be worried about you –'

He must be referring to the night we spent together, which made me squirm.

'You already know my opinion about this *quest* you think you're on to find Patrick.'

He was now managing to sound like my dad, but I listened meekly. 'I couldn't get any sense out of you last night. I'm worried all this stress is making you a bit . . .'

'Crazy?' I suggested helpfully.

'You're crazy for agreeing to work at that place,' he said. 'Did you see any sign of Patrick yesterday or any more of his stupid clues?'

I held up a hand in protest. 'I discovered lots of useful stuff – Benedict House was first a church, which echoes Patrick's message. Mrs Benedict views Sister Catherine as some kind of permanent guardian of the estate and the house will pass to the Church again when the Benedict line dies out.'

Harry didn't react.

'Can we leave now?' I asked.

He shook his head and looked at me pointedly. 'I've been doing some research of my own.' He took a folded piece of paper out of his pocket and carefully smoothed it open. 'Station Island has another name: *Saint Patrick's Purgatory*. Does that mean anything to you?'

I pursed my lips. 'I remember my mum telling me

purgatory is that halfway place between heaven and hell where you kind of . . . wait to be redeemed. She thinks it's full of pain, torture and repentance.'

'Patrick's so conceited,' Harry said. 'I thought it might mean something else.'

I tapped a front tooth with one finger. 'Like the other clues, it connects with the afterlife, but . . . Patrick did tell me, in one of his depressed moments . . . his addiction felt like purgatory. Maybe that's another piece of the puzzle.'

Harry handed the paper to me and I saw that he'd highlighted a few lines of text. I read it aloud:

'"In the fifth century after Saint Patrick was shown the cave and the image of hell, other people followed his footsteps . . ."' Remembering Patrick's game, I stopped, then hurried on. '"These people, penitents they were called, would prepare for fourteen days and on the fifteenth day descend underground for their souls to be judged.'

I sensed that Harry hadn't taken his eyes off me for a second. I looked up warily, knowing what he was about to say.

'Sister Catherine asked you to work Benedict House for fourteen days, Sinead! Isn't that weird?'

It *was* weird, and my throat tightened, but I shook off the uneasy feeling. The fourteen-day trial had something to do with James. It was too much of a coincidence otherwise. I stayed perfectly calm, knowing that Harry was still looking for a reason to stop me going back there. 'The only significance of any of this,' I said, 'is what it tells me about Patrick's game.'

Harry shook his head in disagreement. 'I think you're out of your depth, Sinead, and deep down you know it. You said yourself something's wrong about this whole Patrick-going-missing thing. This time is different from the others.'

I kept my voice quietly monotone. 'I grew up with religious superstition and narrow-mindedness – Patrick's attempts to frighten me with tales of an abyss or fathomless pit. That's what I'm trying to escape from.'

Harry looked through me as if I wasn't there. 'I'm worried Patrick's going to drag you down into an abyss of his own.'

'Then don't desert me, Harry. Stick with me while I find the answers and break free.'

He still looked angry, but I devoured the rest of the text, hopeful I'd won him round. 'It says here that time in purgatory is meaningless, one second can feel like a hundred years. That echoes Patrick's message too. And Saint Patrick and the Benedict estate both date from the fifth century.' I bounced to my feet. 'We can talk in the car.'

Harry refused to move, his bottom lip pushed out. 'I don't want you to go back there . . . In fact, I'm not going to take you.'

I hadn't bargained on Harry being so strong, and he went up in my estimation. There was something else I knew about him – he was easy to manipulate.

'I have to go back and fetch my bike at least.'

'Promise that's all you'll do – fetch your bike and get out of there.'

'I'll get out as soon as I can,' I said, not committing myself. I steered him towards the door and picked up my bag, which contained supplies for the day – a huge bottle of water, tuna sandwiches, a couple of energy bars and fruit, plus some rubber gloves because my hands were already like sandpaper. Harry didn't protest again.

The heat was intense. In fact it was hard to remember what cold felt like, and there were already warnings of a hosepipe ban. Dad used to talk about the endless summers of his childhood, when the tar bubbled on the roads and he spent all day at the seaside searching for crabs and starfish in rock pools. I had always felt envious when he reminisced like that. Did passing time make everything seem rosier? The roads weren't bubbling yet, but urgent warnings had been issued on the TV and in newspapers about the dangers of the heatwave. Harry's car had no air conditioning and some of the windows didn't open. It was like being inside a microwave. I made a tired noise, wriggling into the seat and pretending to doze. I was worried that Harry would refuse to take me all the way there. I'd seen no buses and imagined that even if there were any then they'd only run about once a day. We reached the outskirts of the village before I stirred, gave a languorous stretch and stole a glance at Harry's grim profile.

'Why so miserable?' I asked.

His hands gripped the steering wheel tightly. 'Explain to me again exactly what that nun said?'

'I've told you before. Sister Catherine made it clear she knows what I'm looking for and I'll find answers to the mystery of Patrick's disappearance at the house.'

Harry took his eyes from the road for a second. 'As I was driving it occurred to me there's another possibility.'

'What?'

'This is not really about Patrick at all. What if you're really a target, Sinead? It's all set up for you.'

I laughed and shook my head. 'What do you mean?'

Harry stared straight ahead, unblinking. I knew how difficult I could be, but he was way off mark. 'This has nothing to do with me,' I said. 'Nothing in my family has ever been about me. Patrick is at the centre of everything.'

'He *might* be at the centre of it,' Harry said. 'He might be part of the plot to lure you to this weird house . . . the Latin clues and the picture on the wall, the cryptic advert in the newspaper and the Saint Christopher. What if Patrick isn't really missing at all but part of a ruse to entice you there?'

This made me pause for thought. Deep down I knew Patrick would have enjoyed turning our childhood game into something more sinister. It would be an added bonus if I was made to suffer in some way. But there was a definite flaw in Harry's idea.

'Why didn't something happen yesterday?' I demanded. 'How come I wasn't captured and locked up somewhere?'

'I don't know,' Harry replied, chewing his lip.

'Stop here. James showed me a secret entrance yesterday so I don't have to battle with those huge gates.'

The driver behind us honked his horn in annoyance and I resisted the urge to make a rude gesture.

'Who's James?' Harry asked.

'The son of the former squire,' I said. 'I mean, he doesn't have the title, although Sister Catherine insists on calling him Squire James and sometimes Master James . . . Didn't I tell you all this last night?'

'You fell asleep mid-sentence,' Harry reminded me.

I cringed and squeezed his hand. I couldn't remember what I'd told him. I was so exhausted last night that my mouth refused to work and all the words came out slurred. He'd offered to cook for me, but I'd awoken to find myself alone with a plate of cold macaroni cheese on the coffee table.

'It's the same guy we met in the police station and at the coffee shop,' I added. 'The one I had a go at.'

'That's a coincidence,' Harry said suspiciously, 'unless he's somehow involved.'

'Don't be silly. He's only staying a few weeks and then he flies back home to . . . the other side of the world.'

Harry digested this for a minute and it was impossible to tell what he was thinking. He must have sensed my impatience as I edged further towards the passenger door, one hand wrapped around the handle of my bag.

'Don't go, Sinead,' he said. 'I've got a bad feeling about this.'

'There's nothing to worry about,' I assured him.

'I think you should turn around. Walk away and forget Benedict House.'

I frowned. 'Why are you so adamant?'

'You seem to have changed,' he complained. 'In just one day.'

Harry wasn't as unobservant as I'd imagined; he'd felt the difference in me. The only thing I remembered about last night was that when he kissed me, I'd wished he was someone else – I'd wished he was James.

# Sixteen

'You can concentrate on the drawing room today, Sinead. Master James has expressed a wish that you work no more than six hours and take a proper lunch break.'

I swallowed hard because she looked me up and down with such contempt that I actually felt naked. Did she think I'd worked my charms on James just to get preferential treatment? Under her scrutiny I felt so dirty that I had a terrible urge to yell at her that I was still a virgin, but I didn't, and dutifully trailed after her.

'How's my trial going?' I asked.

'It's early days,' she replied noncommittally.

Harry's words were still buzzing in my head and I spoke before I'd had time to think. 'I suppose you must have heard the legend surrounding Benedict House.'

She froze and turned to me slowly. I was forced to examine her close up, her dried-up skin looking as though all the life had been squeezed from her, and her thin mouth just a slash in her shrivelled features.

Nerves made me babble. 'The one about the evil squire selling his soul to the Devil and how the house lures people in to judge them.'

After a lengthy, stomach-turning stare, she chose to answer. 'That's not the full legend, Sinead. People are not lured in, they are invited, but more importantly, they have a chance of redemption, an opportunity to save their soul.'

When her back was turned again I made a gruesomely comical face. On my first visit Sister Catherine had seemed shocked that I'd managed to get in without an invitation. Was she crazy enough to believe in the legend? I could see how Benedict House got its otherworldly reputation, but I was determined not to be spooked.

I trailed after Sister Catherine. The drawing room was more formal than the dining room, with many paintings, ornaments and a general air of ostentation. There were a number of wing chairs, two enormous sofas in green and cerise chenille, a gold and black lacquer screen and a small piano. The range of furniture was French style, high gloss with delicate bow legs, taller and more elegant than the heavy, squat furniture in the other room. The wallpaper was textured and decorated with peacock feathers; I felt as if hundreds of eyes were watching me.

Sister Catherine left me alone without any explanation of what she expected, although there was the usual array of cleaning materials as well as an additional jar of wax. The label gave instructions on how to seal a wooden floor. I looked down and baulked; the floor consisted of hundreds of tiny blocks of wood that fitted together like a jigsaw. Some were black with age, some cracked or chipped, but overall the effect was quite beautiful. I knew machines existed to polish and protect floors like this, but it was obvious I was supposed to tackle this one by hand. She seemed determined to make me suffer.

I waited until she had left and watched from the window as she began her tour of the grounds. Now was my chance. I took Patrick's key from my bag and darted in and out of rooms, checking all the doors, cringing at the general squalor and mustiness and noting an unpleasant scorched smell that lingered. I took a look in the scullery again, and the kitchen with its ancient Aga. In one corner there was a velvet curtain hanging from a brass rail. I swished it open and found a woodwormy door that looked as old as the house. My heart beat faster. With sweaty fingers I inserted the key, expecting to meet the usual resistance, but it fitted. My breath caught in my throat and I paused for a moment, feeling a definite sense of triumph. I was going to find Patrick on my second day. I turned the key shaft, but the lock wouldn't move. I jiggled it and then used both hands, hoping that brute force would work. Annoyed, I gave the door a kick and it bounced open. It hadn't even been locked.

Hesitantly I stepped into a narrow corridor. The floor sloped downward, the temperature growing colder as I descended. It was so dark I could barely see a few inches in front of me. My mind was feverish with thoughts of finding a jail, dungeon or torture chamber. I kept turning around, imagining I could feel fetid breath on the back of my neck. I stopped myself just in time before I ran into shelves of dusty old bottles of all shapes and sizes. This must be the wine store. It was a dead end. My shoulders slumped. I shouldn't have underestimated Patrick. This had been too obvious for him, not enough of a challenge.

I didn't dare venture upstairs and had no choice but to get back to work. The windows in the drawing room overlooked the rear of the house, with wooden shutters that folded back against the wall and rested on cushioned window seats built into the alcoves. This ceiling wasn't open to the rafters but lower and smooth except for the most incredibly detailed cornice and overblown plaster mouldings of grapes and flowers with massive petals. Brandishing the feather duster I climbed the ladder and tackled the chandelier, listening to the glass tinkle and having visions of it falling to the ground and smashing all over the floor like crushed ice.

It was thirty minutes before Sister Catherine made her next appearance. I tried hard to appear industrious and made a mental note of the time, thinking I could log her comings and goings.

'Everything OK?' I asked, and received a frosty look. She turned and left the room.

I listened carefully. Sister Catherine's footsteps stopped in the hallway. I poked my head out into the vast space. It was as if she had vanished. The fancy oak panelling ran along every wall, but I figured there had to be a disguised door somewhere. It was virtually compulsory in this type of dilapidated old house. I whistled softly to myself, thinking what to do. It was exactly twenty-one minutes before I heard her footsteps again.

It should be easy to find a concealed doorway, no matter how tightly it was fitted, but there were splits running down the entire series of panelling, which confused my eye. And the minutes were ticking by. Sister Catherine could return and realize that I was snooping. There might be steps behind the door to the cellar, and she would push me down them and leave me there. My spine prickled. *Those beneath the earth cry out for release.* I had visions of decomposing corpses, maggots wriggling out of the mouth and the eyes. Or she would be waiting for me when I opened the door, arms extended, ready to pounce and wrap her claw-like hands around my neck and strangle me.

What was the matter with me? Sister Catherine was a frail nun, and the only other person here apart from James was his sick gran. The hairs on the back of my neck rose; there was that noise again, a long mournful sigh. If I closed my eyes it was the strangest sound – hypnotic and mesmerizing. There was a draught wafting from somewhere as though the voice was being carried on the wind. I didn't want to listen to it and yet I didn't want it to stop. My hands felt along the wood panelling and one of my fingers grazed a small bump, a doorknob of the exact same hue, imperceptible except to the touch. The blood was pumping fast around my body, roaring in my ears like the sea. My hands were impossibly clammy and tiny beads of sweat broke out on my forehead.

Harry's words came back to me. *What if you're really a target, Sinead?* What better plan than to entice me in here of my own free will? But the door was such a temptation that I couldn't have backed down even if my life was in danger. I opened it and went through. There was a pull cord to my left which illuminated a cupboard measuring no more than two metres square. The panelling continued into here and it all looked very ordinary. On one side, coats and jackets hung on a series of large brass hooks, and on the other, shoes, walking boots and wellies filled a rickety rack. The floor appeared to be solid stone with no discernible trapdoors or hatches. It smelt damp and musty. Immediately in front of me was another door, made of honeyed pine. This made sense – a passageway to another part of the house. I looked for a keyhole and, failing to find one, rattled the handle. The door opened easily, but on to a solid wall. I made a noise of frustration and instinctively reached out to touch the bricks.

The sighing was getting louder now; in fact, it wasn't sighing, it was closer to whispering. I was sure I could almost make out words, and there were different voices and pitches – incessant, pleading and desperate, growing faster and more urgent until it felt as though they were inside my head. Was Harry right? Was I going crazy? I switched off the light and stepped back into the hall, trying to work out where the passageway must once have led. It looked as though the wall formed a buttress to a different part of the house. Following on was the west wing, which James had mentioned was out of bounds, almost ready to fall down. But James had been away for eight years and would believe anything he was told. And what better place to carry on something secret? I needed to get inside and take a look, but first I'd have to shake off Sister Catherine.

I took out my lunch and positioned myself outside on the same bench as the previous day. Sister Catherine brushed past me with complete disdain. It seemed to me that she never sat down, ate, relaxed or spoke unless it was absolutely necessary. I watched her as she began another journey around the grounds. She didn't look back, but my eyes doggedly followed her until she was lost inside the foliage. Then I ran around the back of the house to the west wing, where I was confronted by notices warning that it was unsafe to enter. It didn't take long to work out a possible way inside. The conservatory was in a sorry state, although I could envisage how beautiful it once had been, with its ornamental glass roof. The main structure was made of wood, but the timber had rotted and panes of glass were missing. When I peered inside it was like a tropical rainforest, with giant ferns, their leaves radiating outwards to form massive umbrellas, and vines strangling anything in their path. I carefully lifted one leg through the gap, feeling all around for shards of glass. The other leg quickly followed and I tried to find a space to stand upright. My hair was limp within seconds, my breath shallow. Moisture dripped from everywhere.

I covered my mouth and nose as the sweet, sickly scent of decaying vegetation grew stronger. There were waxy plants with leaves the size and shape of elephant ears, huge swaying blades of lofty grasses and beautiful orchids – notorious for being delicate – yet they'd survived in this abandoned place. As I shuffled forward, I nervously glanced around. My imagination was in overdrive again and images of killer plants, moving by stealth to surround me, clouded my judgement. My breath froze. Right in the centre was a bloated monstrosity with two curved petals open like the mouth of a carp, topped with a yellow and red bonnet of veined leaves surrounding the drooling lips. It had to be carnivorous. Beside it were five or six little replicas, looking up with expectant mouths as if hoping for leftovers. In my haste to get past, I nicked myself on a cactus spike and red spots dripped on to my T-shirt.

At the end of the conservatory was a set of double doors. They weren't closed and the jungle had begun to march through there as well. I couldn't wait to leave the humidity behind and I burst through the opening with a loud gasp. This room had been stripped of everything, but the glitter ball and sprung wooden floor gave me some clues – with fantastic light and elegant proportions, it must have once been the ballroom. I could almost hear the swishing of ladies' frocks, the sound of champagne corks popping and tinkling laughter. But the room was now infested with some kind of decay. Puffballs oozed from the ceiling, large sections of which had fallen down and lay smashed across the floor, soft like chalk. The plaster on the walls had also crumbled as the white fungus forced its way out. This room was being eaten from within. As I took a step back my foot slipped through a joist in the floor, scraping the skin around my ankle. The expensive sprung floor had disintegrated. I started to think I should have taken more notice of the warnings.

I reminded myself of the reason I was here – the entrance from the boot room. The corresponding wall was directly in front of me and there was no evidence of a doorway. I froze as another chunk of masonry fell, just missing me. I stared down at a smashed cherub, its rosebud mouth a gaping hole and its remaining curls looking like horns. I was worried that my movements had set off an avalanche and began to crawl slowly back towards the conservatory. Something distracted me. I was temporarily blinded as a light shone in my eye, the reflection off a tin box nestled in one corner. It was the only thing left in the room but it appeared temptingly bright and untarnished. I knew I should run but all I could think about was finding another of Patrick's clues.

Inch by inch I shuffled forward, the palms of my hands and my knees scraping the wooden floor, all the time listening for warning sounds of falling debris. I reached the box and crouched. The lid opened easily but it was empty, and I sighed with disappointment. A speck of colour flitted in front of my eyes and I blinked. It was a black and red insect with a barbed tail, its wings fluttering so fast that it made me think of a tiny fan. Its beady eyes focused on me. It hovered in front of my face and I instinctively swatted it away. Suddenly there were five of them, ten, twenty, an entire swarm, a red and black mass clouding my vision and in my hair and on my neck, crawling around my mouth. I tried to scream but there was one on my tongue, grazing the roof of my mouth. My throat began to gurgle and I knew that any minute I'd have to swallow.

And suddenly I was back in my room, in my nightmare, choking on the weight of my fear. The swirling darkness overcame me and there was no way I could fight against it. I was floating out of my body as my life ebbed away.

'Are you going to tell me why you're really here?' a voice demanded.

# Seventeen

'It was just a dragonfly, Sinead.'

'There was more than one of them,' I insisted, still gagging. 'They were all over me, even in my mouth.'

James tried to suppress a grin. 'There was one small insect and you were flapping about like you'd sat on a hornet's nest.'

'I want to get out of here,' I said, overcome with self-pity and embarrassment. I pushed my way back through the conservatory, puzzled that the plants didn't seem quite so overgrown or threatening now and even the man-eating flower looked smaller and harmless. I covered my head with my hands, wondering what was happening to my mind.

'Come on, let's walk,' he said. 'I'll square it with Sister Catherine.'

I followed him into the wood, grateful that the trees were closely planted and provided shade.

'You don't think it's weird,' I asked slowly, 'the

west wing being in ruins like that? It looks like it's been abandoned for at least a century.'

'Suppose,' James deliberated, 'but Gran says it's dry rot, and once that takes hold it spreads like wildfire . . . everything literally falls apart, crumbles into dust. You really shouldn't have been in there.' He turned and confronted me with a knowing smile. 'And? Will you tell me why you're really here? If you're not following me.'

'I told you, I need the job.'

'You're lying,' James said with complete confidence. 'You didn't even ask about the salary, and you don't look the type to take orders from Sister Catherine.'

He was right and my guilty face said everything.

I took a deep breath that hurt my lungs. 'OK, I'll come clean. It's my brother, Patrick. He hasn't been seen for a few weeks and everyone's really worried. He told his neighbours about getting a new job and he had a copy of the local paper with a circled advert for Benedict House.'

'So . . . you came here expecting to find him?'

I nodded. 'Sister Catherine hinted she knew something about him, but she won't tell me unless I agree to—'

'I can't believe she'd do that,' James cut in. 'Not when she knows how worried you are.'

I had to bite back anger. 'It's true. She keeps saying all this weird stuff about answers being revealed and how if I work here I'll find what I'm looking for.'

He shook his head incredulously. 'Why would she say

that, and why would you go along with her? You've no evidence Patrick's even been here.'

'I have. He left a kind of . . . trail for me to follow. I also found his medallion in the grounds.'

James still looked sceptical. 'Tell me about this trail.'

I was hot and bothered and my throat tickled horribly. 'We used to play a game when we were children. He'd leave me clues and I'd follow him to solve them. He's still doing it now. He's even left me a key and I have to find the door it fits.'

'OK . . . but Sister Catherine wouldn't get involved in childish stuff like that.'

'You don't actually know anything about her,' I burst out. 'She could have some kind of hold over your gran. I mean, why does your gran say she's always been around when she clearly hasn't?'

James suddenly hung his head. 'I didn't realize until I came back, but Gran . . . she forgets things and gets confused –' He shrugged, looking unhappy.

I winced. No wonder Sister Catherine had said Mrs Benedict didn't receive visitors. I threw James a sympathetic glance, not really knowing what to say.

'It's really sad,' he went on. 'She's fixated on the past and thinks my dad is still here, at the house.'

'And where is he?' I asked for the second time since I'd met him.

James looked away into the wood, his eyes remote. 'The truth is, I don't know. He walked out on Mum and me and hasn't been in contact since. That's why we emigrated. I came back here hoping Gran would be able to help, but . . . she can't and now I don't know where to look and I don't have much time –'

I felt sorry for James. He'd travelled from the other side of the world looking for answers and come up against a brick wall. I knew how that felt. His eyes looked glassy and he changed the subject. 'What was the job Sister Catherine advertised?'

I scrunched my face. 'It was vague . . . something about a life-changing opportunity. If Sister Catherine was counselling Patrick, it might make sense.'

'Counselling Patrick because . . . ?'

'He's an addict,' I replied, surprised how easily it rolled off my tongue. 'And he has other . . . psychological problems. Dad was always threatening to check him into rehab, and Sister Catherine made a pointed comment about lost souls –' I cringed, realizing how weird this sounded.

'I'm sorry about your brother, Sinead, but I can't see Sister Catherine putting up with messed-up teenagers.'

I grimaced. 'She's not exactly Mother Teresa, is she?'

We walked on in silence, but now that we'd talked it felt comfortable between us. Inside the trees' natural arbour the temperature was at least ten degrees cooler and I could breathe again.

'I missed it here,' James said unexpectedly.

'What? The sun and surf weren't a match for rainy old England?'

'Surprisingly, no,' he answered with touching honesty. 'I missed the rain most of all. Sometimes I'd wake in Melbourne in the blistering heat, convinced I was back here on a dewy morning, my shoes and socks wet and the wood smelling damp and earthy.'

'It must have been an idyllic childhood,' I said with envy.

He gazed into the distance. 'So I've been told, but . . . I wouldn't really know.'

I did an about-turn. 'You don't remember?'

He looked me straight in the eye, his mouth set firm. 'I have this blank . . . a dead part of my brain that I can't access, and only vague flashes of memory . . . but I don't even know if they're real.'

'James, that's awful,' I said. He looked so lost that I wanted to reach out to him. I had to ball my hands into fists to stop myself.

He sucked in a breath. 'It feels as if my life only began when I reached Australia. Mum's told me things about living at Benedict House, but . . . I can't connect with them.'

'Has your mum ever talked about returning together to help you . . . connect?'

James shook his head. 'She doesn't even know I'm here; she would have stopped me.'

'But . . . why didn't she want you to come back?'

'That's what I'm here to find out,' he said grimly. 'I'm eighteen now. I can make my own decisions and go wherever I choose.'

'And . . . you might come back someday?' I asked, hope blooming inside me.

'Never say never,' he quipped, and there was that sadness again. He leaned against a silver birch and picked a few tiny leaves from a lower stem. We hadn't walked very far but he was quite out of breath. I wondered if the humidity had got to him. I flopped on to a pile of pink blossom that still covered the ground. He did the same.

'You OK?'

He closed his eyes tightly, opened them wide and then repeated this twice more. 'Yeah. Sometimes I get dizzy ever since I had . . . glandular fever in the winter. It's made me a bit run-down.'

'Had your bloods checked?'

'Not lately,' he replied, with an enquiring lift of his eyebrows.

'My dad's a doctor,' I explained, 'but . . . I don't get to see him either.' I knelt up, pretended to roll up my non-existent sleeves and reached for his wrist. 'Wow, your pulse is slow! No wonder you feel faint.'

He grinned. 'It should be beating faster.'

I peered at his arm all the way past his elbow, taking in the scars, bruises and needle tracks. He saw where my eyes were drawn and flushed. 'I was ill already, picked up food poisoning and ended up in hospital.'

I knew enough about addicts to be almost certain he wasn't one, but something was odd, some of the needle marks looked years old. I gazed into his eyes to check that his pupils weren't dilated. How had I never noticed them before? I mean really noticed them – the beautiful shade of hazel reflected the surrounding wood and gave them an almost golden tinge. Something rose in my throat and stayed there. I couldn't move, blink or even breathe, but then neither did he, and one of us had to eventually break away. I briskly pulled the skin below his eyes as if nothing had passed between us. It was pale, almost white, instead of a healthy pink. Dad had told me this could be an indicator of anaemia.

'You really *should* get a blood test,' I said. 'You might be low on iron.'

James gave me a salute and rolled over on to his back, staring up at the thick branches, only a small patch of blue sky visible. I wanted to lean over and kiss him, so badly that it hurt. Another moment and his lips parted slightly, his eyes flickered and he was asleep, his breathing now soft and regular. With anybody else I might have felt slighted, but it was obvious that he was exhausted, probably still jet-lagged. It was hard to resist an urge to take out my phone and capture an image of him sleeping but I couldn't have faced Harry after such a betrayal.

I gazed around the wood just to be certain that no one was watching and then allowed myself to study every last detail of James's features. There was a scar above his beautifully formed upper lip and a tiny blemish on his chin. I took in the curve of his cheek and his sweeping brow; even his hairline was enthralling. If I'd stayed longer

I could have counted every pore and imperfection in his skin, each one of which was all the more touching because of his overwhelming beauty. If I pictured an angel in my mind's eyes it would be James, asleep in the remains of the spring blossom, facing up to heaven. And if I rearranged the petals and bunched them slightly together, they even resembled wings.

For once my mind wasn't frantically galloping ahead to something else or worrying about Patrick. I was perfectly happy to stay here watching James and thinking about the things he'd told me. He wasn't here for a holiday. He'd come back to Benedict House to try to find his dad and to regain some memory of his childhood. Every now and then he would twitch and his forehead crease as if with pain. I wanted to run my hand across it to iron out the furrows. He gave a little moan, his eyes fluttered open and he took a breath.

'The white knight. Even here I can't escape from him.'

'White knight?'

James rubbed his eyes with his fists. 'Just a stupid dream I have.' He raised himself to a sitting position. 'There's a guy dressed all in white with a red cross on his chest like a crusader or something. There's a dead hare lying next to him.'

'Sounds like a nightmare.'

He screwed up his mouth. 'Mum thought so too. She was so worried she even took me to the school counsellor.'

'And?'

He frowned. 'The dream only happened after we emigrated. The counsellor said the white knight was my dad, who'd turned into this kind of heroic figure because I idolized him . . . and the dead hare was a symbol of my loss because we were separated.'

'That's plausible.'

'But the dream is really disturbing without knowing why. The guy doesn't move or speak . . . just stares through me. It used to drive me crazy because sometimes it felt like a hazy memory more than a dream.'

I hugged my knees, feeling an immediate empathy with this. 'I had asthma. I still dream about the first time I couldn't breathe, when I was little . . . I thought I was dying.'

'How old were you?'

'Four . . . maybe five.'

'Tell me what happened,' James said simply.

I glanced at him and looked away, realizing I'd never even told Harry details of that night. I began hesitantly. 'I woke from a really deep sleep and knew something was different in my room . . . I stayed really still and then . . . I was fighting for breath –' My throat scratched again and I swallowed, remembering the sensation as the air was sucked from me and I lashed out with my fists. I stared down at the ground. 'The other day Mum hinted it had all been in my head.'

'I'm sure it wasn't,' he said.

I was about to remind him of my encounter with the

dragonflies, but I clamped my mouth shut. I didn't want James thinking I was borderline insane.

After a thoughtful silence he said, 'We seem to have a lot in common. We've discovered we're both looking for missing family and –' he laughed – 'we both have really bad dreams . . . maybe we can help each other.'

His words dragged me back to reality. Had I really just divulged my life story to someone I'd only known for two days? What was it about James that made him so easy to confide in? His suggestion lifted my spirits. Talking to Harry lately had become so confrontational; it would be good to have an ally, someone else who was stumbling around in the dark, just like me. I couldn't get my head around how strange it was that we'd ended up in the same place at the same time, both looking for answers. But I was still determined to keep my distance, so I shrugged nonchalantly.

'Tell me more about Patrick's clues,' he asked. 'If they're connected to Benedict House, I might be able to help.'

I took a crumpled piece of paper out of my pocket. I'd created my very own mind map of all Patrick's clues, the latest arrow connecting Benedict House to the first church. I'd also added Saint Patrick's Purgatory and the fifth century. Wary of his reaction, I also described the weird wall mural.

He didn't look at me as if I was crazy. 'You must think a lot of your brother to go through all this,' he said.

'I do,' I answered hesitantly, 'but this is a kind of

goodbye . . . I mean, goodbye to chasing after Patrick and looking out for him. I'm ready to let him go, if I can only solve his clues.'

After a few minutes James's forehead wrinkled. He repeated a few words to himself and then got to his feet. 'Will you come with me, Sinead?'

'Where to?'

'There's a temple I'd like to show you.'

He held out his hand and I took it. As our eyes locked all my good intentions flew out of the window. For one heart-stopping moment I would have followed him to the ends of the earth.

# Eighteen

We walked through the wood together, side by side, stumbling over tree roots and being hit by branches because the path was single file only. But I didn't complain because I didn't want James to let go of my hand.

'I thought it must have been demolished,' he said, his stride increasing. 'This used to be a clearing without anything blocking the view and the temple could be seen from the house. That's one thing I remember.'

I looked around, puzzled. These trees looked old to me and I wanted to ask James how they could have sprung up in the eight years he'd been away. But he was probably just mistaken. He had left as a boy and returned as a man, so everything would be distorted in his eyes. He stopped dead and I did the same, my gaze following his. I could just make out the impressive grey slabs of an oblong building, crowns of laurel leaves topping the classical columns. But it was swamped by greenery as if the wood had claimed it for its own. Ivy curled and writhed around its columns like a giant serpent and on to the domed glass roof. After my recent experience any excessive growth made me nervous and a felled tree nearby didn't lessen that feeling. It had been overtaken by the same ivy, which erupted from its trunk, making it seem alive with tendril arms reaching out for me.

'Wow! Most people have a little summer house or maybe a garden room . . . you have a temple.'

'Yes, but look what's written on it.'

I looked up at the monolithic structure. There were letters carved across the top and one word caught my eye – *Gloria*. The rest was obscured by the thick covering of waxy pointed leaves, but I guessed immediately what it must say.

'*Sic transit gloria mundi* – so passes away earthly glory,' I said, and blew out slowly. Patrick! I could feel his presence trying to pull me back to him. He must have stood on this very spot plotting his next move or challenge for me. Suddenly the wood seemed really hostile. At this moment I could really believe this wasn't a game, that Patrick wished me harm.

'Do you think your brother's been here, Sinead?'

I nodded.

James's voice was calmly pragmatic. 'In that case, we should investigate.'

It was so dark inside that I had to squint to make out any details. I walked gingerly because the floor was matted with years of rotted leaves, grass and berries and I didn't want to imagine how many animals had made this place their home in the harsh winters. Stone plinths of different heights were dotted around.

'The temple paid homage to Greek culture,' James said. 'There used to be a collection of marble statues displayed here, but they were donated to a museum.'

It would have been lovely in here before the trees and climbers took over – I could imagine light flooding the dome, hitting the white marble and bouncing off the walls. The only ornamentation I could now see was carved figures on the walls; they reminded me of crude Stone Age art.

'What are these?' I asked.

'It's the story of the underworld. Here's the king, Hades, with his wife, Persephone.'

I ran my fingers across the images, parts of which were missing because the stone was porous and crumbly.

'Does it give you any clues, Sinead?'

'The underworld, and the cave revealed to Saint Patrick,' I reflected, talking mostly to myself. 'They're both visions of the afterlife, one pagan, one Christian. It probably makes sense to Patrick's warped mind but not to me . . . and then there's all the stuff about time fleeing, which is weird because . . . it seems to slow down here.'

'No one can slow down time,' James said, but he sounded like he would have liked to be wrong.

I looked around again, not sure why I disliked the temple so much. It struck me as a decadent reminder of a bygone era, but there was also something creepy about the empty interior. I was about to leave when I spotted some branches placed on one of the plinths. They'd been carefully arranged in a triangle shape, so I knew they hadn't blown in from outside. I picked one up, noticing it had been whittled smooth with a knife. Sweat pooled at the base of my spine and I tried to keep my voice steady. 'This is a sign from Patrick.'

'It's easy to see *signs* everywhere,' James said gently.

'A *secret* sign,' I emphasized. 'Whenever I was in trouble at home or Mum and Dad had had a row, Patrick would leave a warning by the front door . . . some branches in the shape of a triangle. It's the international symbol of distress. Patrick learned it in the Scouts or somewhere.'

'And what does it mean?'

'It's an SOS.'

James's brows arched. 'Save our souls.'

I shivered in the gloom of the temple. I pulled James outside with me and cupped my hands over my face. 'These clues are so morbid, and Patrick's mental state is shaky . . . but . . . as long as I'm following him, I think he's safe. I don't know why he's doing all this, or why Sister Catherine is holding out on me, but I feel I'm getting closer.'

James threw back his head as if expecting answers to drop from the sky. 'I can't think of any other leads, Sinead.'

I was disappointed, but didn't want to show it. 'You've got me this far. You told me about Benedict House first being a church, and I'd never have found the temple on my own. I thought about following Sister Catherine –'

'Don't bother,' he said. 'She does the same walk day in, day out. It would drive anyone else crazy.'

I scowled in agreement. 'Well . . . maybe . . . you could try out the key for me tomorrow on the upstairs doors. I haven't made it that far yet.'

James nodded easily, as if this was a perfectly normal request. He looked up again at the Latin words.

'You recognized the phrase, James.'

'It's the strangest thing,' he said. 'I know my way around the house and the grounds. I can remember the seasons and how the landscape changed –' he paused – 'particularly in autumn; the whole place is dazzling when the leaves change colour and die in an incredible blaze of glory.' He blinked rapidly. 'But everything else is like . . . fighting shadows.'

I tried to reassure him. 'You'll remember more things now you're home. Your mum must have helped to fill in the blanks.'

'Yeah, she's told me how inseparable Dad and me were and how we'd roamed the estate together doing guy stuff.'

'And what did the counsellor say about your blank memory?'

He sighed. 'Probably brought on by the trauma of leaving my friends, my family, the place I was brought up. It's weird because I've spent the last eight years being someone, but I don't know if that person is me.'

'Memory loss can't alter your personality,' I insisted. 'It can't change what's inside.'

James took a faded photograph out of his pocket and handed it to me. It showed a youngish, well-dressed man standing in front of a red two-seater sports car. He didn't have to tell me that this was his father, the resemblance was undeniable; the bone structure, and the hairline, even the stance was James's. But there was arrogance, almost a sneer, in the smile that James didn't have, and there was something about the eyes that made me uneasy.

'I'm trying to get under Dad's skin,' he said, with a rueful laugh. 'That's why I hired the classic car.'

'Has it brought anything back?'

He rolled his eyes. 'Only he used to drive like a demon. I've had to stop myself from copying him more than once.'

Remembering my scary spin in the car I gave a weak smile. I knew we should have been heading back, but I wanted to help James, and I didn't want to end our time together. Our talk about our dreams was still fresh in my mind. I had an idea.

'Will you try something for me?' I suggested.

'What?'

I looked down at the springy forest floor. 'Will you lie down?'

James didn't even ask why. He even seemed grateful to drop to the ground. The floor was cushioned with the latticework of a rope-like plant. I knelt next to him and tugged on a strand to feel how tightly it was anchored. I told him to close his eyes and waited until he was settled. When I covered his lids with my hands his lashes fluttered against my palms.

'I was really scared of the dark,' I said, 'but Mum would never let me have a nightlight. I used to lie awake for ages and . . . because I couldn't see, my sense of smell and hearing were heightened. That's how I remember so much about the night I got ill. I thought we could maybe see if it works for you . . . to jog your memory.'

'You're experimenting on me,' James teased.

I pressed my hands tighter against his eyes. 'Just lie still. Let your mind wander and your senses reach out.'

I waited for a few minutes, intently watching the expression on his face. It gradually changed from amused scepticism, to mildly serious and then to concentrated.

'I can smell woodsmoke,' he said, his tongue moistening his lips. 'I can hear birds beating their wings and footsteps crunching through the dry leaves. The footsteps are heavy and they're getting closer . . . A woman is crying –' He flinched. 'I can feel hot breath on the back of my neck, a dog panting, and drool spattering my skin. There's squealing . . . it sounds like an animal in pain, it's high-pitched and desperate –'

James's eyes suddenly flew open and he stared at me as if I was a stranger. 'I was back here again, and I remembered Dad's dog, Cerberus.'

'Cerberus?'

'The three-headed beast that protected the entrance to

the underworld,' he said, sitting up. 'Dad's joke about his favourite pet. He used him mainly as a guard dog but they were devoted to each other –' He stopped abruptly.

'Anything else?'

He shook his head in frustration. 'The rest is still shadows . . . shapes moving through a mist. It feels as if I'm trapped in a kind of . . . halfway place.'

'Halfway between what?'

'Reality and delusion,' he said flatly.

I squeezed James's shoulder and helped him up. We walked back to the house together and I hoped that he might grab my hand again but he seemed far away, lost in his thoughts. He left me with a dejected smile and a promise to stop by tomorrow and pick up Patrick's key. I expected a lecture from Sister Catherine, but she seemed strangely impassive.

'I'm still following Patrick,' I said, almost in defiance. 'I've found more signs that he's been here.' She stared straight ahead without acknowledging my words. 'You can't expect me to slog away here for fourteen days without giving me something to work on.'

For a moment I actually thought there was the trace of a smile on her lips. 'You should concentrate on proving you have the endurance necessary to see this task through.'

'I have enough *endurance* to find Patrick,' I assured her.

She wrinkled her nose. 'Perhaps you should ask yourself

if you belong here at all . . . if you have the right qualities to remain at Benedict House.'

'Remain!' I cried, incensed. 'I'm only here for Patrick. I'm not going to stay here one minute longer than I have to. I'm not a prisoner. I could leave right now and never look back.'

She clutched my arm, her bony fingers hurting my flesh. 'When you find your heart's desire, Sinead, don't look back; you must never look back.'

As if worried that she had said too much she put one finger across her lips and walked quickly away. I tried to shake off her strange words. By the time I'd finished cleaning the drawing room my legs were rubber and I could barely lift my head. I cried off meeting Harry, desperate to unwind alone and think about the day. My evening meal was a sad microwave dish for one, bought in the corner shop and consisting of reconstituted meat floating in some kind of sauce. It looked and tasted like spicy glue.

My mother had left me four messages. I had to speak to her and persuade her I was making progress and that Patrick had been at Benedict House. She still hadn't been to the police. It was almost as if she believed in Patrick's game so strongly that she viewed me as the only one who could bring him home. I pondered Patrick's clues again and thought about helping James, but the memory of my visions kept returning – malevolent plants, predatory fungus and a swarm of angry dragonflies. Dragonflies – I'd never seen one before, but the first time I did, hundreds had attacked me.

I Googled 'dragonfly' and baulked at the various names for them, mostly malign – water witch, devil's needle, devil's horse, horse stinger, hobgoblin fly. There were old superstitions that a dragonfly could pluck out your eyeballs or sew your eyelids together. In Sweden it was believed they were used by the Devil to weigh your soul. If one flew around your head, then this was what it was doing. Benedict House seemed to be doing things to my mind, not helped by Sister Catherine saying weird stuff about me remaining there. As if anyone would stay a minute longer than they had to. I tried to switch off, but it was impossible. Her urgent voice still echoed in my head like some strange omen. *When you find your heart's desire, Sinead, don't look back; you must never look back.*

# Nineteen

James's irises were melted caramel today and his pupils huge dark orbs. Each time I saw him I had to stop my heart from fluttering like a trapped butterfly. He took the key from me and stuffed it in his pocket.

'Any plans today?' I asked, trying to sound nonchalant.

'I'm going into the village later on to talk to some of the families I used to know. I'm hoping someone might remember something about Dad . . . or me. I might even find out who I used to be.'

I smiled encouragingly. 'Good idea.'

'Any more thoughts on Patrick?'

I twisted my head to one side. 'I wondered if there was a basement in the house. One of Patrick's sayings was *Those beneath the earth cry out for release*.'

James scrunched up his face doubtfully. 'I know every inch of this house and there aren't any underground rooms.'

'Patrick's SOS clue links with Benedict House once being a church,' I went on. 'I had another idea there might be a part of the house that's more sacred than the rest, something in its history.'

My words seemed to register with James and he stared at me intently. 'There is a special place.'

My heart began to race. 'Where?'

'Benedict House has its own priest's hole. Have you heard of them?'

I put my hands on my hips with mock indignation. 'My mother is Catholic *and* Irish. Of course I know what they are . . . secret places to hide Catholic priests during the Reformation.'

'Wouldn't it fit? A place of penance, save our souls . . .'

My eyes lit up. 'When can we go there?'

'We'll have to wait until there's no chance of Sister Catherine coming back.'

'Why?

His eyebrows spiked. 'Because she's made the space her own.'

My eyes darted nervously about but James assured me that we were alone.

'It's fine, Sinead. Sister Catherine goes to visit Gran at the same time every day and spends more than half an hour with her.'

'She's weird with her timing, isn't she?' I asked, aware that I could be talking about myself. 'Everything's so precise and measured, as if it all means something.'

'Gran told me she comes from a closed order where

they shun the outside world but pray all the time. She rises at four a.m. and begins her walk in the dark.

'Really? But how does she see?'

James shrugged. 'She knows the place so well she must feel her way along. Don't get hung up on Sister Catherine – I think deep down she has a good heart.'

My lip curled, unwilling to attribute any unselfish motives to my surly namesake. I turned my attention to James. The last few hours waiting to see him had dragged so much. He had a small smear of something by the side of his mouth, perhaps from his lunch, and I wanted to reach out and wipe it off. His skin smelt of apple or some kind of fruit juice and I inhaled deeply. He was drawing me in and I was struggling to stop it from happening. There was something about him that belied the brash, flirty exterior. And he noticed things that most people didn't, with eyes that seemed to see deep into my soul.

I jiggled impatiently on the spot. 'OK, where is it?'

James smiled enigmatically and went straight to the concealed doorway in the hall. I followed him through and we stood, almost touching, in the small space.

'I knew this place was odd,' I said. 'Sister Catherine spends ages in here, and when I sneaked a look I saw the doorway's been bricked up.'

James turned to me with mischievous eyes and then slowly crouched and examined the wood panelling. There was a slight creak and one of the sections of the panelling actually slid upwards in the same way as a sash window moves. We both stared into a space.

'Come on,' he urged. 'Every ancient house has to have a secret staircase.'

I felt a tingle of excitement following James. He ran like a small boy, his feet turned outwards and clattering on each step. We climbed so high I figured we must have been close to the roof space. How would an old woman like Sister Catherine manage these stairs? I wondered. There was an answer to one mystery though; there must be a vent somewhere because I could feel a shaft of air and hear a rushing sound which would account for the strange sighing. I also remembered those desperate voices and realized that I was seeing *and* hearing things that weren't there.

There was another tiny door on the right-hand side. My eyes automatically searched for a keyhole. I looked to James for direction and he pushed open the door, urging me to go first. I took a tentative step inside. The room contained little more than a single bed, a chest of drawers and tiny lattice chair. I noticed a spare nun's habit resting on the back of the chair as if it was waiting for someone to put it on. Everything was painted white and the crisp bed sheets were tucked in very tightly without the faintest wrinkle. Immediately in front of us was a fabulous painted trompe l'œil of an arched window, depicting a girl with short dark hair standing beside a lake looking up to the sky. Her hands were held aloft as a flock of doves flew upwards. A semicircle of sunlight illuminated the painting, radiating outwards and fading as it reached the girl. I was blown away. It was bizarre to conceal something this beautiful. The only other decoration in the room was an icon of a lady dressed in white robes. Above her head was a halo and faint lettering – Saint Catherine of Genoa.

I asked the question even though I instinctively knew the answer. 'Sister Catherine sleeps here? She'd rather hole up in this tiny room than in the palatial house?'

James shrugged. 'Guess so.'

The space was a blank canvas. It reminded me of Patrick's bedroom after its transformation. I scratched my nose thoughtfully.

'Patrick's flat's been given an amazing clean – it was literally dazzling. What would you make of that?'

James shrugged. 'He's trying to turn over a new leaf, cleaning up his space and . . . maybe himself?'

'That's what Harry thought . . . but I was so disbelieving. Maybe Patrick is trying to change and become a new person.'

'Hope so,' James said.

'I'm still no closer to finding him,' I said with regret. 'The priest's hole is a great lead, but I don't think Patrick's been here.'

'This isn't the priest's hole, Sinead. This was meant to look like a servant's bedroom.'

I frowned. 'Where is it then?'

James made me face the doorway. I heard some kind of metal catch opening and he turned me around by the shoulders with the look of a boy showing me his secret den. I could see that the painting disguised a cavity just big enough for an adult to hunker down inside. I walked over, desperate to find one of Patrick's clues, but the space was empty. Despite my disappointment, I couldn't help but admire how ingeniously the thick wall had been excavated. The painting had been applied to a heavy slab of wood with cleverly concealed locks that were flush with the wall. Grinning, James squeezed himself into the hole and I wondered how often he'd done this as a child. It must have been a fantastic place to hide. I couldn't resist the urge to shut him in.

'You can stay in there until Sister Catherine gets back,' I called.

James's muffled speech sounded as if he was getting annoyed, which made me grin to myself. But then he hammered on the wood so frantically that I knew something was wrong. I hastily tried to open the locks but my fingers were sweaty and it took me several goes to master them. His agitation made me fumble even more. Seeing him shocked me. He was crouched inside, cowering, his hands covering his head.

'James, I'm sorry, it was just a bit of fun –'

He climbed out, his face ashen and his breathing laboured. I could see he was trembling. 'I get a bit claus- trophobic,' he muttered, clearly embarrassed. 'I suddenly remembered how much I hated being in there, but it was too late; you'd locked me in.'

Since I was a child I'd hated confined spaces too. I apologized again, kicking myself for being so insensitive and thinking how dangerous it was that the priest's hole couldn't be opened from the inside. As I put the painting back into position I noticed the back of the wood: there were many deep scratches as if someone had used their nails to try to claw their way out. I shivered. James was already outside the door as if he couldn't wait to leave. I took one final look around to make sure that nothing had been disturbed. My eyes rested on the benevolent features of Saint Catherine, her halo an iridescent band of gold, her head bowed in modesty. I sighed inwardly. There was nothing at all to indicate Patrick had been here.

I followed James down the stairs. He had just slid the panelling back into place when we heard the distinctive sound of footsteps. I stiffened, looking around for somewhere to hide. He pushed me into one corner behind two thick coats suspended from a hook, but our legs were still visible and there was no way we wouldn't be spotted. As if in recognition of this, James turned to the side and pulled me towards him until our faces were pressed together, our lips almost touching. I could feel his heartbeat. Even shaking with nerves I was determined to enjoy every second. A narrow beam of light entered the space, telling me that the door must have opened a fraction.

My breathing was so irregular that James put one finger across my lips and kept it there.

The purposeful footsteps stopped only inches from us. I almost giggled because my nerves were so jagged, but I managed to stop myself. I didn't dare peek out but closed my eyes. Sister Catherine hadn't made another sound, which meant she was probably staring in disbelief, waiting for us to show ourselves. The only comforting thought was that if she did lock me in here for all eternity, at least I'd be with James.

*Concentrate, Sinead. You might never get this close to him again.*

My eyes were screwed so tightly shut that I could see stars that blotted out everything but the touch and smell of him. Sara had asked me what I was going to do with all the time that I frantically saved, and now I had the answer – stay here with James, never having to move or speak again. This was pure heaven.

There was a slight rumble, a rustling sound and the distinctive thud of someone climbing, shoes hitting bare wood. Somehow Sister Catherine couldn't have seen us hiding. She had gone. I opened my eyes and stared directly into James's. We were so close that his lashes brushed my cheek. He still didn't move and neither did I. Being hidden in this way made me feel safe and lessened my nervousness. Our breathing synchronized and his warm breath entered my mouth. James slid his finger from my lip and traced the line of my chin down to my neck. A surge of desire ran through me and I closed my eyes again, waiting for him to kiss me. Nothing happened. My hand slowly reached out and felt rough material but there was no solid flesh. I blinked my lids open and found myself alone, clutching some kind of woollen duffel coat. I hadn't heard James leave.

His voice eventually brought me back to reality, an impatient hiss that came from outside the boot room. 'Hurry up, Sinead. Let's go before she comes back.'

*You puckered your lips . . . you puckered you lips at him and he ran a mile.*

Frantically pedalling, to get as far away from Benedict House as fast as possible, I alternated between growing hot and then cold thinking about it. I practically threw myself at him and he walked away. All I could imagine was how pathetic I must have looked, eyes closed, lips pursed, swaying towards him, ready to swoon into his arms. It would have been nice to crawl into a cave to hide. *You puckered your lips!* I silently screamed to a passing lorry, whose backdraught made me wobble dangerously. My face felt on fire, like a bad case of prickly heat.

*This was why you never bothered dating, always kept guys at arm's length or as friends. In the space of a week you've completely messed up with two guys – made a fool of yourself over one and unforgivably hurt the other.*

I was so mortified I didn't even answer my phone or update my mother. When I checked there were twelve missed calls. I couldn't help but reflect on how badly everything was going. I hadn't discovered any more of Patrick's clues, and James had found out little about his past except that he was claustrophobic, like me. It was easy to avoid Harry's calls, but my mother wouldn't give up. Eventually I was forced to answer my phone, my stomach curdling.

'Sorry, Mum. I lost signal.'

'I had a dream about Patrick,' she said tearfully. 'He was a little boy again and we were in the city together, but I let go of his hand and couldn't find him. It was *devastating*. I know what my subconscious is trying to tell me – I've let down my only son. He's out there, alone and without protection, a sheep among wolves.'

'I'm sorry,' I mumbled again. 'I think I'm getting closer. He wants to be found, Mum, I know that now. In a way he's helping me.'

'It's his cry of despair,' she went on. 'Patrick's so gifted – that's part of his trouble. He can never be ordinary; we should never expect him to live a mundane life like other people. When he's home we must find an outlet for his extraordinary talents.'

I spaced out as she listed his many talents, as if I didn't already know them all off by heart. She finished with her usual refrain: 'Don't let me down, Sinead.'

I answered automatically. 'I won't.'

# Twenty

Next morning I was given the privilege of cleaning the dark and gloomy study. My mood hadn't improved and Sister Catherine always managed to get my back up. She couldn't possibly know about my scary visions, but her manner was definitely meant to intimidate. I was determined to let her know she wouldn't succeed.

'Nothing about this place scares me,' I said. 'And I can survive any endurance tests you throw at me or any of the other *weird* things that go on here. I'll see this through until I know where Patrick is.'

'Nothing here can hurt you, Sinead,' she answered. 'I'm glad you're not afraid. The only thing to fear is fear itself.'

'Very profound,' I muttered under my breath.

Sister Catherine must have heard. 'Would you prefer it if I told you to face your demons? That this is the time?'

I glared to let her know how much she was annoying me, but a fleeting look of something almost like affection crossed her face. It quickly vanished. 'I'll leave you to your work,' she said curtly.

I looked around the study. There was a collection of murky gold-framed oil paintings on the wall. One was a hunting scene, with lots of red-coated figures on horseback chasing a fox, the master blowing a horn. A smaller painting depicted a dog with a dead pheasant in its mouth and a hare lying on the ground, blood oozing from its wounds. I worked all morning, jittery at the thought of seeing James again, but the hours dragged and he didn't appear. It hurt that he didn't seek me out; he'd seemed so keen to help. But that was before I threw myself at him.

In my lunch break, I headed into the wood with a heavy heart, making for the temple. It was the last place I knew where Patrick had definitely been and I had no further ideas beyond going back to it. At first I'd been afraid of getting lost, but now I could see that the entire estate was circular, and if I doubted my sense of direction I had only to look for the wooded wall. As I walked I recognized markers, remembering how James had taken my hand here only two days ago, and it had felt so natural. I stopped abruptly when I came across a figure lying in the grass, the sun glinting off his blond hair. It had to be James, but he wasn't moving. My heart froze. Filled with dry-mouthed dread I walked closer, but then I saw that his eyes were open and his chest was rising and falling. Relief flooded through me.

'James, you gave me such a fright.'

'Did I?'

His expression was utterly depressed, his eyes dull and his mouth turned down. 'What's wrong?' I asked.

He waved his arm. 'Can't you see? . . . It's this place. There's something . . . hidden that strangles all beauty.'

His words came completely out of the blue, but as I sat down by him and I looked around I could see what he meant; on the surface everything was alive and in full bloom, with the lush tracery of the trees protecting us, but a network of weeds lurked beneath, stealthily destroying everything in their path.

He directed his gaze towards a massive oak tree. 'I've remembered something else, Sinead. I've remembered how deadly the estate can be.' He held out his hands, and in each was an olive-green mushroom. He watched my face closely. 'One's edible, a common field mushroom, the other is a death cap, the most lethal of all fungi. Death can occur in less than twenty-four hours.'

'You can't be that certain.'

'I can,' he insisted. 'It's easy to confuse them, but the death cap has a distinctive smell, like rose petals.'

'Rose petals,' I repeated faintly.

'Still don't believe me?' James brought one slowly towards his lips. I watched, mesmerized, certain that he was joking until he opened his mouth and the mushroom hovered above his furled tongue.

'What are you doing,' I yelled, knocking his hand and sending it tumbling. 'I believe you – there's no need to do something stupid.'

James rolled over on to his back and stared up at me, an unreadable smile on his face. 'I could die in your arms, Sinead.'

'I'd rather you stayed alive,' I said, trying to sound normal. 'It would be a horrible, drawn-out and agonizing death.'

He threaded his fingers together and put his hands behind his head. 'I can think of worse ones . . . slower, infinitely more painful, until you beg never to see another sunrise.'

I was angry with him for him for talking like this. 'I could never imagine wanting to cut short my life,' I said. 'It's so precious – time is precious.'

James's head lolled to one side and I noticed that even upside down he was still beautiful. 'Time's only precious when it's running out, Sinead.'

'What's wrong?' I asked again. 'Did something happen in the village?'

He sighed. 'Nothing happened in the village – that's the point. Everyone I spoke to said my dad was some kind of saint that everyone loved, a great squire, friend and regular Santa Claus . . . oh, and he and my mum were blissfully happy together.'

'Maybe that's the truth then. Why would they lie?'

'Because they don't want to upset me. But I know they're lying – they can't look me in the eye.' He screwed up his face. 'You know . . . I came home expecting to find my hero, the white knight, and I'm scared of what's happening.

I'm scared of my mind, the dark places where bad things lurk.'

'We all have those places,' I tried to reassure him. 'Maybe your mind is confused and is . . . kind of punishing your dad for leaving you?'

James took a shaky breath and I realized how difficult this was for him. 'When I was locked in the priest's hole . . . I was a little boy again and I could smell something on my clothes that made my stomach turn . . . whisky and cigarettes . . . it was in my nostrils, choking me . . . I think it was his smell. I think he used to put me in there, shut me in the dark, and I gouged the wood until my fingers bled trying to get out.'

'You don't remember him doing that?'

James shook his head.

'But . . . you could have been accidentally locked in there, by a friend playing a joke, like I did.'

His eyes were huge and haunted. 'Something else . . . The other day, in the wood . . . when you covered my eyes . . . I was terrified of something . . . or someone . . . thrashing through the trees . . . The shadows are getting closer, and they're frightening me.' He looked so tragic that my heart constricted.

'You must wish you'd never come back.'

He angled his head to look at me. 'I could never wish that. I'm just beginning to realize why I did come back.'

I tore my eyes away. *Don't look at him, Sinead, he's*

*working his magic again. Remember why you're here.*
*Remember Patrick.*

'I'm going to the temple to look for more clues,' I said
abruptly.

I got to my feet and headed further into the wood. I
didn't wait to find out whether James was going to follow
me but I could hear his footsteps behind me. I deliberately
kept my pace brisk and walked in the centre of the path
so we couldn't walk side by side. As soon as we entered
the temple I sensed the oppressive atmosphere. It felt as if
the wood had come alive again, as if the climbers might
break through the glass roof and choke me. I mooched
about, talking through Patrick's clues, keeping my face
expressionless. I knocked his sticks off the plinth, annoyed
because this had proved such a dead end.

'Which statue used to stand here?' I asked James
casually.

He didn't have to think. 'Eurydice. She was my
favourite.'

'What does she look like?'

'She's gorgeous,' James said, and I almost felt jealous.
'Long dress, flowers in her hair, graceful . . . hand on her
forehead –'

My heart missed a beat. 'I saw a statue like that in the
grounds when I first arrived.'

'But . . . I'm sure they were all given to the museum.'

My forehead creased. 'I don't think I imagined it. She
was luminously white and she had one hand on her brow.

She really spooked me at first because I thought she was real.'

'Could you find her again?'

'I . . . think so. She wasn't that far from the main gates.'

We set off together and I maintained a fast pace, annoyed with myself for missing something so obvious. Patrick had chosen that particular plinth for a reason, and I needed to find out why. After a while James was almost panting and I noticed again how exhausted he still was, beads of sweat shining on his upper lip. His lethargy and the marks on his arms still bothered me and I kept throwing him covert looks.

I tried to remember when I'd first noticed the marble lady. It was hard to be exact, but we reached the enormous gates without any sign of her.

'She was definitely visible from the path,' I said.

James looked at me sceptically, which made me wonder if I'd dreamed the whole thing. I ran forward, thinking back to when I was riding my bike and I saw her head shining through the greenery. She wasn't anywhere to be seen. Puzzled, I delved into the undergrowth. It didn't take me long to see the white marble form. My voice was high with excitement.

'Here she is. She must have moved. No . . . that's not possible. The bushes must have fanned out and covered her.'

James ducked his head through the leaves and joined me. He grinned broadly and ran his hands across the smooth marble. 'Eurydice,' he said proudly. He looked around. 'But where's Orpheus? They never should have been separated.'

'Are they a couple?'

'Of course. Don't you know the myth?'

I shook my head.

'Orpheus and Eurydice,' James said. 'Greek legend tells that she died on her wedding day. Orpheus was overwhelmed with grief and played such mournful songs on his lyre that the ferryman allowed him to cross the River Styx alive and descend to the underworld. The king and queen of the underworld were also moved by his music and allowed Eurydice to return to earth . . . but there was one condition. Orpheus should not look back at her until he reached the mortal world. But . . . he looked, and she was taken from him for the second time and he couldn't see her again until he died.'

I couldn't take my eyes from the statue. It had weathered with age and eroded in places, but was still beautiful, rust-coloured veins running through the almost white marble. I was transfixed by the curves and the fluid shapes, amazed that anyone could sculpt anything quite so lifelike, from the bloom of the flowers in her hair and the folds in her long dress, to her perfectly sculpted fingers and toes. Eurydice, lamenting, was already half turned as if she was about to be spirited away.

'What's that wrapped around the base?' I asked suddenly.

James bent down to investigate. 'It's a grass snake. Don't panic – it's dead.'

I stared down with disgust at the scaly green skin with distinctive black bars.

'What a weird coincidence,' James said. 'Eurydice died because she was bitten on the foot by a snake.'

My face darkened. 'I don't believe in coincidences any more. I bet Patrick's left it there for me.'

'Why would he do that?'

I scrunched my face. 'Erm . . . Eurydice is another link to the underworld . . . Saint Patrick was supposed to have chased all the snakes from Ireland . . . the wall mural showed people with hair made of serpents . . . Patrick's still showing me different images of the afterlife.' I threw up my hands. 'Or maybe I'm just clutching at straws.'

'Orpheus spent his life mourning Eurydice,' James said pensively, 'just waiting to die. He should be here. They're eternally linked.'

'Orpheus could be Patrick's next clue,' I said hopefully.

I was glad the trail hadn't gone completely cold, but Patrick was still testing my patience. I walked around in circles, trying to make my brain work, to slot the pieces into place. James tried to help but he was listless, picking daisies and making them into a chain. I walked over to him, unable to fathom his melancholia.

'All this talk of the afterlife,' he said quietly. 'Do you ever wonder what happens . . . after you die?'

I shrugged. 'Doesn't everyone? But . . . it's always going to stay a mystery.'

'But what do you believe . . . really?' he persisted.

I took a deep breath. 'If I said I believe we're just part of the nitrogen cycle and we rot in the earth to nourish the soil, would you believe me?'

'No,' he answered.

I stuck out my chin. 'OK . . . I think something survives – memories or consciousness or . . . the soul if you have to call it something.'

'And what about love? Can that survive death?'

'I don't know.'

'But what would be the point of love if it wasn't everlasting?' James took hold of my fingers and rubbed them.

'You know I have a boyfriend,' I reminded him, still smarting at his rejection and guilt-ridden over Harry.

'He's not right for you,' James said simply.

'What about those girls I saw you with?'

James winced. 'They meant nothing. It's been a long time since any girl looked at me and . . . I went a little crazy –'

I rolled my eyes in disbelief. Girls must hit on him all the time.

'I'm not lying,' he protested. 'You know I've been ill. The truth is, I've never even had a steady girlfriend.' He pressed his forehead against mine. 'Yesterday . . . I was so scared . . . I've never felt this way before and I panicked.

I spent all night wishing I'd kissed you and couldn't sleep, thinking about you.'

My stomach flipped.

'But I don't want to hurt you, Sinead. You know I can't stay –'

These words suddenly hit home and I wrenched myself away. 'You leave in . . . ten days.'

James's shoulders stiffened and he looked at me with reproach. 'Don't remind me again. I can't let you go, and I can't be selfish enough to ask you to follow me –' He closed his eyes in despair. 'I promise you every moment I have left is yours. We could live a lifetime in ten days.'

I shook my head emphatically. 'I'm sorry, James. That's just not enough time.'

I turned on my heel and walked away.

# Twenty-One

Harry was feeling hurt. I could tell by his reproachful eyes and the way he chopped the vegetables for our stir-fry; the sound of the knife against the wooden board was too quiet and precise – Harry normally attacked everything with gusto. I made an effort to compliment him on his cooking and to clear my plate, which wasn't that difficult because he was a great cook. I, on the other hand, burnt everything, even toast.

'Thought you were avoiding me,' he said finally.

'Course not. I've been wiped out, working in that creepy mausoleum, but . . . I have some news about Patrick.'

'You've found him?'

'Not exactly . . . but he's still leaving me clues. I found a temple in the grounds of the house with the same Latin motto as the mission house. Inside are drawings of the underworld in Greek mythology and an SOS – save our souls – sign, exactly like the ones he used to put outside our house to warn me.'

I was filled with guilt again because I'd deliberately failed to mention that James was helping me. Harry's face seemed to be permanently disapproving, his lips set in a thin line. I tried to make him snap out of it by sneaking up behind him and tickling his back. He almost managed to smile.

'And I also found a secret room with a concealed priest's hole . . . but that drew a blank. I still don't know what it means. The clues are all connected to the afterlife though, some Christian, some pagan.'

Harry sighed heavily and I realized that this was taking its toll on him too. 'I still think you're in danger,' he said, 'but . . . you're blind to it.'

'I had another of those freaky visions,' I continued lightly, but I needed to share this with someone.

Harry frowned. 'Go on.'

I told him about the dragonfly incident in a half-laughing tone so he didn't think me completely gullible. 'Apparently dragonflies have long been thought of as evil and when they fly around your head they're actually weighing your soul.'

'Your mind is so hung up on death, judgement and the hereafter, Sinead, you're probably seeing things.'

'Probably.' Harry obviously shared my own fears. It would almost be preferable if he had said I *was* insane. 'Sometimes . . . it's stupid . . . but I almost think there's something malevolent in the house . . . or the grounds . . . just watching, biding its time.'

Harry had barely touched his food. He pushed his plate aside whereas I had long finished. He began to plead with me again. 'I don't want to lose you.'

'You won't,' I reassured him, unable to look him in the eye. Still running through my head were James's words. *I've never felt this way before.* Was he sincere? Why had I reacted so badly? Because he'd said the worst possible thing to me – he couldn't give me any more time.

Harry sat beside me on the sofa and began nuzzling my neck. 'Missed you.'

'Missed you too,' I answered robotically.

Harry entwined his fingers with mine and I rested my head on his shoulder. He seemed happy to stay this way, but I was itching to do some research on my laptop. I made a few noises to politely hint at my restlessness, but he kissed my cheek and stroked my hair, forcing my head back into position. I tried to speak and he stopped me by pressing his lips against mine. This gave me an immediate flashback to being close to James. I went through the motions and must have fooled him, because Harry smiled at me and brushed my hair from my face.

My conscience began to prick me again. Harry was happy with so little it just wasn't fair of me. The niggle grew stronger until I felt physically sick. He stroked my arm and I recoiled.

Now he did look puzzled. 'Is something wrong, Sinead?'

It all came to the surface in one hot, bubbling eruption of guilt. 'There is something wrong . . . very wrong.'

He held me at arm's length, searching my face for an answer. I couldn't hold his baby-blue gaze and dropped my head. The seconds ticked by, each more painful than the last, until I just blurted out the truth.

'I have . . . feelings for someone else. I'm sorry . . . it just happened.'

He ran one hand through his curls and gave a hollow laugh. 'Is that all?'

Now I had the courage to look at him. 'Isn't that enough?'

Harry made a circle with his lips as if he was going to whistle but just blew into the air. 'I guessed as much,' he said eventually.

'You guessed?' I was mortified because he also must have guessed *who* I had feelings for.

He nodded. 'You looked at *him*, James, in the coffee shop, and I'd never seen your face that way. It actually lit up . . . like a lantern.'

There wasn't anything I could say to make it better. 'Sorry,' I mumbled.

Harry appeared almost upbeat. 'Thank you for telling me the truth. It can't have been easy.'

I winced because he was letting me off the hook. 'But . . . that doesn't make it any better for you.'

He shrugged and there was determination on his face.

I'd forgotten how stubborn he could be. 'It's OK because . . . he'll be gone in –'

'Ten days,' I prompted, shamefaced.

'Ten days,' he repeated, almost trance-like. 'But I'll still be here for you . . . to scare away the nightmares and hold you close when you're upset. I don't have a tan or a surfboard,' he added with a cynical smile, 'but I'm here.'

'You have an amazing heart,' I told him truthfully, wishing the ground would open up and swallow me. 'I know you don't want me to go back to Benedict House, but nothing will happen between me and James –'

'You're wrong,' he said. 'I wouldn't try to cage you. I have to let you follow your heart and hope it's just for now. If you love someone, you have to set them free and hope they come back to you.'

What else could I say? Apologizing further would only make things worse. I couldn't stop my foot tapping on the floor, each awkward second feeling like a minute.

'The heat doesn't seem to be breaking,' I said at last.

Harry nodded solemnly. 'It's going to be a sticky night.'

'I wish it would rain again.'

'Me too.' 'Harry got up and said with forced cheerfulness, 'Why don't I go to the shop and get you a dessert? You need feeding up.'

I smiled. 'That'd be great.'

He could read my mind so well; any kind of emotional turmoil made me famished and I was desperate for sweet comfort food. When the door closed I buried my face in a cushion and then threw it against the wall. How could Harry be so annoyingly understanding and infuriatingly noble? Why didn't he criticize me, shout or get angry? After a few minutes of beating myself up, I calmed down. A weight had been lifted from me, the weight of my guilt. I'd told him the truth, even though it had been one of the hardest things I'd ever had to do. Harry was honest, dependable and my best friend. If James made my life turbulent, then Harry calmed the waters and brought me back to shore.

Now alone, I knuckled down to the daily task of updating my mother. I couldn't stomach another conversation and stuck to texting meaningless phrases about trying my hardest to search for Patrick and being hopeful of finding him soon. She didn't even bother replying. Harry came back with a raspberry meringue. He scooped a large portion into the only clean bowl he could find, which meant we had to share. This seemed to break the ice between us. We sat side by side on the sofa, my laptop on my knees.

Harry touched my shoulder hesitantly. 'How's the freaky nun? Saint Catherine?'

'You mean *Sister* Catherine.' Something clicked and I stared hard at Harry. 'Actually you could be right. I think she might have taken her name from Saint Catherine of Genoa. I found a holy icon in her bedroom when I was snooping.'

My fingers busily typed 'saint catherine of genoa' and I gave a little flourish with one hand. 'Look at this. "Saint

Catherine of Genoa was shown a vision of what a soul experiences in purgatory. After this she devoted her life to the poor, sick and destitute, suffering the same burdens as them."' I nudged him. 'Purgatory leads back to Station Island and Saint Patrick and all the other clues . . . It's like they're all in this weird circle and I can't find the end.'

'The end is what worries me most,' Harry said bleakly.

I didn't answer, intent on absorbing the details of Saint Catherine's life and wondering how anyone could be so impossibly perfect. Apparently she used to drink water laced with vinegar as a penance. I could still taste the bitter water in Benedict House. It didn't mean anything, I told myself. It was the ancient pipes. Sister Catherine was probably used to the taste and James remembered it from childhood.

'All the allusions lead to the same place,' I reiterated.

'But not to Patrick,' Harry said. 'He seems to have disappeared off the face of the earth.'

A shudder of unease ran through me and for one crazy moment I couldn't suppress the idea that all this was real and my soul was being judged in some way. I felt compelled to pose the question. 'If you had only a few days to live, Harry, would you feel . . . confident your soul was . . . pure?'

Surprisingly he didn't make fun of me. 'I don't know what the measure is, so how can I know?'

I swallowed and said sorrowfully, 'My life is littered with good intentions gone bad . . .'

'But they're still good intentions,' Harry said.

'Mm,' I agreed, biting my lip. 'But I'm a lousy daughter, sister and friend, without any patience or consideration.' I wondered why I was increasingly susceptible to divulging my most intimate thoughts.

'That's rubbish, Sinead. You do nothing but put your family first. And you've done something good. You've made me incredibly happy.'

This was debatable as well, but I smiled weakly at the compliment. My face scrunched up as I struggled to remember anything really selfless that I'd ever done. The amount of effort this took was disturbing, until a light went on in my head.

'Well . . . actually . . . I did save a baby bird once. It had fallen from the nest and couldn't fly.'

Harry grinned. 'That's a start.'

'My mother told me not to bother,' I rushed on, 'that it would be kinder to let it die, so I kept it secret for weeks and fed it round the clock from a small pipette.' I looked away, embarrassed. 'I was so happy when it took its first flight but . . . it wouldn't leave and kept tapping on my window. It broke my heart to ignore it, but I wanted it to be free, soaring in the sky, not trapped in my bedroom.'

'That's two good deeds,' Harry said. 'Saving it, and being generous enough to let it go.'

'Suppose,' I answered, pleased without knowing why.

Harry studied me closely. 'It isn't healthy to be dwelling on all this. You said yourself, Benedict House is like a mausoleum. Stay with the living and with me.'

'I'm so nearly there, Harry. I can feel it happening. There's a new life waiting for me and I'm like . . . that bird waiting to spread my wings.'

This was a bit poetic for me and Harry seemed surprised. He didn't stay and the night seemed to last forever. The heat, my conscience, James's words and all the strange stuff that had happened conspired to disrupt my sleep. I awoke sweating and struggling to get my breath, pushing damp hair from my forehead. My dream was horribly vivid – I was underground, getting deeper and deeper into the earth, unable to turn around. Smoke was clogging my throat and a voice close by was pleading with me to fight. *Don't die, Sinead, it's not your time. Don't die.*

# Twenty-Two

James must have heard my bike wheels cutting into the gravel because his face appeared at one of the upstairs windows. He came out on to the balcony, dressed only in a pair of striped boxers. I shielded my eyes to gaze up at him while he leaned over the balustrade to peer down at me. He raised one hand and then disappeared. I figured he must be getting dressed. I breathed the summer scents and watched an industrious bee collecting pollen. A noise made me look up – someone clearing their throat. I had been wrong about James getting dressed; he was barefoot and still almost naked. His hair was attractively untidy and one side of his face marked from being squashed against a pillow. He moved closer until we were only a metre or so from each other.

It should have been no different from seeing him on the beach or in a swimming pool, except that somehow it was. I studied every sinew of his lean frame – the small v of hairs on his chest, the hollows above his collarbone, his ribs, even his navel, which was a gorgeous indent.

*Why didn't he say something?*

And yet I didn't want him to in case it spoilt the moment – it felt as if everything on the planet had ceased to exist except the pounding of my heart.

I realized the time and panicked. 'You should go before Sister Catherine appears. She'll be horrified to find us like this.'

He leaned in and lifted my chin with his finger. 'Did you know your eyes have a fleck of violet dancing in the sunlight?'

I turned my face away. After yesterday I was more determined than ever not to let him play with my heart.

'I have to find Patrick,' I said firmly. 'That's the only reason I'm here. Nothing else matters and you must concentrate on your own search. Maybe . . . helping each other isn't a good idea.'

This didn't seem to faze James at all. 'If we don't work together,' he said, 'then you won't find out what I know after talking to my gran.'

'But . . . you said she was –'

'She has lucid moments, Sinead, and she was very clear on one thing –' James hesitated. 'Both Eurydice and Orpheus were retained by the estate. Orpheus is definitely still here, in the grounds somewhere. Apparently it was me who decided his position all those years ago . . . but . . . I can't remember.'

'We could look for him later,' I said, my face blanching as I heard footsteps.

My eyes silently begged him to hurry, but with teasing slowness he disappeared back through the main entrance. I lowered my head, trying to compose myself, and when I looked up Sister Catherine was approaching. Guilt must have been written all over my face.

'Will you be able to get the work done in time, Sinead?' Her voice was cracked, like woodsmoke mingled with disapproval.

At the mention of time my lip curled. 'Time drags here. Haven't you noticed?'

'Is that not what you've always longed for – more time?'

I was too stunned to answer. *How did she know about my time obsession?*

She looked me up and down in a probing way. 'I hope very soon you will come to realize that you are in the right place; this is where you want to be.'

*And why did she keep going on about me staying? It wasn't going to happen.*

I fixed her with my hardest stare. 'I know you have some kind of weird *agenda,* but let's get one thing straight . . . nothing and no one will ever persuade me to stay here.'

'Persuasion is not in my nature, Sinead. Your choice will be a willing one. Now follow me into the library.'

She actually crooked one gnarled finger at me. The library was as dull as it sounded: ceiling to floor solid-wood, glass-fronted bookcases that were weirdly empty of books. The more I thought about it, the house was surprisingly bare of personal possessions. It was as if James and his family had never lived here. I set to work, trying to calm down. My pulse still hadn't stopped racing as I pictured James in his boxer shorts, warm with sleep. It only took a small mental leap to imagine him moments earlier in his bed, before he awoke, and me lying beside him. He would have opened his eyes, looked at me as if I was the only girl in the world, enfolded me in his arms and then . . . I shivered. I had to stay strong.

James came back just after midday. The scorching sun took my breath away and I pulled him quickly away from the house. The dry leaves of the wood opened with a rustle to allow us inside. I noticed the giant trunk of a fallen oak tree and sat on it. I got my sandwich out, staring up at the spread of greenery and branches protecting us. James joined me, his long legs dangling above the ground.

'The estate is huge,' I said. 'It'll take us forever to search for one statue. Doesn't your gran have any idea where Orpheus could be?'

James shook his head. 'No, but apparently it was a special place where I liked to come. I waylaid Sister Catherine this morning, sure she would have noticed it on her travels, but she said she never veers off the pathways and her eyes are only ever fixed on God.'

I rolled my eyes. 'She is totally weird.' I tapped my hand against the side of his head. 'It's in there somewhere, James. Think.'

'I can't. I know the paths, but they're all the same to me.'

I picked bits of bark from the tree with my nails. 'Your mum said you were close to your dad and you did things together. What sort of things?'

'Erm . . . she said we used to hang out in the wood playing Robin Hood, making camp fires and sleeping outside.'

The thought of a young James running through the wood with a bow and arrow was especially sweet. It didn't sound like the same dad who would lock him in a dark hole.

'You thought you remembered something crashing through the wood after you. You were only a boy. If you felt threatened you would have run somewhere safe . . . a special place if you had one.'

'Suppose,' he answered, 'but how do I find it?'

'The grounds aren't lit at night,' I said thoughtfully. 'If you slept outside you must have known your way in the dark.'

James still appeared doubtful and more than a little nervous. 'To find it I have to go back, Sinead, and that's what I'm scared of.'

'That's what you're here for,' I told him gently. 'Your mind hasn't forgotten; it's just . . . suppressed some things you don't want to remember. I think you can still find that place if you try.'

James looked at me for a few moments and then stood

up. He squared his shoulders and blew out as if he was about to run a race.

'Try not to think or reason,' I said. 'Just feel your way . . . your body might instinctively remember the route . . . I'll follow behind,' I reassured him.

James set off, looking bewildered and more than a little apprehensive. He glanced back once or twice as if checking I was still there. But then his posture changed and became much more purposeful. He gained speed and I had difficulty keeping up. My feet had to negotiate every bump and crater in the ground, but his didn't falter; they knew the way. When he came to a fork in the path he didn't hesitate. I was right; he could have done this in the dark. When James checked behind him now, his eyes didn't see me; they kept looking around wildly at something unseen. I could see fear on his face and his breath was coming in gasps. I remembered that feeling from when I first arrived, the blind panic that had consumed me when I thought the foliage had come alive and was bearing down on me. I called to James but he was deaf to my voice. He cut his arms on twigs but didn't seem to notice. He ran like a boy again, his head down, his feet churning up the narrow path. On and on he ran until he stopped dead by a weeping willow, out of breath and sweating. He looked around blankly and seemed astonished to see me. He shook himself as if suddenly remembering where he was.

I bent over with my hands on my knees, panting, my chest tight. When I looked up James had triumphantly moved aside the yellow ground-length fronds of the weeping willow and I could see Orpheus in all his glory. I studied the skilfully chiselled features and then looked at James, unsure who was the more perfect. I spaced out for a moment, imagining the two statues back together: Eurydice, desperately tragic because she was about to be spirited away, and Orpheus, forlornly gazing on her for the last time, knowing they were about to be separated again.

I walked past James and slipped inside the fronds to take a closer look, the long dry grass tickling my legs. I could see identical rust-coloured veins running through Orpheus and noticed the same attention to detail; the lyre in his hand was exquisitely sculpted. James stepped inside with me and the natural light faded. No wonder he had liked it in here when he was small – it was completely secluded. I waited for him to explain if he'd remembered anything else or if he knew what he'd been running from, but his expression was curiously peaceful.

'You seem to be able to find the answers better than I can, Sinead.'

'I just used logic,' I replied. 'I'm detached from the situation, so it's easier for me.'

I took a tissue out of my pocket and wiped the blood from his arms. I could feel his eyes on me.

'When you're with me, you chase all the bad stuff away.'

'You're not afraid any more?'

He shook his head. 'This place becomes beautiful

again. You seem to know me better than I know myself,' he added softly.

I tried to distract him. 'Orpheus is so lifelike I can almost hear his music.'

James hadn't taken his eyes off me. 'He was so skilled at playing the lyre he could charm any living creature, even objects like stones and rocks.' Like a magician he plucked something from between Orpheus's fingers. He took hold of my hand and placed a white stone in it. I could feel how smooth it was.

'Please don't run from me,' he said.

I took a few steps back, my arm skimming cold marble. James's sudden piercing voice stopped me in my tracks.

'Stop, Sinead! Whatever you do, don't move backwards another inch. Walk towards me.'

Convinced that a snake was about to bite I froze, unable to move at all, a foot raised in the air. James stepped forward and let me fall into his arms. I twisted my neck and stared down at the ground. Serrated metal teeth grinned up at me.

'It's an animal trap,' he said, his hand cradling the base of my skull, pulling me closer. My heart was still thudding and I wanted to stay in his arms, but very deliberately I extricated myself. I watched him pick up a stick and snap the jaws shut. Realizing what could have happened, I looked away in horror.

'It's all coming back to me now,' he said thickly. 'Dad loved hunting . . . rabbits, hares, foxes . . . These traps have been illegal for years, but he still used them. They wouldn't kill, only maim, and the animal would be left squealing in agony until he came back and put them out of their misery. Sometimes he'd forget, and when I was lying in bed I could hear them crying all night. His study was filled with the animals and birds he'd killed. They were put in glass cabinets and given staring glass eyes. I wouldn't ever go in there – it was filled with death.'

'That's so awful, James,' I said. 'Why did he put a trap so near Orpheus?'

His jaw clenched. 'Because it was my favourite place. He put it there as a punishment because I wouldn't go hunting with him. He liked to crush and maim and kill, Sinead, and he wanted me to be like him.' James's face was filled with anguish. 'I didn't want to kill. I would never kill.'

# Twenty-Three

I was desperate to make this better for him. 'It doesn't mean your dad's a monster. Some people think there's nothing wrong with hunting.'

James tore at the neck of his T-shirt and I could see a rectangular scar faded to silvery lilac. 'He hit me with the butt of his gun because I wouldn't kill a hare. It was howling with pain. I should finish it off . . . I should prove I was a man . . . Mum was screaming in the background and . . . I don't remember anything else . . . I think I blacked out.'

I wanted to put my arms around him but I was scared of getting close again.

'Mum hated the estate, Sinead. She wanted to leave and take me with her. Dad said she'd have to go to the other side of the world for him not to find us.' James flinched. 'I guess that's just what she did.'

'I'm sorry,' I said, realizing how inadequate this sounded.

'Don't be sorry. I'm glad I know the truth, even if it hurts. The truth is so important. It's what I came home for. That and . . . to meet you. 'His gaze was soft and imploring. 'What I feel for you is true, Sinead . . . I couldn't fake it.'

I knew that James was drawing me in again, and I was feeling too weak to fight. His lips moved silently and his eyes flickered. I placed my fingers across his eyelids and forced him to close them. He was physically and emotionally exhausted and was asleep in minutes. This was the second time that he'd fallen asleep on me. I tried to forget the look on his face when he told me that he couldn't fake his feelings for me. No one had ever looked at me that way. Emotion compressed my heart.

I jumped to my feet, more unsettled than ever and desperate to stretch my legs. Poor James. His dad was turning out to be a cruel bully – as far from the white knight as it was possible to be.

I felt a lump in my throat and tried to focus on Patrick's clues. Both statues had been found, but they weren't together. I moved from the willow's shade. The white stone was still in my hand. Strange, there was another on the ground. I hadn't seen any others like this. My skin pricked. Had Patrick left them for me? I walked slowly, my eyes scouring the ground. Each time I found another stone my pulse quickened. The trail took me through the trees until I reached a clearing that felt like coming across an oasis in the desert. The pretty glade was so unexpected I could have believed fairies had arranged everything to blend together so beautifully. The wild flowers were a riot of colour and the surrounding trees young and supple. Two had actually bent towards each other to form an arc, like two lovers desperate to meet. The grass was green and moist, in contrast to the scorched yellow blades elsewhere. The trail stopped. I searched and searched, unable to believe that Patrick would leave me in limbo like this.

I shielded my eyes, gazing further afield. There was a slatted wooden bridge that crossed a narrow, twisted stream that was all but dried up. James's story suddenly came back to me: *Orpheus was allowed to cross the River Styx.* The stones were as smooth as pebbles from a beach, as if polished by water. I walked towards the bridge. There must have been some kind of enclosed garden on the other side. I could see a dense surrounding wall of greenery. A noise made me stiffen, a low menacing growl that made the hairs on the back of my neck stand on end. I froze, all my muscles taut, my legs weakening.

The most enormous black dog had appeared on the other side of the bridge. Its back was arched, hackles raised and teeth bared, its lips drawn back in a savage snarl. It had the barrel-shaped body of a small donkey, and the typical oversized head of a bull mastiff, with wide and dangerous jaws. I didn't dare turn around and run because I was sure this would make me an easy moving target. Quietly and without making any sudden movements I backed away, but each time I took a step the dog advanced, spittle drooling in anticipation. I was certain it was about to run at me.

My hands reached behind me, moving aside the shrubs and bushes until I was hidden. I was still too frightened to turn my back on the creature and continued slowly retreating, trying not to make the slightest sound. I barely allowed myself to breathe. My finger hooked some kind of metal ring hanging from a tiny branch. I took it with me but didn't dare look at it until I was far enough away to feel safe. My blood ran cold. It was a round metal dog tag. Engraved on it was the name *Cerberus*.

James was just emerging from behind the curtain of the weeping willow when I limped back, still violently trembling. 'I-I've just seen Cerberus,' I managed to stutter, 'near the bridge. I thought he was going to attack me.'

With shaking hands I handed over the dog tag.

'This can only mean only one thing,' James said grimly. He looked pale.

'What?'

'That dog would never have left my dad's side. Dad must be back. He's probably found out about my visit and he's skulking somewhere in the village, plucking up the courage to see me.' His lips thinned. 'And I'll be ready.'

I opened my eyes wide. 'After what you've remembered I'm surprised you'd want to see him at all.'

'I'm a man now,' James said, squaring his chin. 'I want to look him in the eye and ask him to explain. If he can't explain, I want the chance to tell him what I think of him.'

I nodded, knowing exactly how James felt. I had similar thoughts about facing Patrick again.

'What were you doing by the bridge anyway?' he asked.

'I found a trail of stones like the one you took from the statue. They're all smooth and round like beach pebbles. I thought of Patrick again and followed them to the bridge.'

James shielded his eyes. 'That's strange because . . . in a way both statues belong over there . . . with the dead.'

My heart jumped. 'The dead?'

James pushed his hair from his face. 'The graveyard.'

Somehow this didn't surprise me, but I did wonder why James hadn't mentioned it before. 'Is it a family plot?'

James shook his head. 'In the Reformation it was illegal to perform Catholic burials, but one of my ancestors ignored the ruling and allowed them to take place on the estate. To keep them secret the graves couldn't be marked. Dad used to tell me it was blessed land and I must never play there; the dead shouldn't be disturbed.'

'Weren't you ever tempted?'

'Of course . . . but a giant wall of holly and poison ivy surrounds the site and I was scared.'

'Of Cerberus or your dad?'

'Both,' James answered, stony-faced.

'Cerberus wouldn't hurt you though?'

Keeping his eyes firmly fixed on me, James arched and twisted his neck. I could see two puncture wounds surrounded by scar tissue. I suddenly realized what he was trying to tell me and my mouth dropped open.

'Mum told me I was savaged by a stray dog who wandered into the estate, but after today I don't believe her any more.'

'But Cerberus knew you. Why would he attack? You still don't remember?'

He shook his head. 'My memories are like . . . subliminal cuts breaking through a film . . . the rest is still hazy.

I pulled James by his T-shirt. 'I have to go back there. The graves might be a link to Patrick's clues about the afterlife.'

James dug in his heels. 'It's too dangerous,' he insisted. 'Cerberus could attack you as well. His jaws would make the animal trap look tame.'

These words really hit home. I thought of my recent escape and had to lean against the nearest tree to steady myself. For a moment all the weird things that had happened to me since I began my search for Patrick flashed before my eyes: my brush with death in the clock tower, the brambles, the dragonflies, the animal trap and now Cerberus. Maybe Harry was right and I was in mortal danger. My mind wouldn't confront the other kind of danger I irrationally feared – the danger to my immortal soul.

My face must have given something away, because James came towards me with a concerned expression. I opened my mouth to speak, but no words would come out. It was as though my throat had locked. The sight of James advancing on me rendered me even less capable of speech. He leaned against the same tree trunk, his head angled to mine and his eyes scanning my face. My legs were even weaker now, but for another reason. One of James's hands gently rubbed my cheek as if to wipe away a tear and then touched my forehead, my eyelids, my nose and lips, as if he was blind.

'I want to remember,' he whispered. 'Even in my sleep, I want to remember your face.'

I didn't know that I was edging towards him until the bark of the tree grazed my skin. Our lips touched but we didn't kiss at first; we stayed together like this until it felt as if I was breathing life into James. His colour heightened and the blood returned to his pale lips. When we finally kissed it was tentative, as if we were both scared of our feelings. We didn't close our eyes, and I could see my own face reflected in his irises. It seemed as if the world had stopped revolving, and I could scarcely bear the strength of my feelings. They rose from deep inside and stayed in my chest, suffocating me. Part of me wanted to run away, except I couldn't have left James if my life depended on it. His kisses grew more intense. These sensations were completely new to me and I was glad of the tree for support. We finally separated and faced each other. I nervously touched my lips, which felt hot and bruised.

'I don't want to hurt you,' James said.

*I'd rather be hurt than not have this; I finally know I'm alive.*

This admission shocked me. It weakened my former resolve and came straight from the heart, without thought or deliberation. But I wasn't ready to let him know this.

'There's Harry to consider,' I said, still wary of letting my guard down.

James's jaw tightened. 'I'm running out of time. Don't go tonight, Sinead. We need to be together.'

I put my hands on either side of his face. 'I can't. There're things I have to do and . . . someone I have to speak to.'

He gave a small nod and kissed my forehead. 'Until tomorrow then.'

We strolled back to the house together and he left me at the main entrance. I threw myself frantically into work, trying to calm my racing mind. When I had been kissing James it had seemed perfectly clear who I should be with, but I was worried about jeopardizing my friendship with Harry, even though he'd been so understanding. And James still couldn't promise me more time. It seemed such a mess, and I was getting distracted from my mission to find Patrick.

When Sister Catherine did her usual home-time inspection her face wasn't as sour as usual. My work had been so diligent that even she couldn't find fault with me. I was dismissed for the day with what might even have been a faint smile. As I emerged from the secret entrance on my bike the late-afternoon sun made me squint. I began to pedal, a sinking feeling in the pit of my stomach about what was ahead. My phone beeped and I pulled over to the side of the road. It was a message from Harry. He was on a day trip to Chester, chaperoning his sister and her Girl Guide pack. The coach had broken down, leaving them stranded. He didn't know what time they'd be back. I pictured Harry surrounded by tired, whiny little girls, patiently trying to keep their spirits up. He had a heart of gold, I thought, selfishly glad to be let off the hook.

Without thinking, I turned my bike around, knowing I had to see James. As I approached the wooded wall even the griffins seemed to be looking at me favourably. I pushed aside the ivy and ducked through the doorway, the pull of James growing stronger. There would be no need for words, which was just as well because I was terrible at expressing myself. As I cycled along the path I recognized the copse that concealed Eurydice. I was overwhelmed by a sudden urge to see her again, threw my bike to the ground and buried my head among the green speckled leaves.

# Twenty-Four

I was cold. It seemed so long since I'd been really cold that the sensation took me by surprise. My clothes felt damp and I shivered. There was an odd noise close by and it took me a minute to realize that it was my own muffled breathing; my face was buried in the moist grass. It must have rained. I managed to sit upright, flexing my muscles to ease my stiff joints. My arm hurt and a quick glance revealed an awesome bruise, the size of a fist. My mind was befuddled and foggy as I tried to recall the sequence of events. I had been making my way back towards the house when I'd stopped to see Eurydice. Had I fallen and hit my head?

Something else was weird – it was getting dark, which meant that I'd lost hours. I really should get home, but I was still groggy and there was a beautiful sunset – shades of violet and pink surrounding a half-circle of radiant fire. I stared for another few minutes, trying to make sense of it all. The halo of fire was rising instead of sinking and warm rays were dappling the grass beneath the trees. I looked at my phone and my heart raced with confusion and bewilderment. It was 5.30 a.m. It wasn't evening, it was morning. I must have been here all night, and that wasn't rain on the grass, filling the upturned flowers like tiny silken pitchers, it was dew. I had lost twelve whole hours.

A deep sense of grief welled up inside me as I recalled my dreams. I'd dreamed that I was trapped here for years, trying to find James again. Every season had passed and still I searched through blistering heat, driving rain, gales and blizzards. The ground was soft underfoot with summer petals and then hard as iron with frost. And Patrick had been in the dream. I felt him as strongly as if he was standing in front of me now. He had a beacon, a flame on the end of a wooden torch that flickered to extinction as he retreated through a series of tunnels. He had tried to show me the way, firstly with encouragement and then with growing anger that I wouldn't obey. His firm hold on my arm had turned into a vice-like grip as the roof of the tunnel became lower. I twisted to get away from him and his fingers hurt my flesh. I was choking with panic and I began to claw at his handsome face, leaving deep gouges in his cheeks and neck as though he'd been savaged by a wild animal.

Shuddering at the memory, I stood up with difficulty. I would make my way to the house to see if James was awake and if he could shed light on my missing hours. I needed to know what had happened to me. There had to be an explanation. I tried to damp down my growing fear that there were no rational explanations any more; this place was beyond the realm of the normal. I swallowed a panicky sob. My hand blindly touched Eurydice's face and my fingers felt perfect marble tears that I hadn't noticed before. A nearby tree was smeared with some dark substance and I stopped to examine it, fearful it was my blood. When I scraped at it with my fingers, flakes became embedded under my nails, but they weren't the colour or texture of blood. What the hell was happening? I stumbled on. James's car was parked at the front of the house and I remembered last night and my urgency to be with him. It hadn't abated, only intensified. If only he would appear on the balcony again, warm with sleep.

The front door was open, but there was no sign of anyone about. I entered the hall and listened, the hairs on the back of my neck standing on end. The sighing was particularly mournful in the silence, and every now and then an indistinct word seemed to filter through. I cautiously moved towards the concealed door, straining to listen. A low voice growled, 'Sinead'. It was Patrick's voice and he'd used the same sharp tone as in my dream. My heart hammered. I knew he was close. It was the same feeling I'd experienced before. As if on cue, a tiny crack opened in the panelling. This was the moment when I'd finally caught up with my brother and he was going to show himself. I had followed his footsteps far enough. The game was over.

\*

A disembodied hand appeared, the skin wrinkled and covered with liver spots, the nails discoloured. I wanted to run away, but found myself glued to the spot in terrified fascination as the crack widened. An ancient, wild-eyed figure with a shock of white hair emerged, dressed in a long ivory nightdress. Her face consisted of deep folds of yellow skin, her cheeks were sunken and her mouth formed an O of surprise. Her feet were bare and in one hand she was carrying an oil lamp. She moved towards me and I resisted the urge to run. One misshapen finger pointed in my direction as if in accusation.

'You're here already,' she gasped, and her chest seemed to rattle with the effort. 'I wasn't expecting you so soon.'

'Mrs . . . Benedict?' I asked cautiously. 'I'm Sinead. Sister Catherine employed me.'

Her hand loomed in front of my face, but as I instinctively withdrew to protect myself it dropped down to her side. She turned towards the sweeping staircase and her body tensed as though in preparation for the climb. I offered her my arm and took the lamp so that she could hold the banister. Her breathing was worryingly laboured but she made it to the top. Once inside her apartment she seemed to collect herself and her expression relaxed. This could be an opportunity to ask her about Patrick.

I showed her his photo. 'Have you seen my brother here recently?'

She shook her head, but didn't seem surprised by my

question. 'I'm sorry. Sister Catherine is the one you should ask. I don't see the people who are invited in.'

*People who are 'invited in'. So it wasn't just Sister Catherine who talked about these strange invitations.*

I put my phone away, disappointed.

'Let me get you some breakfast,' she said.

I held up my hands in protest. 'No . . . really. I couldn't put you to so much trouble.'

'I'll cook some scrambled eggs,' she insisted. Her eyes ran up and down my body. 'You're very fresh-faced, but . . . so terribly skinny.'

'I have lots of nervous energy,' I felt the need to explain. I studied my face in the mirror over the mantel. She was right about my skin – it positively glowed, as if I'd bathed in morning dew, which was fitting because that was exactly what I had done. And my hair didn't look as if I'd been lying in the wet grass all night. It looked better than when I slept on a feather pillow.

This was the first time I'd been upstairs at Benedict House. Several more oil lamps were dotted about and the heat had created flame-shaped stains on the hessian wallpaper that almost flickered in the sunlight. At night it must be like an inferno. Idly I picked up a photograph from a carved sideboard. I identified James's father immediately. His arms were possessively circled around a woman sporting a 1980s bubble perm and a blond boy with a wobbly smile. They had to be James and his mother. They both had the same large hazel eyes, but there was something else – they both looked vulnerable and scared, held in that suffocating grip. James's father looked directly into the lens with an arrogant smile. I studied his face again, wondering if he could really be as cruel as James suspected.

Now that she was in her apartment James's gran seemed quite animated. She motioned me to sit at a small round table. A huge plate of steaming scrambled eggs on thinly sliced brown toast and a cup of tea were placed in front of me. I was desperate for coffee but smiled gratefully. I took a sip of the tea. It tasted fine – no bitter residue of vinegar.

'It must be positively Sisyphean working here,' she said. 'You don't look up to the task.'

'Sisyphean?' I enquired blankly.

She brought her own breakfast to the table and sat opposite me, looking pleased to explain. 'Sisyphus was a deceitful king who was required by the gods to roll a boulder up a hill for all eternity as a punishment. Each time he had climbed halfway up, the boulder would roll back down and his task would begin again.'

'I'm stronger than I look,' I replied, wondering if the whole family was obsessed with myths. 'I believe Benedict House has its own spooky legend.'

She sipped her tea primly. 'Sometimes it's hard to separate history from legend, but we ensure that the entrance always remains open.'

My mouth twitched because she couldn't have been more wrong; Sister Catherine ensured the entrance always stayed closed and fastened with a thick metal chain. James's gran seemed willing to chat though, and I kept my tone conversational.

'The house used to be a church, I believe?'

She laid down her knife and fork. 'That's not strictly true. The church was demolished and Benedict House built afterwards . . . on a different site within the estate grounds.'

My mouth dropped open. 'I was told the house used to be a church, so I thought they were . . . kind of one and the same. Where was the church then?'

She shook her head. 'It could have been anywhere on the estate. Over a thousand years have passed.'

My brain was whirring, trying to make sense of this new information. The first church, the one that Patrick had written about, didn't relate to Benedict House itself. It could be anywhere in the grounds. I screwed up my eyes in frustration.

'Would there be any old maps or books that might pinpoint the exact location?'

'There was a fire in the house,' she said wearily, pressing her forehead with her hand. 'All was lost.'

'What about the local archives?'

She clicked her tongue. 'The Benedict family history has never been given over to the archives. It has always stayed here, where it belonged.'

To go up in smoke, I thought crossly.

I sat for a moment, wondering what else to ask her. It

was impossible not to be drawn again to the photograph of James's father. The conceited smile and knowing eyes made James's resemblance unwelcome.

'Too handsome for his own good,' she laughed, noticing my attention. 'Just like my grandson. Have you met James yet?'

I paid an unusual level of interest to my plate, trying to ignore the fact that James would be sleeping next door. 'Yes . . . we've bumped into each other. James mentioned that he was . . . kind of hoping to meet his dad . . . now he was home.'

I held my breath. 'I hope he doesn't,' she said fervently. 'I really hope he doesn't but . . . it's out of my hands.'

I leaned back in my chair, wondering what to make of this. Was she acknowledging what a horrible father her son had been?

'I . . . thought I saw a black mastiff in the grounds today, close to the bridge. James thought it might be Cerberus, his dad's dog.'

'Ah, poor Cerberus,' she said sadly. 'Such a faithful pet, but he won't have much longer to wait.'

'For what?'

'To be . . . reunited.' She looked around absently. 'I can't let him near the house. If he should hear his master's voice, I'm not sure what would happen.'

A rash of gooseflesh broke out on my arms and legs. 'His master's voice?'

'Yes. I was listening to it in the hallway with the others. Weren't you?'

'I don't know what I was listening to,' I said, my stomach churning.

'But . . . I thought Sister Catherine had explained things and you understood why you were here.'

My knife jumped out of my hand and clattered on to the plate. What had Sister Catherine been saying to a sick old lady? James's gran smiled sweetly and a little knowingly, beckoning me closer. I leaned warily across the table.

'James told me a secret,' she whispered. 'He told me about the special young lady he's met. I'm so pleased for him.'

My heart soared and I tried to contain my grin. James had told his gran about us. He must be so sure of his feelings.

'Did James say anything else about . . . this young lady?'

She laughed gaily. 'He said she was a firebrand and he'd fallen for her the first time he saw her.'

'I wish he could stay longer,' I said, sighing with happiness.

'Whatever do you mean?'

There was something so incredulous in her expression that I feared I'd made a huge faux pas, but it was impossible not to continue. 'He . . . mentioned something about going back to Australia.'

She shook her head and smiled as though humouring

me. 'He was never supposed to leave at all. It was my duty to invite him here, but only to face his trial . . . It's too late for him, you see.'

I stared at her, dumbfounded.

'You do understand, Sinead. No one just leaves –'

I tried to keep my face impassive as I tentatively got up from the table and backed towards the door. The calmer her voice became, the more it chilled me.

She carefully wiped the corners of her mouth with a napkin. 'No, no, no, silly girl. My son discovered that it is impossible to depart this place. James won't be able to, and neither will you. Your arrival heralds a new beginning, and for me an end to this mortal coil.'

*Please let me get out of here. James had tried to warn me his gran wasn't herself. I should have listened. She was totally freaking me out.*

Thankfully I'd reached the door and my hand gratefully clasped the brass handle..

'I really should be getting on. Thank you for breakfast.'

She hadn't finished, and to reinforce her crazy utterances she stood up with her arms raised, her ivory gown shimmering in the rays of sunlight. 'Your destiny is to stay here in a prison of your own choosing. The earth will weep with you and from your tears will spring forth new shoots –'

I bolted from the room and galloped down the stairs.

# Twenty-Five

A nervous laugh escaped from me and I blew out softly, sinking down in the hallway and then rocking backwards to sit on the bottom step. Despite the heat I was shivering. Mrs Benedict's words were so disturbing, especially after hearing Patrick's voice this morning. *I was listening to it in the hallway with the others.* It wasn't just me. She'd heard something too.

What had Harry told me about the legend? *The moans of the damned can still be heard today.*

*Stop it, Sinead. You're overwrought.* I put my head in my hands. The catalogue of weird events was growing and so was my fear. Why didn't James wake? I didn't have the courage to burst into his bedroom unannounced, but I needed to be with him so badly that my desire was turning to a desperation that made me shivery and feverish. I moved outside to the front of the house, but the blind in his room was pulled down.

He must have been confident that it hadn't been going

to rain last night, because he'd left the top down on his car. My fingers trailed across the trim and stopped. There were distinctive horizontal scratches on the left door, silver showing beneath the metallic topcoat. And I could feel a slight dent, damage that hadn't been there the other day. James hadn't mentioned it to me. I took my hand away from the car and caught sight of my nails. They were still embedded with dirt and specks of red where I'd scratched at the tree this morning. Slowly I placed one finger against the paintwork – it was a perfect match.

A memory came flooding back in one hot, desperate surge. I was gazing at Eurydice when a car flew past me at speed, scraping the nearby tree and propelling me into the long grass. But not before I caught a glimpse of James's beautiful profile. And as I breathed in the smell of grass and earth, the sound of laughter resounded in my ears – a girl's laughter. That was the last thing I heard before I passed out.

James had been with another girl. All the time I was lying unconscious, James was with another girl, immediately after declaring his undying love for me. How could I have been so stupid? My teeth actually ground together. I was a terrible judge of character – except for Harry. Thank goodness I hadn't told him about James last night.

Even in my torment a feeling of self-preservation took over. No one knew about my night in the woods and no one would. I breathed deeply to stop the hurt from rising, but my chest throbbed as if I'd been stabbed. Everything was raw, and if my feelings were visible I'd be a candidate for open-heart surgery. *What I feel for you is true, Sinead . . . I couldn't fake it*. James must say the same thing to every girl he met. I should get out of here while there was still time, because I couldn't trust what I might do.

'Sinead . . . you came early.'

I didn't turn around for a few moments, trying to control my anger. James had annihilated me last night, turned me into dust, and he deserved the same. Anger would only play into his hands.

I confronted him now, my eyes bright, and a sweet and trusting expression painted on my face.

'Yes . . . I'm early.'

'I hardly slept a wink,' he sighed, walking towards me. 'You felt so close I could almost have touched you.'

'Yet . . . I slept like the dead,' I drawled, trying not to sneer. James was wearing jogging bottoms and a vest top, but he had obviously just woken because his hair was attractively dishevelled. He must have detected something odd in my voice because a deep crease appeared in his forehead.

'Is everything . . . OK?'

'Everything's just . . . brilliant, James.'

He was right in front of me now, his warm breath like a caress on my face. There was no treachery in his huge hazel eyes and I wavered, rooted to the spot, wanting to believe that I was mistaken. He inclined his head to mine and I didn't pull away. We were cheek to cheek when a scent assaulted my nostrils, a musky perfume that definitely wasn't mine. I took a step backwards.

'Was it painful?' he murmured sympathetically. 'Telling Harry?'

I looked at him in astonishment, feigning ignorance. 'Telling Harry what?'

He appeared wounded and I was glad. 'About us,' he said uncertainly.

I put one hand across my mouth, acting shocked. 'You mean . . . that was serious?'

James's arms folded defensively across his chest. 'I thought so.'

I inched towards him until our noses were almost touching, my expression one of suppressed amusement. Then I planted a kiss on his right cheek, feeling like Judas.

'I was just fooling around, James. I thought you knew that.'

'I do now,' he answered quietly. His eyes lingered for a second longer, studying my face. I saw hurt, confusion and injured pride fighting each other before he turned and walked away.

It was a hollow victory. I was so devastated that my throat contracted and I had to slow down my breathing to get enough air into my lungs. I lowered my head and tried to salvage some vestige of pride.

*James has gone away with the notion that you're just*

*toying with him. How much better is that than for him to believe he's broken your heart?*

This thought shocked even me. I did have a heart, and it had been shattered by a boy I'd known for less than a week. But he wasn't aware of this and he never would be.

Sister Catherine chose the worst moment to materialize.

'Are you close to finding what you came for, Sinead?' she asked.

I raised my head and looked at her murderously. 'You know what I came here for – Patrick and nothing else. You promised me answers.'

Her eyes seemed strangely unfocused. 'Whenever answers elude us, it is because we're looking in the wrong place.'

'My mother is crazy with worry,' I growled. 'Don't you care?'

'Of course, but my role is limited.'

I rubbed my temples, trying not to lose my temper. 'When I first arrived you told me the estate had always belonged to God. I know there was a church here before the house–'

She bowed her head in acknowledgement.

'I want to know where it stood.'

'I can't tell you,' she replied. 'You have to find it for yourself.'

'I can't. The estate is massive.' I threw my hands in the air. 'You want me to be like you, endlessly walking the grounds looking for something that's lost? I won't do it. I'm . . . I'm leaving . . . right now.'

It was as if I'd had my own epiphany. Of course I should leave. Why was I hesitating?

'You promised to stay fourteen days, Sinead.'

'I told you I could walk away any time and that's what I'm going to do.'


Once I'd made my decision I couldn't get away fast enough. I grabbed my bike and set off, half expecting Sister Catherine to try to stop me, but she didn't. On my way out I glared at the griffins, who seemed to be watching me with reproach. When I got back to the flat I expected to feel relieved, but the atmosphere had changed and it wasn't peaceful any longer. There was an odd smell in the air, like meat when it's still pink and all the fat is melting, and the heat had brought with it a dozen or so angry flies. I kept finding them on the floor, buzzing, in their death throes. The light was too much for me. I searched for a packet of tacks and pinned a sheet to the window, the thickest one I could find. Then I slumped on the sofa, the implication of what I'd just done sinking in. I'd lost my temper and walked out without solving Patrick's clues. I'd have to face Mum and explain why I hadn't been able to find him.

But what about me? Surely I deserved some attention and understanding? I was so cut up over James I felt physically sick, but also tired and weepy. In the last week my emotions had gone completely haywire. I really wanted to talk to someone, and my mum was the only person I could think of. I knew we weren't close, but she'd been a teenager once; she must remember how it felt to have your heart broken for the first time. I needed some of her time, and Patrick would have to take a back seat for once. In a weird way this might actually bring us closer. I drank about a litre of coffee before I could pluck up the courage to phone her.

She didn't even say hello before jumping down my throat. 'Have you found Patrick, Sinead?'

'I think his trail's gone cold, Mum. I don't know what else to do. I've tried my best –'

Her voice rose sharply. 'But . . . I don't understand. Patrick would never break off like this. You must have missed something. You need to retrace your footsteps.'

'Thing is, Mum –' Tears streamed down my cheeks unchecked. 'Something happened when I was at Benedict House. I met this boy and—'

'You met a boy?' she interrupted.

'Yes, I met a boy . . . and everything was great between us, but I found out today he's been seeing someone else. I feel so miserable and . . . stupid –'

Her voice became low and almost sinister. 'So let me get this straight. While you were supposed to be looking for your brother you were actually making a fool of yourself chasing some boy.'

'It wasn't like that. We found we had loads in common,

and he knows the Benedict estate and he was helping me look for Patrick.'

There was an ominous pause. 'That's the problem. I can see it now. Patrick left the trail for you and you alone, but you've allowed a stranger to get involved. This is private *family* business, not to be shared with every passing Romeo. You must go back.'

'I don't think I can,' I said feebly. 'I can't face him again – it hurts too much, and I'm tired of the endless work.'

'Stop being so selfish, Sinead. It's a bitter lesson to learn, but this boy has probably seen the real you. It's only possible to keep it hidden for so long.'

I sniffed and pulled some tissues out of my bag. 'What do you mean . . . the real me?'

She didn't hesitate. 'This is a hard thing for a mother to say, but there's something cold and *twisted* in you. I used to think it was my fault, but now I can see it's always been there . . . I've known it since you were small. I'm sorry, Sinead, but you must have realized you're different.'

I didn't even protest. My mother had just confirmed my worst fears. No matter how often Harry told me I was a nice person, I didn't really believe him.

'Now you have a perfect chance to do something good,' she continued, 'to find your brother. I can't believe you're wavering.'

*One, two, three, four . . . come on, Sinead, I'm not far away. Five, six, seven eight . . . follow my footsteps, it isn't difficult.*

'I'll go back,' I said wearily, recognizing that I was beaten. 'Maybe . . . we could have a meal together first. I could come home now and we could—'

My mother's voice was coldly brusque. 'You really shouldn't come home again, Sinead, until you've found your brother – until you bring Patrick back to me.'

I would have to go back to Benedict House after all, but the prospect of shaking off Patrick didn't seem liberating any more. What sort of life would I have to look forward to afterwards? Sara was right: I managed to alienate everyone around me and I was going to end up isolated and lonely. *This boy has probably seen the real you.* Him and everyone else. I couldn't run away from what I was any longer. I curled up on the sofa in a tight ball, my hands hugged around my body, desperate for oblivion.

I zoned out and had the strangest sensation of being awake and dreaming at the same time. I was outside Sister Catherine's white room, trying to walk down the staircase only to find it shifting beneath my feet. I pressed my palms flat against the walls but they were moving too, and hot air was rising from somewhere, fanning my body. I looked down with horror to find myself descending further and further into a black hole, hot gas and ashes flying upwards, and the voices weren't whispering any longer, they were howling in pain. And Patrick was waiting at the bottom of the stairs to greet me, his eyes crazed with hate. My feet were desperately trying to climb back up, but I kept sinking further towards him. I could feel myself growing weaker, overcome by the fumes. I reached into my pocket and took out a tissue, pressing it against my mouth and nose. There was something else in there; my hand closed around his Saint Christopher medal. I threw it into the pit and emerged into sunlight, so dazzling that it blinded me.

The flat bell startled me, a loud, insistent buzz. I was surprised to see that it was evening. I pressed the button, sure that it must be Harry. James's voice made my heart soar and then plummet. I frantically checked my hair and face in the mirror before letting him in. He looked gorgeous but hostile; his face was set like stone, his body language standoffish and his voice clipped. He launched into his obviously well-thought-out speech with the air of someone who was here on sufferance.

'Sister Catherine is concerned by your absence. You shouldn't stay away because of me, Sinead. I know exactly where I stand and I won't bother you again.'

I was so full of conflicting emotions that I simply closed my eyes. James seemed at a loss what to do next.

'This is the wall mural?' he asked. He stepped closer to take a look. 'It looks like Dante's nine circles have been merged into one.'

'Nine circles?'

'Of hell,' he finished.

'What . . . makes you say that?'

'All those bodies writhing around in torment, and the giant snake . . .'

I scrunched up my face. 'I know there were people with serpents in their hair . . . but I don't remember a giant snake.'

He pointed with his finger. 'Here it is . . . a really ugly one with the head of a man and a forked tongue.'

'Let me see.'

I moved James aside and stared at the image. I felt hot, then cold, and an acute weakness swept over my body and drained my little remaining strength.

'That wasn't there before. I'm certain.'

James didn't respond as if I was deranged, although his eyebrows knitted together. 'Your snake connection?'

I gave a small, uneasy nod. 'Maybe . . . but that means someone's been in the flat again. It has to be Patrick, so . . . he must be OK. Right?'

James went over to the door and examined the chain. 'This is useless. Someone could just reach their hand inside and unfasten it. Who fitted it?'

'Harry,' I whispered. 'He's not very practical.'

A fly dived at James and his face was filled with disgust. 'You shouldn't stay here,' he said. 'The gatehouse is empty. Why not come back with me? Stay a couple of days until things die down, or you feel better about everything.'

After what had happened between us I looked at him warily. As if he'd read my mind he said, 'I mean . . . there's no reason why we can't still be friends.'

I nodded gratefully, feeling as if I'd been thrown a lifeline. I couldn't go back home, and I didn't want to stay here. I flapped around, completely disorganized and getting nowhere fast. I had begun to haphazardly throw things into a small holdall when gentle fingers on my arm made me stop.

'There's nothing you need, Sinead.'

I was so drained that I took James at his word and walked out of Patrick's flat in just the clothes I stood up in. James's car was waiting outside, and I gratefully slid inside. James leaned across and fastened my seat belt for me, gently attentive as though I was ill or in pain. He gave me a final searching look before he pulled off into the city traffic.

# Twenty-Six

Sleep that night was unusually deep and refreshing. When I awoke the thin duvet covering me was hardly disturbed, as if I hadn't moved in the night. James had left me with instructions to make sure that all the doors and windows were secured, but these fears seemed ridiculous on an enclosed estate on a bright summer's morning. Inside, the gatehouse had the appearance of a child's playhouse. After the grand scale of Patrick's flat, with its high, echoing ceilings, I expected to feel closed in, but it was like being enfolded in a warm blanket. I padded around in my bare feet, on tiles already warmed by the sun. The surfaces were free from dust, which made me think that someone had lived here recently. It couldn't have been Patrick, because there was a definite feminine smell, something old-fashioned and floral.

It didn't take me long to work out that there was an immediate problem. James had encouraged me to bring nothing. This was one of the rare occasions I regretted not listening to my mother's advice about carrying spare underwear for whatever disaster she envisaged. I thought about asking Sister Catherine for a loan of clothes, but there was little point unless I fancied wearing her spare nun's habit.

A note had been posted when I was showering. It said just two words – *breakfast outside*. I opened the door. On the step had been left a small basket filled with bread rolls, jam, butter and coffee. James was nowhere to be seen, but I sat on the cool stone breaking the crusty rolls into pieces and smearing them with jam. I had company. The birds and hares were tame, eagerly pouncing on any dropped crumbs.

I took a deep breath and got out my phone. I had to get in touch with Harry. I composed a text telling him that I needed some space to get my head sorted and to solve Patrick's disappearance. I'd be in touch soon.

On my way to Benedict House I looked for Eurydice and stopped dead. She was visible again, but this time from the other side of the bush. James had clearly been busy. He was determined she should be reunited with Orpheus and must have been moving them closer. Or was he moving them towards the bridge, where they belonged? No matter what James said about it being too dangerous to go there, I had to take a look in case Patrick had left something for me. Now seemed a good time, before I could be talked out of it again. I made my way to the weeping willow and walked on to the glade. I stayed at a safe distance, and climbed up on to the lower branch of a tree to give me a vantage point.

My stomach lurched. Cerberus was pacing back and forth, even bigger than I remembered. The memory of the puncture wounds in James's neck hadn't faded. Dogs usually went for the throat if they were aiming to kill, and I knew from my father that this breed was different from others. Once they sank their teeth into a victim their jaws locked and were difficult to prise apart. There was no way I was going to be able to cross that bridge. Why had the dog stayed? It didn't make sense. James was adamant Cerberus would never have left his dad's side, which meant his dad had deliberately left him behind. It also meant he couldn't be living close by. Maybe Mrs Benedict hadn't been confused when she said that Cerberus was waiting to be reunited with his master. I needed to tell James.

As I was making my way back to the house something suddenly occurred to me; if I couldn't get over the bridge, then neither could Patrick, so that was one place I wouldn't have to worry about following his footsteps.

My sense of timing hadn't failed. I made it to the house on the dot of ten.

Sister Catherine subjected me to an unusual degree of scrutiny. 'You came back,' she said.

I faced her directly. 'I came back.'

'Are you ready to complete your trial?'

This irritated me, because she obviously thought she'd won. 'Do I have a choice?'

'I've already explained to you, Sinead, that you've always had a choice.' I didn't argue and my silence must have pleased her. I watched her rub her hands together with what looked like satisfaction. 'You'll soon be back to the start.'

*Back to the start*. What did she mean? I wasn't going to redo all the tasks she had set for me. When I reached the last room, I certainly wasn't going to begin all over again. She must be mad to think that.

I waited for her to explain. '*Domus dei*,' she murmured.

'I already know about the first church, remember? And you still haven't helped.'

Her face softened imperceptibly. 'When the time is right I'll be there for you.'

*When the time is right*. Sister Catherine *had* won; I'd thought I could save time and skip her stupid trial, but I could see now this wasn't going to happen. She wasn't going to give me any answers until my fourteen days were up.

'You may begin work upstairs, Sinead.'

Sister Catherine left me at the first door at the top of the grand staircase. I was nervous about bumping into James's gran again and quickly went inside. This room looked to be the master bedroom because of the intricately carved four-poster bed. I endured another interminable morning choking on dust. At midday I took my lunch outside. My mind was more active than ever. Neither the snake connection nor the statues seemed to lead anywhere concrete. The key was a non-starter as well. James had tried it out in every lock upstairs without any luck, so he'd given it back to me. Had Patrick changed tactics? Had he gone to ground? And something was different about Sister Catherine; she seemed almost regretful that she couldn't help more, as if her hands were somehow tied.

My feet kicked up the dusty gravel. I was beginning to feel like James, chasing shadows in this strange place. The first church still felt like my best clue, and in her own weird way Sister Catherine had confirmed this. I would start my search close to the house and work outwards. Perhaps there was still some kind of marker that had been covered up over the centuries, or maybe Patrick would nudge me in the right direction somehow. I tilted my head. The silence here was usually profound, but I could hear whistling and it wasn't a bird. I stood up and followed the sound to the back of the house, to the corner where the wild flowers were rampant. I wandered through an ornamental arch. In contrast to the woods, every plant and flower here was light, airy and delicately overgrown, swaying without the slightest breeze.

I drew back behind a trellis and slowly peered out. James was digging in one part of the garden and whistling. He didn't know he was being watched and seemed engrossed and happy in his work. He was wearing rolled-up jeans and a frayed cotton shirt open to the navel, his hair glinting in the sun. I sighed and a symphony played somewhere in my head. I shouldn't have been peeking, but it would be worse to be discovered tiptoeing away. I gave a small cough.

'Sorry, James, I . . . didn't know you'd be here.'

'Did you sleep well?' he asked, stretching lazily.

I laughed. 'Like the dead again.'

He pointed to his spade. 'I'm trying to tame everything here so Gran can sit outside more. She's cooped up in her flat so much.'

'I met your gran,' I said. 'She cooked me breakfast yesterday morning.'

James seemed a little embarrassed and knelt down, tugging at a weed. 'Was she . . . OK?'

'Erm, she was . . . just fine. Thing is, James . . . I went back to the bridge this morning and Cerberus was still there, pacing about. Your gran told me he was waiting to be reunited with his master. She spoke as if he'd been here for a while.'

'Cerberus is still here?'

I nodded. 'I think your dad must have left him behind and . . . gone far away, even abroad.'

James looked at me, stunned. 'You're right. He never would have left Cerberus unless he had to. He loved that dog so much – more than he loved –'

He left the rest unsaid.

'Why's he hanging around the bridge?' I asked. 'It's almost if he's guarding it.'

James rolled his eyes. 'Dad probably trained him to do it years ago, to stop me from going over there.' His face darkened. 'I was so convinced Dad was close. I've been having more dreams about the white knight . . .'

I had to nudge him to continue.

'Now . . . when I see him . . . he's covered in the hare's blood . . . and his eyes stare at me like they're accusing me of something. I wake up soaked in sweat.'

My heart went out to him. 'James . . . even I can work this out. You feel guilty about your dad killing animals and trying to make you copy him. Subconsciously you think you've got their blood on your hands.'

'I wish I could stop it,' he said, his expression anguished.

'It will stop when you meet your dad again, when you confront him about his behaviour.'

'*If* I ever get to meet him. I thought I had a lead the other day, but it came to nothing.'

'What was it?' I asked.

His mouth twitched at the corners. 'When I was asking around the village one of the girls I went to school with hinted she knew something about my dad and if I took her on a date she'd tell me.'

My stomach muscles clenched. 'Did you . . . take her out in the sports car?'

'Yeah . . . How did you know?'

'Just a . . . kind of . . . lucky guess. Did . . . did she tell you anything?'

James grimaced. 'No, she giggled a lot and went on about how she'd had a crush on me when she was ten. It was a complete waste of time.'

He pushed up his sleeves and sat on a dilapidated bench. With his arms behind his head the gap in his shirt widened to show even more of his chest. I sat next to him, hearing the bleached wood creak ominously. One thought superseded all others. If James had told me about his date, we'd be together now; there was no doubt in my mind. Why hadn't he? Did he think I'd be jealous or had it just slipped his mind? I had a gnawing pain inside to think that I'd messed things up between us and wasted so much time.

'Any more leads on Patrick, Sinead?'

I tried to speak normally. 'I asked your gran about Benedict House first being a church. She said the church was demolished and the house built on a completely different site.' I held up my hands. 'I know the estate is huge, but I'm looking for any sign of where the church might have once stood. In his note Patrick described it as some kind of gateway.'

James gave me a sidelong glance and I wasn't sure if he'd forgiven me yet. 'Will you still help me?' I asked. 'You know the grounds so well.'

He nodded but still seemed distant. We sat for a few more minutes, both ill at ease. My arms were folded tight across my chest, while James was absorbed in picking particles of soil from his fingernails.

'Have you everything you need in the gatehouse?' he asked eventually.

I wondered if he was being funny. He must remember

that I'd left Patrick's flat with nothing. 'Well . . . I don't have any clothes or toiletries or . . . er . . . underwear.'

James smirked. 'We're not that different in height. I'll pass some of my things over.'

I tried to banish the image of James taking off his clothes to hand them to me. 'I wonder who lived there before. The place is immaculate, and I can still smell faint perfume.'

'Sister Catherine,' he answered simply.

For some reason this completely floored me. 'Sister Catherine?' I gasped. 'Why didn't you tell me?'

James looked puzzled. 'Why would I?'

I was unusually flustered. 'It's just that . . . when we explored the priest's hole you didn't mention it.'

He screwed up his face. 'I didn't think it was a big deal.'

He was right. It wasn't a big deal, but I still felt the need to ask: 'When did she leave the gatehouse? Do you know?'

James blew out air unconcernedly. 'A couple of days ago. She said it was time for her to go, and I helped her move a few things.'

'Did she say why?'

'She said we'd be having a new guest to stay and she needed to make room for her.'

My heart was racing. 'She definitely said room for *her*?

'Mmm . . . is that a problem?'

'No problem,' I whispered hoarsely.

# Twenty-Seven

Sister Catherine hadn't known I was going to stay in the gatehouse. How could she? I was just being paranoid. She probably *invited* guests to stay all the time and it was nothing to do with me. Even so, my stomach fluttered with disquiet. And what about James? I'd messed things up between us so badly, but it wasn't too late. Why didn't I just go to him? My heartbeat was driving me crazy. I covered it with one hand, but that did nothing to quell the relentless boom that sounded out my loneliness, my desire to be with him and every miserable second that I wasn't. Why didn't James come to me? Because he didn't know the reason why I'd given him the brush-off and probably thought I was horrible. I could leave the gatehouse now in the moonlight, walk to the main house and throw stones at his window. It was that easy, so why didn't I just do it?

It was after midnight when I finally got off to sleep. I dreamed that I was standing in front of a row of identical wooden doors, holding Patrick's key. I inserted it into the first lock and the door opened on to an empty space, pristinely white and clinical. In despair, I ran to the next one. When I looked into the distance the doors had joined in a circle and I was back to the beginning. But I couldn't stop looking. It felt as if this fruitless search went on all night. In despair I began to bang on the wood with my fists.

I sat bolt upright in bed, my heart thumping with the impact of the dream. I flinched. The knocking on the door was real and James was shouting my name. I looked around for something to put on. Wrapping the white cotton bed sheet around me I stumbled into the bathroom, rinsed my mouth with toothpaste and hurried to open the door.

'You look like Eurydice.' James smiled, taking in my makeshift robe. He offered me another basket of food. 'It's after nine. You were still zonked.'

I didn't ask how he knew this, because there was only one way. The gatehouse was tiny, and the flimsy curtains didn't meet properly – he must have looked in on me while I was sleeping. I put the basket down, catching the sheet just before it slipped off. 'I didn't bring a dressing gown, or a towel,' I said shyly.

James produced a carrier bag from behind his back. 'There's a towel in here, and the other things I promised.' I muttered an embarrassed thank-you. He walked about ten metres and couldn't resist looking back, his eyes half-closed in the sun. Now was the time to say something. I could run into his arms, remembering to keep hold of the sheet. I was so full of yearning that I was dumbstruck and stood like an idiot looking at him. James gave me a regretful smile and turned to go. I watched him walk away, hurt rising in my throat. This was how it would feel when he left to go back home, and I made up my mind right there and then not to watch him go. My heart would stop beating with the pain.

*But he wasn't on his way back to Australia. He was only walking to the main house. Another golden opportunity wasted. Why was I so inert, so incapable of seizing happiness? I knew he still had feelings for me. He couldn't make it any more obvious. What had happened to my determination to capture every moment?*

With a huge adrenalin rush, I slammed the door shut, emptied James's bag on to the floor and snatched up a pair of long shorts and a sports vest. It took no more than thirty seconds to wriggle into them and slip on my trainers. James had only a small head start but he was already out of sight. With my long legs I had always been good at sprinting and was confident of catching him easily. But I ran and ran, giddy with my own nerve, until I reached the place where the trees thinned out and I could see the house and forecourt. He wasn't in front of me. I looked all around and he wasn't anywhere. My chest hurt and I was furious with myself again. He must have gone another way.

I limped back towards the gatehouse, my heart in the pit of my stomach, and came face to face with Eurydice. 'I've lost him again,' I said. I touched her face but couldn't feel the delicate bumpy tears. *Weird*. The marble was completely smooth.

'Why did I let him go?' I moaned. 'And why am I asking you? You're just a lump of stone.'

I stared into her blank eyes, pathetically looking for a reaction. I even touched her nose with mine, willing her to give me an answer. 'You don't know how it feels to even have a heart,' I told her scornfully.

'No, but I do.'

I almost jumped into the air as James spoke. I turned around to see him appear from behind a tree.

'What are you doing?' I asked shakily.

'Waiting for you, Sinead. Why were you running?'

James was advancing towards me, his face serious and intense. Pathetically I began to back away, squeaking, 'You didn't bring any . . . milk.'

'And that's the reason you came rushing after me?'

'Yes,' I fibbed.

'Who have you lost, Sinead?'

I didn't reply, and my retreat ended when I bumped against the statue. My hands reached out and clasped her cold dress. 'Her tears have disappeared,' I said, puzzled. 'They were there the other day.'

'You know that's impossible.' James was now only inches from my face. 'You haven't lost me,' he whispered. 'I've been waiting since I first set eyes on you.' His arms extended to embrace Eurydice, trapping me between them both. 'Don't tell me to go again.'

I shook my head and glanced down to study her feet with their perfect toes. He put a hand under my chin, forcing me to look at him.

'Will you stay with me?'

'I'll stay with you,' I echoed.

'For how long?'

'Forever,' I answered lightly.

'That's what I wanted to hear,' James said. He inclined his head to mine and pinned me against the marble statue. I couldn't have moved anyway, but I didn't want to. This time was different; this time there was no distance or uncertainty between us. It wasn't just the kiss that made my body melt; the honesty of it reached deep into my weary soul. I should have trusted my instincts before – this *was* impossible to fake. When we pulled apart I tried to explain about seeing him with that girl, but he barely listened, just greedily kissed my lips between each word.

I felt a huge pang, realizing how bittersweet this was because time was so short for us. 'I won't watch you leave,' I told him fiercely. 'I won't watch you walk away from me.'

James took my hand and placed it across his heart. 'I can't leave you, no matter where I go or what I do. Do you understand?'

I was drawn into his eyes again and saw everything that I'd ever wanted from life but hadn't known existed. I was overwhelmed by the knowledge that this was mine and I would jealously guard it. No one would cut short our time together. If anyone tried, they'd have a fight on their hands.

\*

The rest of the day passed in a kind of dreamy haze. Thought was impossible and speech incoherent. Sister Catherine might have given me instructions or she might have just moved her lips. I worked like a machine, with no idea how I was functioning. My limbs seemed not to belong to my body and I looked at them in bewilderment. The feeling of separation from James was already acute, but there was a consolation: I was wearing his clothes and they still carried his scent. Each time I breathed, he was with me. This was how love or madness felt, or maybe both.

At the first opportunity I walked straight out of the house towards the flower garden. Anticipation flooded through me, but when I was about halfway there something changed and a sense of bereavement, like nothing I'd ever known, overwhelmed me. I ran the rest of the way, terrified that James had gone. But he was still there, beautifully introspective and busy tilling away at the soil. The relief was overwhelming and I took a minute to watch him work. I was perfectly quiet, but he must have sensed that something had changed and looked up. He noticed me and put down the hoe. We didn't speak but stayed a distance apart like two blocks of stone. I couldn't hold out as long as he could and walked into his arms.

We sat on the rickety bench, touching each other's faces before settling into a long, lingering kiss. In the extreme quiet of this place, summer made a noise beyond the birdsong, a heavy and sultry hum of its own. Even the heat had a kind of vibration. It was such a balmy evening that we stayed outside and didn't think about food. No matter how much we kissed I couldn't get enough of him, and it was so secluded here that all my inhibitions seemed to disappear. I traced my fingers against the roughness of his chin and felt the hard line of his jaw. My lips grazed his cheeks and caressed the beautiful groove above his mouth before moving down to his neck. I kissed from his ear to his collarbone and tasted salty sweat. My hair brushed his chest and I felt him shudder. I changed position because my body was aching to get closer to him. My long legs straddled him and I arched my back as he kissed my throat. The heat from us was enough to start a blaze. I turned my head to one side and he lightly blew on the back of my neck as my body twisted into him. My T-shirt had ridden up and I heard him groan as our bare skin touched. The oppressive heat only increased my desire; I felt intoxicated and filled with complete abandonment.

James was watching me attentively and the tension was too much to bear. I traced one finger along his arm and stopped at his wrist, feeling his pulse quickening. Every part of me was throbbing, waiting for him to make that move, the one that crossed the line between what we were doing now and what we were about to do. I thought I'd made it clear to James what I wanted, but I felt as if he needed some kind of definite sign. I wasn't sure if I was brave enough to say the words.

When I eventually spoke my voice was scratchy and

my face stayed firmly buried in his chest. 'We could . . . go back to the gatehouse. You don't have to leave tonight. I mean . . . you could . . . stay . . . with me –'

James stood up suddenly. I adjusted my clothes and tried to look nonchalant, but inside I was burning with embarrassment.

James wouldn't look at me, but I heard him say without the slightest doubt, 'That's not a good idea, Sinead. I couldn't trust myself.'

# Twenty-Eight

I thumped the pillow so hard that the filling separated and left me with uneven lumps and bumps that hurt my head. *Couldn't trust himself.* The only worse thing James could have said was that he respected me too much. I'd thrown myself at him and he couldn't accept because he had scruples and moral fortitude and other totally annoying qualities. Sleep was difficult, and when it eventually came it was filled with tortured dreams about James in which he had absolutely no morals at all. I was desperate to see him again and woke early. I waited impatiently by the window until I saw him approach the gatehouse, and I opened the door before he could reach it. We were both a little awkward after last night, and when he discovered I still intended to work his face fell.

'You're not serious?' he asked. 'Spend the day with me, Sinead. You know we don't that have much . . .' He stopped abruptly and the word *time* was left unsaid. I was grateful.

I rested my cheek against his, my fingers tugging at his hair, now torn between duty and desire. 'I can't forget about Patrick,' I said. 'Sister Catherine's won, and she knows it. She told me I'd have to work for fourteen days before I found my answers. Without any other clues from Patrick, I can't do anything else.'

James stroked my neck and sent an immediate shiver down my spine. He screwed his mouth in deliberation. 'I'll help you then. We'll get through the work more quickly together.'

'I have to do this alone,' I answered carefully. 'It feels like this is my task, and my task only.' My furrowed brow indicated that I didn't even understand this myself.

I expected James to protest again, but he cupped my face in his hands and brought it closer to his. The moment before we kissed was always the best; the expectancy and longing made everything feel as if it was happening in slow motion. As our lips met my hands clutched the back of his head and my body moulded into his. We fitted together perfectly, two parts of the same whole. I smiled to myself, thinking that he must have changed his mind about leaving last night and was intent on making up for it now. With one swift movement James backed me up against the wall, one of his legs pressed between mine. Delicious sensations coursed through my body. I dropped a hand and snaked it under his T-shirt, my fingers walking across his back, feeling it ripple. My mind was momentarily clouded by a blissful image of James taking me in his arms and carrying me into the bedroom. He would stare at me with his gorgeous hazel eyes before . . .

But the dream ended as abruptly as before. James disentangled himself and gave a forced cough. 'I didn't realize the time, Sinead. We should go now – Sister Catherine is probably waiting.'

*Sister Catherine is probably waiting. What difference would a few minutes make? All she ever did was wait.* And why was James so reluctant? Was it me? Maybe I was doing everything wrong. I sucked in my cheeks, pondering the issue as we made our way towards the main house. We parted by the steps to the entrance.

Sister Catherine was waiting for me just inside, but I was taken aback because she was looking inexplicably . . . pleasant.

'Good morning, Sinead.'

This was the first time she had greeted me politely, and I was convinced that she was still gloating about getting me back here. Weirdly she didn't give me any instructions, which meant I was free to work wherever I liked. But I didn't even think of slacking off. I flew through the house as if I had wings. If this was the only way to find out what had happened to Patrick, then I was ready to knuckle down to the job.

When I caught up with James again we navigated the estate, trying to map out the likeliest places for a church to be positioned. I think we both knew deep down we were unlikely to find any remains. The passing centuries would have erased all trace, but I remained alert for further clues. I agreed with my mother: Patrick would never break off completely. His ego wouldn't allow him to.

The sun was at its highest and James was definitely struggling with the heat.

'Still tired?' I asked with concern.

'I'm much better here,' he answered slowly. 'Back home I was hanging around, waiting to . . . recover.'

I looked at him doubtfully. His tan was fading and he seemed to grow paler by the day.

'Fancy cooling off?' he said, wiping his brow. 'I know a little place.'

I thought he was flirting, until he wiped my cheek and showed me the dirt on his hand. I was as grubby as a street urchin. As we cut through the trees my hand wormed into his and I felt his thumb digging into my palm. This path was denser than anywhere he'd previously taken me, and bright emerald moss stained the ground. Our hips bumped together as we tried to walk two abreast. I could smell water before we arrived, that slightly moist scent of decaying vegetation. The ground grew softer and my trainers stuck in places.

'It isn't exactly a lake,' he said, 'more a pond.'

'I knew there was water here,' I exclaimed. 'I saw steam rising and heard a bubbling noise.'

'Hardly.' He laughed. 'This is the coolest part of the

estate. The summer's been so hot the water level's dropped, but it's OK for a dip.'

I still hesitated. There was the dilemma of taking off my clothes. Underneath I was wearing a perfectly sensible bra and a pair of James's boxer shorts, which were surprisingly comfortable, but I still felt self-conscious. James bent down and rubbed some mud between his thumb and finger before smearing two streaks of earth on either side of my face.

'Now you have to come in.'

He waded in, cutting through the surface. The water was deeper than I'd expected, up to his waist. When his back was turned I ripped off my T-shirt and cut-offs and followed him. My toes gingerly wrapped around stones and some kind of pondweed but it was shockingly cool and refreshing. I crouched down, trying to hide my semi-nakedness, but James pulled me up again and looked down at me admiringly. He bent his head to nibble my skin from my throat down to my navel. He cupped water over my hair and pushed it back off my forehead. Droplets ran down my face and into my mouth as I kissed him.

'You're so beautiful,' he breathed.

I hadn't looked in a mirror since I arrived at the gatehouse, but the odd thing was that I suddenly believed him; instead of being gawky and awkward I *was* beautiful. And my body was no longer clumsy and uncoordinated, it was strong and graceful. This was the most confident I'd felt and I was determined to persuade James to abandon his principles. My arms clasped his neck, my hands pointed upwards. I was certain that James wasn't faking his feelings; his eyes were tightly shut, his breathing rapid and his body taut with desire. But as if he sensed my thoughts he pulled away from me, which felt doubly brutal.

We faced each other, still panting slightly. I looked down at the water and up again, my eyes shifting uncomfortably. Eventually I stuttered, 'J-just because I . . . haven't *before* . . . doesn't mean I . . . don't want to now.'

I could see James's muscles stiffen and his face was as stubborn as it had been last night. 'It wouldn't be fair.'

'Why?' I asked petulantly.

'Because you know I can't stay, no matter how much I want to.'

'Life's not fair,' I said. 'Didn't anyone ever tell you?'

James bit his lips until they turned white and his hands clenched by his sides. 'I didn't realize how unjust things were until I met you. It's like being given a glimpse of heaven only to have it snatched away again.'

'If we really want to be with each other,' I said desperately, 'it can't be impossible. Ten thousand miles isn't *that* far.'

James smiled sadly and hung his head. I didn't doubt his feelings for me any more, but he seemed reluctant to give me hope that we had any sort of future together. More than ever I didn't want to spoil the time we had left. I moved closer again, my eyes pleading with him. 'I'm here right now. This moment is all that matters.'

I could see that he was trying to swallow and couldn't.

This was agony. I wanted to cling to him until we both drew our last breath, but he seemed set on keeping this distance between us.

'I'll fetch a towel,' he finally muttered.

I stared at James's back as he walked away from me again. I was still frustrated with him, although I understood his reservations better. He wanted to protect me from something I didn't want to be protected from. I was just about to get out of the water when something bubbled under the surface. I was puzzled but a little triumphant; when I'd told James about the strange noise he'd dismissed it out of hand. The sound grew louder, until many gurgling pockets of air were all around me like tiny whirlpools.

I hurried towards the bank, spooked. My foot slipped and my head went under the water for the first time. It was a densely blackish green except for the grainy silt floating in front of my eyes. I stood up, gasping, and felt my legs go from under me. I went down again before I could even take a breath. This time I couldn't get up. It felt as if there were shackles around my ankles, and no matter how hard I tried to move they held me fast. The water was little more than a metre deep but I was lying on the pond floor twisting and writhing, trying to grab hold of anything to help me. I was choking as water filled my lungs.

Out of the darkness came a light, but it was only in my consciousness. Dad was bending over me blowing air into my mouth, screaming at me to breathe. But his face was floating further away. With my last ounce of strength I managed to raise my head slightly and lift one hand out of the water. It was clasped by an iron grip that dragged me from the watery tomb. James turned me on my side and I spluttered water like a gargoyle.

'What happened?' he asked, nuzzling my hair and gently wiping my face with the towel.

'I slipped and must have caught my foot in some weeds,' I gasped.

He screwed his face in disbelief. 'Talk about a freak accident. It seems impossible in such shallow water.'

He must have realized how shaken I was because he patted my skin all over like a baby. This was my closest ever brush with death. I felt certain that if he hadn't returned I would have drowned. My throat was still raw and my chest hurt like hell. I scrambled to my feet.

'I have to get away from here.'

James supported me and I leaned against him as we walked. He seemed unnaturally quiet. I flopped down under the shade of an oak tree and lay on my back looking up at the daubed sky.

'Are you going to tell me what really went on back there?' he asked.

'Your guess is as good as mine.'

'There's something you're holding back from me . . . isn't there?'

I kept gulping in air as if I'd forgotten how to breathe. It was a while before I could speak. 'Remember the time I conjured up the swarm of dragonflies? Well . . . other things have bothered me here. Things I've seen or felt that aren't . . . can't be real, including what just happened in the pool.'

James exhaled in a long rush. 'Have you told anyone else?'

'Mm . . . Harry. He thinks I'm stressed.'

'But you don't agree?'

I gave a cynical laugh. 'Maybe it's me who's in need of the psychiatric help, not Patrick.'

'I don't think so,' James said firmly. 'You seem sane to me.'

I sat with my knees under me. 'You've never thought there was anything . . . *unexplained* here?'

'Unexplained?'

'Like . . . erm . . . not of this world?'

'You mean supernatural?' He smiled ruefully. 'The estate's so old and steeped in history, it can make you conjure things that aren't real.'

I should have been reassured, but I couldn't shrug off the feeling of foreboding. My hair had already dried in the sun. I shook it impatiently and tried to clear my dry throat. 'I have an off-the-wall idea that all this is some kind of weird test – as well as having to work in the house to find Patrick, I have to conquer my obsession with time and . . . my own terror of death.'

James narrowed his eyes. 'That sounds deep.'

I shrugged one shoulder. 'Sister Catherine is so maddening, but she told me to face my demons –'

James's face immediately fell. I realized what I'd said and reached for his hand. 'I'm sorry . . . I know how hard it's been for you coming back and being forced to confront yours.'

He shook his head. 'If I hadn't, I wouldn't have met you, Sinead. I was dead inside.' He gently traced the outline of my face with his fingers. 'I'd do anything for you . . . even walk through fire.'

I smiled dubiously. 'Really?'

'And I'd sell my soul to Satan,' he added recklessly, 'for one more hour with you.'

'You won't have to,' I said, 'because there's nothing to keep me here. Wherever you go, I'll follow.' I felt the truth of this. There was nobody to really miss me and nowhere that felt like home.

A fleeting look of pain crossed James's face. 'There're some places even you can't go.'

'You obviously don't know me. You'd find it easier to shake off Satan.'

I shuffled closer and massaged his shoulders carefully, kneading my fingers into his tension knots. He continued talking, but it was as if he'd forgotten that I was there. 'You see, Sinead, once you allow the possibility that your time is finite, even if you run hard and far, nothing can save you – it will devour you like a wild beast. Don't measure the time you have left.'

He twisted his neck to gaze at me and his eyes met mine with a tortured desperation that I didn't understand.

# Twenty-Nine

I took James at his word. I stopped measuring time: the seconds, the minutes, the hours. If I didn't count them, then they couldn't run out for us. I refused to look at my watch or to notice the height of the sun at midday and the lengthening shadows of late afternoon. I didn't calculate the endless hours I worked in Benedict House or how long I searched the grounds looking for more of Patrick's clues. And I refused to acknowledge how many nights I fretted alone, wishing James would stay with me. Benedict House possessed some kind of power that enabled time to be on our side. It wasn't logical, but I no longer tried to analyse it. Even if we had only days left, we would make them last a lifetime, and I didn't know how but we would find a way to be together again.

I couldn't help feeling a certain sense of triumph. Whatever I had to suffer in this place, and for whatever reason, there was one thing that no one had bargained for: my meeting James. This one factor made everything seem less of an ordeal. I gazed affectionately at Eurydice who seemed to agree with this sentiment. I liked to lie in the warm grass with her watching over me. James hadn't commented on the fact that she'd moved, which made me more convinced he had done it.

'Why did you move Eurydice?' I asked one evening, tickling his face with a blade of grass.

He looked at me askance. 'I didn't. Why would I?'

I pinched his arm. 'To make me think she was trying to reach Orpheus.'

'It wasn't me, honest.'

I smiled wryly, still not believing him. 'Maybe it was Sister Catherine,' I suggested, laughing.

'Hardly.'

'What if . . . she's an incurable romantic and wants them back together again?'

'She's not allowed to be romantic,' James pointed out.

'She's only human,' I countered, which was ironic because at first I'd genuinely doubted this. Night was moving in, and sequins of the setting sun shimmered through the trees. I wasn't even aware that I'd closed my eyes, but I must have drifted off for a few moments. When I opened them my expression was dazed.

'Sinead?'

'The most incredible dream,' I breathed. James shifted but my head still rested on his chest, next to his heart. 'We got old. I saw us walking among the trees, hand in hand. I was wearing nylon trousers and my face was baggy . . .'

I prodded James in the ribs but he didn't even smile. 'And you were just as handsome with grey and white hair, but you had on old men's slacks and slip-on shoes.'

I pulled at his T-shirt but he still hadn't reacted, and I could feel that his whole body had gone rigid. I reached around to kiss him and his cheek was wet. I pretended not to notice. His eyes were hugely sorrowful and he stared at me intently as though to jealously stamp every last inch of my features to memory. He kissed my fingers and examined each in turn as if they were works of art. He smoothed my hair from my face and began kissing my forehead, down to my nose, with its patch of sunburn, to my chin, my neck, even my ear lobes. His lips skimmed my arms, my stomach and my navel, down to my knees and ankles. When he reached my toes I laughed and wriggled my feet away.

'Shall we stay here and watch the sunset?' I suggested.

James pulled a face. 'I prefer the sunrise.'

'Me too,' I agreed, reflecting how quiet he was. And yet I was glad, because some things were beyond words. It was another few minutes before he spoke again.

'So, Sinead – why don't we?'

'What?'

'Watch the sunrise.'

My voice was croakily confused. 'But . . . to see the sunrise . . . you'll have to stay with me—'

'For how long?' he interrupted.

My breath caught in my throat. 'Until dawn.'

James stood in one swift movement and used

both hands to pull me to my feet. 'I think that can be arranged.'

'Do you trust yourself?' I whispered.

I wasn't sure James had heard, until I caught his resolute reply. 'Not for a second.'

When we got back to the gatehouse James didn't turn on any of the lights and I was glad. Despite my conviction that this was what I wanted, I was scared because it meant so much to me. My heart had taken on a boom of its own that drowned out every other sound. I led James into the small bedroom and stopped abruptly, causing him to bump against me. I could see by the rise and fall of his chest that he wasn't relaxed about this either, which made me feel better. We stood by the window watching each other uncertainly, trying to control our breathing. The anticipation was killing me. I took a step towards him and rested my head on his chest. I wanted to savour every second, but my hunger for James wouldn't allow me to. His arms encircled me and I pulled him down with me on to the bed. I lay on my back staring up at him. His eyes looked even more dazzling from this angle, almost amber, the whites startlingly clear. I knew I would never forget the way he was looking at me now.

The heat lingered like a layer of fog. We slept on top of the duvet without even a sheet covering us. The only thing I was conscious of was James lying next to me and the feel of his skin against mine. We lay with our faces touching, but I resented sleep, resented anything that blotted out his features. Fear gripped my heart. It wasn't possible to love this much. It burned within me, consuming me. I'd always found it hard to trust, yet now I had no defences left; my life was in James's hands. It was terrifying to be so vulnerable.

James pointed towards the window. We had deliberately left the curtains open and now the swirling steel-grey night clouds parted like a crack in the heavens. I must have dozed, and when I opened my eyes James was still watching me. Now he did smile and forced my lids to close by pressing his lips to them. The next time I woke the sun was streaming in and I was alone. With a luxuriant stretch I looked around, expecting to hear the door open and see James appear, his arms laden with food. I wanted so badly to hold him that my body ached. I was now confident James would stay. He could extend his visa; he had family living here and seemed to have no money worries. Maybe that was what his gran and Sister Catherine had meant when they said he was home for good.

My expectancy reached fever point until I couldn't wait any longer. After a quick wash I threw on some clothes and went in search of him. He wasn't on the path to the main house or in the flower garden, although I searched every nook, expecting him to jump out on me. I reached the gravel forecourt and looked up at James's window, remembering when he'd come out on to the balcony. I heard a noise behind me and my heart leaped. He was trying to surprise me.

I hesitated before turning around, wanting to relish the moment when we came face to face. Slowly I swivelled on one foot, my grin absurdly wide, but my world came crashing down around my ears. Sister Catherine was looking right at me and there was something terrifying in her eyes, something I hadn't seen before: pity. I opened my mouth to speak but no words came out. I tried to swallow, but my dry throat had closed over. My breath was ragged and full of anguish as I ran into the hallway of Benedict House, up the grand staircase and into James's bedroom. I stopped as the full realization hit me like a sledgehammer – the room was bare, the bed already stripped. James had gone. My eyes darted around wildly, trying to escape from the truth. I took a breath. His scent was here and I wanted to stay and bury my nose in the bedding and howl like an animal. It couldn't be time for him to leave; I would have known.

*You refused to acknowledge the dawn of a new day, and thought that you could cheat time. But it made no difference. No one can beat the ticking of the clock. You've simply been deceiving yourself.*

Sister Catherine had followed me.

'Did he leave me a note?' I panted.

She shook her head. Uncontrollable distress was making me hyperventilate and I sat on the bed and tried to stop wheezing. For once I didn't care how pathetic I looked. It was my fault. James had taken me at my word. I told him that I wouldn't watch him leave, that I refused to see him walk away from me. He had gone without saying goodbye and could already be in the sky now. I had no address, no contact number and my only link was his gran, who wasn't exactly rational.

I stumbled downstairs and ran across the forecourt into the woods. My face was soon scorched by tears and my vision blurred, but I was driven on, compelled to visit every place we'd been together. Every path and every inch of ground assumed new significance because we had trodden them together. Hungry and thirsty, I soon felt weak, but I limped on. In the bare earth by the temple were the remnants of the daisy chain that James had made. I picked it up and slipped it over my wrist.

This was self-inflicted torture, but there didn't seem to be any other way to ease my grief. Without direction I ventured into dark pockets of undergrowth, completely shaded and filled with sharp briars that snagged my clothes and cut my flesh. I knew I should leave, but there was no place I belonged. At least here I felt close to James. My feet felt as though they had covered fifty miles. Eventually I had to admit defeat and try to rest. The only way back to the gatehouse was past Eurydice, and for some reason I dreaded seeing her more than anything.

My eyes must have been playing tricks on me. I squeezed them tightly shut and opened them again, blinking. There was a figure standing next to her. It felt as if there was a bullet ricocheting off my heart. It couldn't be. This was another illusion. I wanted to run, but I forced myself to walk slowly, still convinced that this was a manic case of wish-fulfilment, but even when I was only a metre away, the figure hadn't yet moved. My hands reached out to make sure that it was real.

'I knew you couldn't leave,' I whispered.

'How could I?' James said.

'Where's your luggage?' I asked, still terrified he might change his mind.

He gave a careless shrug and I grinned, weak with joy. He wasn't leaving. There would be no more fear of the hours slipping away from us as now we had all the time in the world. I dragged James into the gatehouse. My eyes never left him, worried he might evaporate.

'I shouldn't have gone,' he said over and over.

There were two bright spots on his cheeks, and his skin was pallid and clammy. I put one hand across his forehead, fearful that he was ill again.

'James, you must lie down,' I insisted.

He took hold of my hand and I had to incline my ear to his lips. 'No, I can't. Don't let me sleep, Sinead. I mustn't sleep.'

I was ecstatic to have him back and brushed aside this strange behaviour. After an hour or so inside he insisted on going out because the heat was still stifling. It was hard to believe it was already evening. I must have been walking for most of the day.

James's mood didn't pick up. As I hugged him he was feverish and trembling.

'I'm sorry, Sinead. It shouldn't have to end like this.'

I gently prodded him in rebuke. 'Nothing's ending. This is the beginning for us.'

He didn't appear to be listening. 'You're the answer to my prayers, Sinead, to fall in love before –' He broke off.

'You're the only thing that matters to me,' I said truthfully. 'I spent all day wandering the estate and realized there was nothing else in the world I really care about but you.'

James seemed deeply affected by these words. He covered his face. 'Don't say that, please.'

I prised his fingers away and held his head, forcing him to look at me. 'You told me once there were places I couldn't follow you, but there aren't. There's nowhere I won't go to be with you. Do you believe me?'

James looked deep into my eyes and nodded, but I couldn't see any happiness there and I wondered why his feelings were in such turmoil. As the night drew in we lapsed into silence. His breathing became more regular and his trembling calmed. The dying sun cast a red and orange glow that was reflected in his eyes. Mine filled with tears again, without knowing why. We stayed there until the light had faded and the black umbrella of night covered us. I couldn't see any stars and the moon was hiding, translucent, behind a cloud. The wood looked different somehow, full of dark shapes, the trees bent and twisted. At night the smells were more pungent and a little overpowering. We came upon the weeping willow and I stopped dead.

'Look at Orpheus,' I said, squeezing James's arm.

The statue was out of the shade, the sweeping fronds now behind him. The clouds stole silently across the sky, revealing the moon at that very moment. It lit up the statue, which glowed like phosphorous, illuminating the criss-cross of deep veins.

'The white knight,' James cried.

His face was stricken with horror and he fell to the ground, his arms grasping smooth cold marble.

# Thirty

I tried to calm him, but his chest was heaving and his speech rapid. 'Dad wanted me to shoot, Sinead, to put the hare out of its misery . . . the noise was terrible, it sounded human. I should act like a man and stop crying, stop hiding behind my mother's apron.'

'It doesn't matter,' I murmured, stroking his hair. 'He was a bully, but he can't hurt you any more.'

'Real men knew how to kill. It was time to grow up, time to be like him . . . I pulled the trigger –'

'You only did it because you were forced to, James. You mustn't feel guilty.'

'Orpheus was covered in blood and so was I –'

'It was a kindness. Your father would have killed the hare himself – it must have been suffering.'

He pressed his hands either side of my face, his eyes rolling wildly. 'You don't understand, Sinead. You don't understand. I was covered in *his* blood! I didn't mean to . . . but I turned the gun on *him*.'

I shook myself free. 'No, James. You just think you did. You wanted to and you've imagined you did. That's not true, it can't be true –'

He ran his fingers through his hair. 'I did do it. I know I did. I can see him now lying on the ground, and then Cerberus went for my throat. Mum had to beat him with a stick to get him off me.'

My eyes were huge with horror and disbelief. 'But what happened after? What did your mum do?'

'I don't know. I must have blacked out . . . Mum tried to convince me it hadn't happened . . . she told me Dad had walked out after a row. She's been telling me lies ever since, inventing a perfect father for me . . .'

His words were slowly sinking in, and I knew that what he was remembering was the truth. 'James, you weren't responsible, you were just a boy—'

'I killed my father, Sinead, I killed my father.'

He repeated this until I put my finger across his lips.

I stroked his cheek with the back of my hand and cradled him in my arms until his terrible outpouring gradually dried up. I was staggered by his revelation, but it didn't change my feelings for him. Not one bit. Not for one second. He was a beautiful, sensitive person who'd been driven to do something so awful it was impossible to comprehend. No wonder he'd looked so haunted and full of sorrow. I was determined to help him find a way to live with what he'd done. If it took forever I'd make him realize he wasn't guilty.

James struggled to stay awake but he was exhausted and his eyes simply wouldn't stay open. It took all my effort to persuade him to stop fighting and give in.

'I'm so sorry,' he said, before finally succumbing to sleep. 'Don't think too badly of me, Sinead. I tried so hard not to love you . . . for your sake . . . but it wasn't possible.'

We lay so closely together that our bodies seemed fused. There was nowhere else I wanted to be but here, on a soft bed of leaves, wrapped around James. He stirred and I pulled him closer. He was restful now, but his revelation seemed to have brought on my own episode of soul-searching. My trial was almost at an end. Sister Catherine had promised me answers, and I was finally going to catch up with Patrick. James's love would set me free, and together we could face anything. I finally had a future. I stroked James's hair, revelling in a new-found peace and contentment. Sleep came easily.

It was pitch dark. I flinched – something must have woken me. A snowy owl in the branches of a large oak was staring directly at me. Then it launched itself into the air and swooped noiselessly at something on the ground, talons extended. I marvelled at the awesome wingspan and the beauty of its flight, but my admiration was tinged with sadness, trying not to contemplate its prey. There was a crick in my neck and it was impossible to move without disturbing James. But I could still feel his skin next to mine and was relieved to find that his temperature was much cooler. Without any effort I dozed again.

*

'James?'

It was first light and my arm was completely numb. We'd slept all night, but I needed to get up and stretch. I laughed as I tried to escape from his embrace and found it impossible. I shook him.

'James? Wake up.'

He was in an unbelievably deep sleep and I still wasn't able to move him or to see his face properly. My free hand could caress his cheek though, and there was no hint of fever or the awful clamminess of last night. My fingers moved to his lips, sketching their outline, willing him to roll over and kiss me. He didn't react and I put my hand across his mouth to feel his warm breath. My heart began to thunder in my chest.

Within seconds I managed to free myself and crouch over James's body. He was lying on his back and there was a pulse, but it was so faint that my fingers had to press hard to detect anything. His face was the colour of chalk and his lips already bluish. I had to get air into his lungs, but I was so nervous that it took me three attempts to begin resuscitation. All my instincts had frozen and I had to distance myself and pretend that this wasn't James; pretend I was still practising on a dummy. If I thought about how much I loved him, I'd be useless. A faint colour returned to his cheeks and his eyes flickered open. The relief was so intense that I broke into hysterical laughter or it might have been crying, I wasn't sure.

'You gave me such a fright. You were hardly breathing.'

He was groggy and confused, which was entirely natural, but there was something in his eyes that made my heart beat even faster. He looked almost disappointed, as if he wasn't glad to be alive.

'James? Say something.'

His gaze dropped. 'I'm so sorry,' he muttered at last, but it wasn't clear what he was apologizing for.

My voice was as authoritative as I could manage. 'You need to go to hospital.'

I took out my phone to dial the emergency services, but James's hand wrapped around my wrist and squeezed tightly. 'If you love me at all, don't do that.'

'You're not making any sense,' I said fiercely. I lay down beside him and forced him to look at me. 'I've only just found you and now . . . I don't understand. It's like you have a death wish.'

My stomach lurched at these words because I remembered some of our deeper conversations. Was James really filled with hopelessness and despair? All the light had gone from his eyes and I couldn't bear to see him like this. I stared up at the gently rustling trees and patches of pale grey sky. They all seemed to be spinning, or it might have been my head.

'Don't you want to stay with me?' I begged.

'You know I do,' he answered, clearly moved. 'More than anything in the whole world.'

'Then trust me.' I propped myself up on one arm. 'Let

me take you to a doctor. You're kind of . . . pale.'

Pale was a massive understatement. His breathing was erratic and there was a strange gurgle in his throat that terrified me.

It seemed like ages before James spoke. 'I can't go back to hospital, Sinead.'

My voice became briskly impatient to hide my growing trepidation. 'Go *back*? What do you mean?'

'You do know,' he continued sadly. 'You've known since the beginning, but you didn't want to see it.'

I adopted my best no-nonsense voice. 'You're not making any sense, James, and this conversation is . . . ridiculous.'

I sat up so as not to look at him and madly twisted my watch round and round my wrist. 'Anyone would think you were really ill.'

The silence was so profound that it roared in my ears, or that could have been the sound of my blood pumping furiously around my body as terror seized me. It was as if these words opened my mind to the truth that I'd tried to ignore – the scars that were years old, the needle tracks, the lethargy, obvious anaemia and general malaise. His strange obsession and almost fatalistic acceptance of death. *I could die in your arms, Sinead*. I couldn't turn around because the expression in his eyes might suddenly make sense and throw light on the real reason why he couldn't stay.

'I've been dying since I left this place.'

I put my hands over my ears, hoping that blocking out

the words might make their meaning go away. But James was behind me now, his chest pressed against my back. He gently put his arms around my neck to stop me from trying to escape. The pain was visceral, as if every nerve ending in my body was being stabbed simultaneously.

'I've been dying for so long, Sinead. Almost half my life.'

'Don't say it,' I begged.

'Chronic myeloid leukaemia,' he whispered.

My tongue stuck to the roof of my mouth and I turned around, my first defence anger. 'You weren't going to tell me?'

'It would have been easier not to . . .'

'For you, maybe,' I growled.

'You really think so?' he answered, overcome with emotion. 'But the truth is . . . I was glad not to. It was important to know you didn't just feel sorry for me.'

I rubbed my eyes, which felt raw, as if they'd never seen daylight before. 'Bone-marrow transplant?'

He gave a hollow laugh. 'Been there, done that. As well as radiation therapy, chemo, blood transfusions, even stem-cell transplant . . . They all eventually failed and I was back to the start . . . except . . . there's nowhere left to go.'

'Don't be stupid,' I snapped, with increasing desperation. 'There's always something new to try.'

'Eight years.' He grimaced. 'That's how long I've been having treatment. I barely remember a time before . . . a time when I wasn't ill.'

We were silent for a few minutes, my breathing now as erratic as his. I was clutching at straws, dwindling hope making me desperate. Medical mistakes happened all the time. James's condition was misdiagnosed from the very outset. He didn't look as though he was drawing his last breath.

'I've seen the terminally ill, James. They don't look like you –'

'I know,' he interrupted with pride. 'This time with you is the reason I had to return here . . . to remember how it feels to really live and to fall in love. You're my destiny, Sinead, but from the second we met, I was leaving you. I tried to go home to spare you this.'

Acute shock hadn't totally taken away my powers of reasoning. I flexed my fingers. 'Is there anything more that medicine could offer you, anything at all?'

James began pulling up tufts of grass, playing for time, his forehead a mass of deep creases. 'With more invasive procedures, maybe a few weeks. They can give me more time, but not *quality* time.' His eyes sought mine. 'I'm dead already, Sinead.'

I tried to compose myself as his words hit home. Dad told me once that part of being a good doctor was knowing when to stop trying, that dying well was as important as living well. I selfishly wanted to shout or stamp my feet, to rage at the world. I wanted to beg James to have more treatment for my sake, to take every second offered to him. But when I could finally bring myself to look deep into his eyes I knew what he was asking me to do – to accept the truth of this. If you love someone, you have to set them free, Harry had told me. And that's what James was asking me to do now. But he was mad if he thought I was going to let him go without me.

'I'll come with you –'

James visibly shuddered and wrapped his arms tightly around his body. 'You mustn't give up your life for me.'

I yanked my hair, my voice rising hysterically. 'Maybe I want to. Maybe there's nothing else here for me.'

'You'll have a great career, meet someone else and—'

'I don't have a future,' I interrupted with stubborn fury.

'Promise me you won't try and follow me. Promise me you won't . . .' James's breathing became increasingly laboured.

This was all wrong. I'd made James even more agitated. I had to be strong for him. My one secret solace was that I wouldn't let him go without me, although I would strenuously deny my intention. I crossed my fingers behind my back and made soothing noises to reassure him that I wasn't serious. The cruelty of this moment hit me like a blow to the stomach. I had gone to sleep planning our life together and awoke to find we had only hours left before we had to say goodbye forever.

I smiled through unshed tears. 'We got old. Remember my dream? We had more than two weeks – we had a lifetime.'

'We had a lifetime.' He grinned, and his face looked boyish again.

'Some people reach old age,' I whispered thickly, 'but they don't really live, they just exist.' I pulled him down on to the grass with me, face to face, squinting in the burgeoning light. 'The sun isn't up yet. Are you in any pain?'

'Not when I'm with you,' he murmured with gratitude. 'You can never know what this means. I've imagined tubes and drips . . . a breathing mask . . . machines to record every heartbeat. If I'd ever thought it could be this way, I wouldn't have been afraid.'

'And why should you be?' I insisted, each word killing me a little more. 'There's nothing to fear.'

'When you tell me that, suddenly I believe it.'

It took every last bit of my reserve to continue. 'I almost didn't meet you again. I had an accident at Patrick's flat and nearly died. It was so weird because . . . right at the end . . . I accepted it.' I caught my tear before it splashed on to him. 'One day with you is worth a lifetime.'

'That's so sweet,' he answered, with a tired sigh.

A disturbing thought suddenly came to me, chilling me to the core. 'James? Your mum . . . !'

'We've already spoken,' he said with unbearable effort. 'She had a kind of . . . sixth sense that something was wrong and she's at the airport now. I told her about you.'

'What if . . . ?' My throat closed over.

'If she doesn't make it?' James finished, and his eyes

were glassy pools of grief. 'She told me the strangest thing, Sinead – that she had said goodbye every single day of my illness and . . . each extra second was a gift.'

A sea of salty tears gushed down my face. I'd been desperate to have a heart and now I knew how it felt when it shattered into a million pieces. After a while James slipped out of consciousness but I continued talking. The last sense to disappear is hearing, Dad had told me. I wanted James to listen to my voice, to take it with him wherever he went. I told him how the clouds were looking today and how the sunlight felt on my skin. I described the trees and the flowers that he loved. I'd been so blind to the beauty all around, but now I could see them through his eyes and describe each petal and leaf. I told him again and again that I loved him. He was more than just comfortable – that awful phrase used to describe end-of-life patients; his face was suffused with happiness and peace.

I wept silently. '*What would be the point of love if it wasn't everlasting?*'

These were the final words I spoke to him. He opened his eyes and took a deep juddering breath. I didn't need a heart monitor to tell me it was his last. Inside I was imploding in one long silent scream, but I stayed with James in my arms, stroking his golden hair and resting my cheek against his until he grew cool to the touch. Right until the end I prayed for a miracle, but they didn't happen for people like me.

# Thirty-One

It didn't seem possible, but it was a beautiful new day. I tried to get my head around an inexplicable new reality – the sun would rise and set, the moon still wax and wane and the world keep spinning on its axis even though James was no longer living in it. I left him lying on a carpet of leaves, looking like an angel. Only this time he wasn't sleeping. Despair now enveloped me like a black suffocating cloud. I wouldn't delay my plan to follow him. He might get too far ahead of me. I didn't know how death worked, but I wasn't taking any chances. My feet took me further into the wood until the earthy dank smell reached me. I staggered on, desperate to reach the pond. My actions were totally premeditated and focused. Death had tried to claim me before – now I was giving myself to it. I waded into the water without undressing, hoping that my clothes would weigh me down and make this easier. Today there'd be no one to save me. I wouldn't even take a gulp of air before being pulled under.

I tensed, expecting to hear the first underwater rumblings, but nothing disturbed the still surface. My body stayed immobile and poised for what felt like forever, willing the end to come swiftly. I submerged my head in the cloudy depths again and again, but each time I spluttered to the surface. Eventually I had to limp out. Foolishness was replaced by anger when I realized how futile this was. There was nothing here to injure me. It had always been my mind simply playing tricks. But now that there was no way to reach James, the impact of his death hit me anew.

The scream came from deep within me and it was a relief to let go. Even the trees seemed to understand and their lush canopy of leaves and branches didn't deaden my scream but appeared to open to release my fury and impotence into the atmosphere. My teeth ground together and must have nicked my tongue because I could taste blood. I struck the nearest tree with my fist, the bark split open like a cracked nut, the diamond pattern imprinting itself in my flesh. I reeled slightly, the physical pain momentarily overshadowing the acute pain inside. Where would I go and what would I do without James? I couldn't leave Benedict House because I felt close to him here. I'd be compelled to tour the estate mourning him, hot tears burning my cheeks, even though it felt like a life sentence. A shudder ran down my spine.

'Your destiny is to stay here in a prison of your own choosing. The earth will weep with you and from your tears will spring forth new shoots.'

James's gran must have known of his condition and predicted my suffering, almost taunted me.

Sister Catherine's voice made me jump. 'This isn't the answer, Sinead.'

She was standing close by, her hands linked before her. She must have heard me scream but didn't ask why. By her expression, it seemed as if she already knew about James, and that I was trying to join him.

My fingers traced the abrasion on my fist. 'Then what is?' I asked heatedly.

'True love cannot be torn asunder.'

Her words didn't comfort me. 'I don't have your faith. And I've no idea where James is.'

Her smile was beatific. 'James is waiting for you.'

'How can he be?' I choked out. 'I watched him die.'

She shook her head slowly but didn't explain. 'Your trial has finished, Sinead. You must now achieve what you came here for and find your brother.'

'Of course . . . but I can't forget James . . . I can't just leave him –'

'You don't have to. Your answers lie in the same place.'

Her words only confused me more. 'We had a deal,' I cried out. 'You promised you'd tell me—'

'*Guide* you,' she interjected, 'when the time was right.'

'Then tell me where the first church stood.'

She pressed her lips together and spoke carefully. 'The site is sacred, Sinead. That should suffice.'

'If . . . *When* I find the site, what should I do?'

'Don't enter in haste or with animosity, Sinead. Clear your conscience first.'

'How can I enter at all? It was demolished years ago.'

'The foundations of the church can never be destroyed. You'll find a way.'

'What if I can't?'

'Face your fears. Your freedom is almost in sight. But don't delay. You don't have much time.'

I screwed up my eyes in despair. When I opened them again I was alone.

I returned to the weeping willow to discover that James's body had gone, although I could still see its impression on the flattened grass. Sister Catherine couldn't have moved him and there was no one else here capable of helping, unless – my knees gave way and I sank to the ground – *James is waiting for you*. There was only one way that James could be waiting for me – if he wasn't dead. Maybe I'd been wrong and his heart hadn't stopped beating. James's protracted illness could have somehow slowed his pulse to mimic death. Sister Catherine surely couldn't be that cruel. If he was alive, she would have told me right away, instead of baffling me again with her strange words. Or would she?

I felt woozy and took slow breaths through my mouth to calm my racing heartbeat. Was Sister Catherine testing my love for James, or my sense of duty towards my brother? Were their fates now bound together? Nothing made sense, but I had to cling to the belief that James was still alive, and in finding Patrick I would be reunited with him. Everything hinged on finding the first church, but in the last few days James and I had covered almost every inch of this estate. All Sister Catherine would tell me was that the site was sacred, as if that should be enough for me to find it. But what if it wasn't enough? What if I wasn't up to the task? The thought of what was at stake was terrifying.

I walked and walked, but every path seemed to lead back to the weeping willow. When I found myself back there for the third time I threw my arms around Orpheus, glad of something to hold on to. I smiled sadly, remembering how James had moved him to play a joke on me. He thought that he belonged over the bridge with the dead. There was no blinding flash of light. When the answer came to me, it was a slow, gentle realization that made me almost believe James had whispered the words in my ear. He hadn't been allowed to play near the graves because the land was blessed. The first church and the burial site must be one and the same. Sister Catherine had waited until my trial was over to give me the final piece of the puzzle. I trembled at the thought of what might lie ahead.

I made my way to the glade and my eyes scanned the bridge. I heard a low warning growl and my stomach pitched with fear. Sister Catherine hadn't told me how to get past Cerberus, but she had warned me that I didn't have much time. I had to do this and I had to do it now. I walked towards the giant dog, trying to appear as meek and unthreatening as possible. Cerberus's ears immediately went back and he bared his teeth. My legs turned to jelly and my heart was thumping so loudly that it almost drowned out the sinister growling. I put one tentative foot on the first wooden slat, my mind teeming with unwelcome thoughts. James's dad had been gone for eight years, but the dog must have remained, surviving on wild rabbits and game. Now he would be used to killing and eating his prey raw. He lowered his front legs threateningly into the crouch position, which I knew was usually a prelude to attack. Even the snarl had changed into more of an excited yelp as though he had smelled blood. My vision began to mist and I took a step back, knowing I wasn't brave enough to do this. In that instant I heard a voice inside my head, 'Face your demons, Sinead.'

Dogs can smell fear. I slowed my breathing and pictured James's beautiful face, then walked determinedly towards Cerberus, saying his name with as much authority as I could summon. And the strangest thing happened: as I approached, he began to retreat with a series of whimpers until he was on the other side of the bridge. Then he sat down and didn't move a muscle. I concentrated on nothing else but putting one foot in front of the other. As I drew closer Cerberus didn't react. He allowed me to pass unharmed. I was still terrified, imagining I could feel hot breath on the back of my legs.

The circular wall of holly loomed before me. It must have been over three metres high. Looking up at it made me a little disorientated. I did a full circuit before I noticed a small gap, almost a doorway, as regular as if it had been especially cut out. I slipped inside. It felt like entering another world. There was a circle of blue sky, but the light was diffused and the air heavy and sultry, as if it was holding its breath. I gazed around, lulled by the silence. There weren't any headstones – the graves remained unmarked – but I noticed some kind of monument. I walked over curiously to examine it.

The brick structure was surprisingly solid with a door in one wall and a pitched roof. As I read the inscription a bolt of terror and elation shot through me. 'I will give unto you the keys to the kingdom of heaven.' I knew those words. I was taken back to the day I'd begun my search for Patrick, the day I almost fell from the clock tower. The message I'd risked my life to retrieve had led me to the church of Saint Peter. The priest had told me that Saint Peter had been given the keys to the kingdom of heaven. He'd hoped that Patrick's key would lead me to the same place. I'd committed the design to memory. The distinctive fleur-de-lis decoration of its handle exactly matched the design around the lock mounted into the door facing me.

I shivered at my discovery. Everything was falling into place. I should have been ecstatic but I couldn't forget Sister Catherine's words. *'Don't enter in haste or with animosity, Sinead. Clear your conscience first.'*

There was somewhere I had to go, and there wasn't much time.

# Thirty-Two

I stood by the roadside with my thumb in the air. Only five vehicles had passed, when a car slammed on its brakes and then its hazard lights. Two elderly ladies were sitting in the front seats and they had a brief conversation before opening the window. I told them a sob story about having a row with my boyfriend and being abandoned in the countryside without any money. They clucked and tutted, their dresses rustling, and I felt awful for deceiving them. They refused to simply drop me in town but went out of their way to take me right to my own doorstep.

It was an odd sensation to be back. My house looked utterly familiar and yet so distant from me. Mum answered the door within seconds, and stared at me as if I was a stranger. I suddenly wondered if she had always made me feel this way.

'Do you have any further news of your brother?' she asked.

Instead of being furious with her, I just felt incredibly

sad. I went into the living room and sat down on the sofa. It was a high-backed one that forced you to sit with a poker-straight spine, about as comfortable as being under interrogation. The room was spotless as usual.

Mum followed me in, still waiting for a reply. I answered her question with one of my own. 'Weren't you worried when I stopped calling?'

She moved her hand in a gesture like swatting a fly. 'Did you go back and look for Patrick?'

'I looked.' Her peevish expression indicated that my efforts weren't enough. 'I think I might have found the . . . er . . . key to where he is, but . . . there's something I have to ask you first.'

My mother's pencilled brows shot up. I ran my tongue over my lips nervously. 'I wanted to ask what you meant when you said I was . . . twisted. It's really important I know.'

She sighed. 'Why bring this up now? The damage has already been done.'

'What damage?'

'Damage to your brother, Sinead, damage to Patrick.'

'I don't understand,' I said, shaking my head. 'How have I damaged Patrick?'

My mother massaged her neck with a pained expression. 'Do you really want to know?'

My eyes narrowed. 'I really want to know.'

She folded her arms across her chest. 'If you hadn't

been such an attention seeker, Patrick's life might have turned out differently.'

'Attention seeker?' I gulped in amazement. 'I was invisible to you. For years you ignored me – you covered me with a blanket!'

I'd returned home to clear the air, desperate to put our differences behind us. Instead I was still the fall guy, but this time something had changed; I had detected a new bitterness in her voice.

'Don't let's argue, Mum,' I said contritely. 'This is hard to explain. I know you don't usually worry about me, but there's been some weird stuff happening—'

'Weird stuff happening,' she mimicked in a horribly piercing voice. 'You were always the same, even as a little girl, inventing stories, trying to make yourself important. That's the reason . . .'

She clapped her hands over her mouth and turned away from me. But I could see her reflection in the mirror, her face contorted with pent-up emotion.

'Reason for what?' I asked, bewildered.

'The reason why Patrick is . . . so vulnerable.'

I groaned inwardly, hating it when she trivialized Patrick's problems and made out that he was blameless. 'So . . . you're saying it's my fault he became a raving addict?'

She winced at the harshness of my words. 'Cast your mind back, Sinead, and face the truth of what you did.'

There were plenty of things on my conscience at this

moment, but my treatment of Patrick wasn't one of them. I hadn't expected her to roll out the red carpet for me, but I was genuinely perplexed at the ferocity and nature of this attack.

'No, you've still lost me, Mum.' Despite all my intentions to stay calm, I was growing hot and bothered. 'Remind me.'

Her eyes blazed. 'That childish *lie* you told about Patrick, Sinead.'

This was growing more bizarre. Patrick's disappearance must have seriously unhinged my mother. I never made up childish lies about him because she wouldn't have believed me. For years she'd refused to believe he was an addict, even when the evidence was staring her in the face. Dad had eventually forced her to confront it, but she couldn't forgive him.

'That night you couldn't breathe,' she continued, her own voice sounding strangled with repressed fury.

I had a sense that my mother's rage had been suppressed for a long time and the floodgates were about to open.

'I was . . . five years old,' I said hesitantly, 'and I had a bad asthma attack . . . You know I did.'

She shook her head determinedly and her face was strangely gloating. 'You didn't have asthma.'

'Yes, I did. I had an inhaler.'

'Your inhaler was empty – it was just a pacifier.'

The panicky feeling was returning to my throat as though my air supply was being slowly cut off. 'Then why did you tell me I did have asthma and that Dad was making it better?'

She ignored my question and declared with a vehemence that shocked me, 'Your *lie* changed the course of Patrick's life.'

This was incomprehensible to me, but something significant was taking place. I'd never seen my mother so darkly incensed. My eyes closed and I was back in my bedroom, waking from a deep sleep. It was a windy night and the branches of the horse-chestnut tree outside my bedroom tapped on the glass and the rain sounded like gravel against the windows. The curtains must have been open just a little, because a tiny bright chink shone through from the street light, and I stayed really still because I knew something wasn't right. It came from nowhere, a soft, downy weight muffling my nose and mouth. I was frantically inhaling, desperate to draw air into my lungs, but there was no air, as though the darkness itself was smothering me. Then Dad was blowing into my mouth and begging me to breathe.

'I didn't make it up . . . Dad had to give me mouth-to-mouth.'

Her glacial stare sent shivers up and down my spine. Patrick had my mother's eyes. I saw him in hers just then, and in that instant I knew what had been different about that night.

'There was someone else in the room,' I whispered, 'someone hiding in the shadows. Oh my God!' I covered my face with my hands, my stomach heaving. 'Patrick had a pillow over my face. It was the middle of the night,' I managed to croak. 'He was pressing harder and harder. I couldn't get him off, he was too strong, and then . . . I gave up . . . I gave up . . . I gave up fighting –'

'It was just a game,' my mother insisted through clenched teeth. 'Patrick told me you did the same to him. There was nothing sinister about it.'

I looked at her in utter horror. 'He nearly killed me, and you believed his pathetic story about playing some kind of game?'

'You were just children,' she protested. 'You shouldn't have made such a fuss.'

At these words another memory slowly filtered through and my eyes kept on staring, unable to even blink. 'I told you what had happened . . . I told you the truth but you said if I ever repeated my story Patrick would disappear into a black hole and he'd never get out again.' A sob escaped from me. 'I've spent my life plagued by nightmares about what he did to me, counting time because I thought I was going to die –'

My mother's face was stained with shame but at the same time she hadn't dropped her armour of self-righteousness. '*I know about difficult choices and how you have to trust your instincts to protect your child.*' She had said these words to me the last time I was home. But she hadn't protected me; she'd only ever protected Patrick. A terrible weakness swept over me. I stood up and walked towards her, dazed like a sleepwalker. 'You . . . didn't believe him, did you?' I asked, bile rising in my throat. 'You knew what he'd done, you knew what he was, but . . . you still blamed me. Even now you blame me. How could any mother do that?'

She didn't even try to deny it. 'Patrick was never the same after your accusation . . . all the light went from his eyes; something died inside him.'

*Something died inside me*, I wanted to scream. I suddenly remembered my father. Where did he fit into all this? I had a momentary flashback to Dad's laughing face as he lifted me high in the air to swing me around. He was always so much fun and so loving. He wouldn't have stood by if he'd known what Patrick had done.

'You never told Dad, did you? You frightened me into keeping quiet and made sure I never repeated the truth to anyone.'

My mother wrinkled her nose. 'Your father knew how highly strung you were and thought you'd had some kind of anxiety attack. He told you it was asthma to set your mind at rest.'

I hung my head for a minute, trying to collect myself. Everything had become appallingly clear, but the biggest shock was the way it made me feel. Together with the disgust and nausea at my mother's actions I was overcome with an unexpected sense of freedom. She'd sacrificed me for Patrick and didn't deserve my loyalty or my love. In coming here today I had faced my biggest demon of all.

My mother moved closer to scrutinize me and for once I didn't recoil. 'You could only ever see the bad in people, Sinead.'

'I was five years old,' I repeated, matching her stare. 'I didn't know evil existed. You should have tackled Patrick's jealousy, but you fed it instead. Maybe *you're* the reason he turned out as he did.'

My mother drew herself up to her full height and tilted her chin away from me. 'As a little boy he loved me so much, he couldn't bear to share me. He simply wanted things to be the way they used to be . . . when it was just the two of us.'

'Patrick stole my childhood, almost took my life, and you allowed it to happen.'

Her brow creased as if this was all mildly puzzling to her. 'You came between us . . . I made a tough choice, but it was the right one. Patrick's always needed me more.'

'You never gave me the chance to need you –' I broke off, recognizing this was futile. It was pointless for us to continue trading insults and I needed to conserve my strength. I knew there was little hope of us being reconciled.

She looked past me into the distance and spoke almost carelessly. 'Often, Sinead, I regret the day that you were born.'

This seemed like a fitting end to the last sixteen years of my life – my mother's desire never to have had me. Her revelation actually made things easier in a way; there wasn't anything here for me, nothing to leave behind. But I still needed to find a way back to Benedict House. I'd asked her for so little; there was one thing she could do for me now.

'Could you lend me some money for a taxi, Mum? There's somewhere I have to go.'

She reached for her purse and pressed some coins into my hand. I took one last look around the house where I had grown up and murmured that I had to leave. My mother rubbed her hands together as if she was washing them.

'Wherever you have to go, Sinead, you go alone.'

I turned to her with a half-smile and whispered, 'I know.'

# Thirty-Three

It would be so much more difficult to face Patrick now. What on earth would I say to him? Did he even remember what he'd done, or had my mother brainwashed him too? The church of Saint Peter loomed into view. I considered going inside but thought better of it – all that gilt, decoration and pomp just wasn't for me. I'd texted Harry to meet me outside and bounced the toes of my trainers against the wall, nervously waiting for him to appear. When he saw me he actually broke into a run, which made me smile inside. I flung my arms around him and squeezed the life out of him. He smelled so good, so fantastically innocent of all the rubbish in the world.

'You OK?' he asked with concern. 'You're as white as a ghost.'

Tears pricked my eyes. There wasn't time to savour our meeting, which might be a blessing as seeing Harry again felt too painful.

'I don't have much time,' I said weakly.

'Story of your life,' he quipped.

I bit my lip and stared down at the ground, bracing myself for my confession. 'There's something I should have told you weeks ago, Harry. Sara is completely crazy about you . . . and I kept it from you.'

He attempted to touch my cheek, but I took a step away from him. 'I'll always love you . . . but only as a friend. She'll love you so much her heart will feel like it's breaking when you're apart, and her face will light up whenever she—'

'I don't want anyone but you,' he cut in, but I hushed him.

I remembered the way James used to look at me, and it was another minute before I could trust myself to speak. 'When someone returns your love, the feeling is so amazing your heart sings and everything in the world changes colour . . . you want to hold the moment forever. That's what you deserve, and that's what you can have. Don't waste it –grab it with both hands, because you never know how much time you have.'

Harry didn't reply, but I could hear his pained shallow breathing. I deliberately avoided looking at him because I didn't want to remember him bereft and suffering.

I tried to swallow and made a horrible noise with my throat. 'Please go, before you see me cry.'

He whispered, 'Look after yourself, Sinead.' Then he smiled the shy, crooked smile I loved and turned to go.

I took a few steps forward and wrapped both arms

around him, hugging him tightly. My head rested against his spine. Then my arms were empty and I was hugging only air. I didn't look up until I was certain that he was completely out of sight.

Coming back to Benedict House felt so right, like returning to my real home. The atmosphere was electric and I noticed the long shadows and quickened my pace. I wanted to see Sister Catherine, to gain some kind of affirmation that I was on the right track, but she was nowhere close to the house. The front door was open and I went inside. I baulked at the sight that greeted me. The magnificent hallway, which I had polished and buffed to perfection, was now filthy, the marble chipped and stained. The sweeping staircase was gouged and split. I went into the main living room and found it in total disarray, the furniture and fittings damaged and the windows smeared with grime. The rest of the downstairs was the same, and water penetration had left damp rivulets down the walls. Despite my fourteen days' hard labour, the house was in a far worse state than when I arrived. It smelled of decay and neglect, as if it had been unoccupied for years.

What was going on? And where was Sister Catherine? I went outside to take stock, heaving for breath as though I'd run a marathon. I glanced upward; the elegant facade had disintegrated as well, the window frames rotted and patches of the roof missing, blackened rafters visible as though fire had ripped through the building. Nothing here should have surprised me any more, but my mind was reeling. I needed to return to the monument, the only real thing my mind could grasp right now.

It was early evening and the sky had darkened in the last few minutes, black and grey clouds swirling angrily overhead, almost extinguishing the last vestiges of sunlight. Because of the prolonged humidity a series of thunderstorms had been predicted and a clap sounded in the distance like the crash of cymbals. The wind picked up, reminding me of the day I started to look for Patrick, when I almost fell from the clock tower, and the day I first met James. This already seemed like a lifetime ago. By the time I reached the glade the rain was battering the ground. The wind had intensified and I had to walk against it. Every step felt as if I was trying to climb a mountain. I rubbed my eyes in disbelief. The ground must have been so dry that the rain had run off into the nearest channel. The dried-up stream was now filled with rising water, a surging torrent almost level with the bridge. I had to get across quickly.

I stepped on to the first plank, but it rocked violently and my hands gripped both sides. My feet were sliding, which forced me to my knees. The wind felt like the roar of a hurricane in my ears, buffeting me from side to side like a rag doll. I wanted to curl up to escape from it, but if I let go of the ropes I'd be thrown into the water. My chin nuzzled my chest to protect my face as I blindly shuffled forward an inch at a time. Something whizzed past my ear, grazing my cheek. It seemed to have the solidarity of stone, as though rocks were being hurled in my direction, and still the water rose, covering my feet and calves as I crawled along. It's a two-metre-wide stream, reason told me, not a raging river, but this felt as real as any of my previous ordeals.

At last I was at the other side, whipped and exhausted but unbowed. It would take more than this to stop me, I thought with pride. I could see the dark outline of Cerberus skulking at the side of the monument. He hadn't growled, but I was still fearful of him. It would be awful if he stopped me now, just when I was so close. I tried to move purposefully, glad when my hands met solid brick. With fumbling fingers I reached into my pocket, took out the heavy iron key and inserted it into the lock. I wasn't surprised that it was a perfect fit, and it turned with ease. I plucked up the courage to look over my shoulder and gaze into Cerberus's eyes. At dusk the dying sun reflected in them like tiny dancing flames, but he didn't appear aggressive any longer. He was lying full-length on the ground, alert and watchful, almost as if he'd been instructed to stand guard.

The door was carved from ancient gnarled wood, at least ten centimetres thick and still strong. It blew shut behind me and I was immediately plunged into darkness, trembling like a leaf in my sodden clothes. After a few minutes my eyes adjusted and the darkness seemed to be composed of shades of green, purple and charcoal. Somewhere there was a tiny dot of white light. I looked down, thankful I hadn't tried to move, because there were steps directly in front of me. There was no choice but to descend, with the terrifying certainty that this was where I had always been meant to come.

The steep steps felt as if they'd been carved into the earth itself. Being underground gave me a horrible claustrophobic sensation. The air was stuffy and my ears felt as if they were plugged with cotton wool. As I descended lower I could see a small room ahead, measuring no more than three square metres, and the source of the light revealed itself, a single candle held in a small glass container resting on a simple stone altar. Who would have come down here to light it? There was a wooden crucifix hanging above. The walls and ceiling were made of rusty brown earth held up by arched stone supports. There was only one other item in the room: a pale leather-bound book. It had escaped me at first because the binding was the same colour as the altar. I opened it at the beginning and there was a full page of Latin text in illuminated writing. Some of the words were vaguely familiar and then it hit me: this was where Patrick had lifted the passage from. The word *infernus* jumped off the page. The priest had implied that it could mean subterranean or hell. If Patrick was trying to frighten me, he was succeeding.

I was scared and frustrated. There was nothing else here. I'd followed my brother's footsteps to the letter and I couldn't stay much longer because I was feeling faint – every cell of my body was screaming to be out in the open. The only way forward was for me to resurface and find Sister

Catherine to ask her why I'd failed. I'd done everything right and I still didn't have the answers she'd promised me. It seemed to take longer climbing back up; the steps seemed to go on forever. My eyes had adjusted to the dark and now I had limited vision. I pressed my ear to the door, listening for any sounds, but my hearing was still muffled. I gently pushed against the wood, but it didn't move. I pushed harder and then used my full weight, but the door held fast; there wasn't even a creak. Hot, wet panic engulfed me. A tomb – that was what this place had become. No one knew where I was and no one would come looking. I'd willingly entrapped myself here to die slowly of thirst and hunger. And I suddenly realized it was scorching beneath the earth.

I'm not certain whether I blacked out for a few minutes or if panic sent me flying into my own orbit, detached from the world. But there was a voice calling me and it seemed real, a voice echoing somewhere in the distance but growing louder. I cocked my head to one side. It wasn't coming from outside. It seemed impossible, but the sounds were emanating from below. My feet took the stairs again so fast that I stumbled more than once.

There was a figure standing in the shadows. I would have recognized him anywhere.

# Thirty-Four

Patrick had a huge grin across his face and I was so shocked to see him that I was struck dumb. He looked so handsome, better than he had done for ages, his complexion vibrant and full of colour, his voice eagerly warm. I expected to feel relief but I was consumed with fear. My trembling worsened and my teeth chattered uncontrollably.

'I knew you'd find me, Sinead. Well done.'

I spread my fingers across my cheeks. 'But where . . . I mean, how did you get past me?'

Patrick moved to one side and held out the palm of his hand in an old-fashioned gesture as though inviting me to dance with him. I stared at the wall until he took a step towards it and, with an impish expression, a step through it. I gaped in amazement. It was an optical illusion. What appeared to be solid earth had actually been hollowed out. Sister Catherine had told me that the foundations of the church remained; they must form a series of tunnels, maybe catacombs. Patrick had a flaming torch in his hand to light our way. This was surreal. I rubbed my eyes in case I was hallucinating again.

'What took you so long?' he asked.

Patrick was acting as if nothing was wrong, which made me so much more afraid. 'Your clues were so . . . bizarre,' I said. 'I was really worried about you.'

'But you solved them all, Sinead . . . except for the snake. I saved that until last.'

'I don't need to know,' I said, dread coiled deep within me.

'You have to know,' he insisted. 'It's important. It's what I've been waiting for.'

I tried but failed to tear my eyes from Patrick. He ripped open his shirt and I could see a red and black snake tattooed diagonally from his waist to his shoulder. His muscles rippled and the snake seemed to come to life, its scaly body undulating across his chest. It was chilling.

'Mum hates tattoos,' I said warily. 'What made you do it?'

'It's the new me,' he replied. 'Haven't you ever longed to break free and become the person you've dreamed of?'

'I've changed as well in the last few weeks –'

'Don't lag behind,' he urged, striding ahead.

My breathing was slow and heavy. 'Why did you make me go through this, Patrick? And why here? At Benedict House.'

He didn't answer. My dread was increasing, yet I was

still compelled to follow him. 'Patrick! Slow down. You're going too fast and I can't keep up.'

Something else was worrying me – the ceiling of the tunnel was getting lower and I had to stoop. My claustrophobia was worsening too, the familiar closed-in feeling filling my mouth and choking me as if the roof was caving in. There were footsteps up above, a backwards and forwards movement that told me we must be underneath Sister Catherine's interminable pacing. I stopped dead as another sound reached me and my heart somersaulted.

'I have to go back,' I shouted out. 'I heard James's voice.'

Patrick turned slightly. I could see only a portion of his face, but the light from the torch made his skin glow a burnt orange. 'It isn't him, Sinead. He's dead, you know that.'

'I don't know that,' I cried. 'His body disappeared and Sister Catherine said he was waiting for me.'

Patrick's tone grew sharper. 'Sister Catherine lied, and if you leave me now, you'll never see me again.'

'Don't be silly . . . I'll follow after you and . . . meet you at the house.'

Patrick angrily made his way back to me. 'You can't just abandon me again, Sinead.'

I was used to his violent mood swings and tried to calm him. 'I'm not abandoning you –'

He pulled a sneering face that made me retreat – he had never looked quite so menacing. 'You know what I tried to do when we were children. What must you think of me now?'

Patrick must have talked to Mum in the last few hours. She must have told him that I knew what had happened all those years ago and he was no doubt filled with remorse. Every fibre of my body was aching to search for James, but the customary loyalty made me hesitate.

'I forgive you,' I said quickly. 'What you did . . . it wasn't completely your fault. Mum should have tried harder to see what was under her nose.'

Patrick grasped my wrist and his fingers seemed to burn into my skin. I cried out in pain.

'You're not going back, Sinead. You've come too far and you've been lost for too long.'

There was no saliva in my mouth and my voice came out thick and claggy. 'I've been confused and aimless maybe, but not lost . . . and since I met James—'

'He isn't enough to save you,' Patrick cut in.

His words chilled me to the bone. 'I've changed,' I yelled as if to convince myself. 'Since I met James I'm a different person.'

'You haven't changed enough,' Patrick said smugly, his eyes glowing like hot coals.

James was calling my name again. On impulse I turned around to make a run for it, and was beaten back by a wall of flames.

'It isn't him,' Patrick insisted. 'He's trying to trick you. You're only safe with me.'

And then James's calm and soothing voice was inside my head. 'Don't listen to Patrick. If you follow him, you'll truly lose your way. Walk through the fire – it won't burn you.'

*I couldn't walk through fire; it would be impossible. Even if this wasn't real, like the other times, and my body remained unscathed, I would still feel the pain. And what if Patrick was right and this was a trick? I hadn't yet seen James with my own eyes.*

'You have to believe you can do it, Sinead. Concentrate your mind. There's nothing to fear.'

My breath was a series of violent gasps, my mind a fog of doubt. Patrick claimed I belonged in this place. Why try to fight it? I'd been following him for so long. Something caught my eye – a moving speck of white in the dark tunnel. I looked up and saw a feather twirling and spinning in the air until it landed on my shoulder, soft and velvety against my neck. I felt an immediate surge of strength. With my eyes tightly closed, the flames still flickering in my consciousness, I took a step forward.

The fire was so close now that my eyebrows were singed and the skin on my face felt like it was peeling; closer again and there were embers in my hair making it sizzle and filling my throat with the smell of sulphur. I reached a shaking hand into the wall of flames, but the searing heat actually turned my body to ice until I was numb all over. My eyes didn't open as my whole body passed through the furnace. There wasn't even a wisp of smoke from my clothes, although I patted myself down furiously.

When I dared to open one eye I still couldn't see James, though I could still hear his voice, now coming from behind me.

'Make your way to the entrance. Whatever you do, don't look back.'

Obediently I began walking. I wouldn't turn around. No matter how badly I wanted to see him again, I wouldn't turn around. My head felt as if it was being twisted on my neck like a corkscrew by an unseen force as I struggled to keep looking ahead. James was so close to me that I could feel the warmth of his body through my clothes, his breath on my neck. If I stretched out my hand I could touch him; if I turned my head fractionally I might sneak a tiny glimpse of him. But I repeated to myself like a mantra, *Don't look back, Sinead; don't look back . . .*

I reached the top of the steps and faced the ancient carved door, wondering what I would do if it didn't open this time around. But it did, and I lurched outside into the light, both arms across my face to defuse the glare. Everywhere was calm: the storm had abated.

'James? I – Is all this . . . real?' I faltered.

'It's real, Sinead.'

There was one overriding question I had to ask. 'Did you . . . die?'

He hesitated for only a moment. 'I did.'

'Then how can—'

I broke off. I'd watched James take his last breath. I was burning to ask how he could be with me now, but I was too overcome. It was minutes before I could speak.

'Your body, how was it moved?'

'Sister Catherine can move heaven and earth,' James answered softly. 'I knew you wouldn't look back,' he added, and there was laughter in his voice.

I still couldn't, terrified of what I might see. It will still be James, the voice inside my head vowed. No matter how he looks, it will still be James. You love his soul. He smelled like warm rain mixed with summer fruits. His fingers caressed my cheek, and my head nuzzled into the hollow of his neck, but I couldn't yet face him. Eventually his hands gripped my shoulders and forced me to turn around. My heart was thumping so loudly with joy and fear that I thought it would burst. Part of me willed it to.

He was as beautiful as ever – no, more beautiful because his skin glowed with vitality and his hair shone like the sun. I threw my arms around him and we embraced for so long that I felt frozen in this position. If he moved away I'd be certain to stay this way, constantly mourning the gap where his body had been. As if in recognition of this James took my arms from around his neck and lowered them to my sides.

A sense of euphoria swept over me. Sister Catherine had told me he was waiting. There must be a way we could be together. Somehow, in this crazy place, there had to be a means to cheat death. 'Now you can stay with me?' I asked with desperate hope.

James's face clouded over. 'It isn't that easy.'

'I survived all the tests,' I gushed. 'I'll love you until the mountains crumble, every star in the heavens has faded and the sun dies.'

James's jaw tightened and he looked with despair into the distance. 'I love you for eternity, Sinead, but there's somewhere I have to go before I can be with you.'

My voice wavered. 'Don't be silly. We found each other again. I defy anyone to prise me from you.'

'But you're still alive.'

'Is that all?' I answered easily, winding my fingers through his. 'I feel like I've always been living on borrowed time. I've already tried to pre-empt death.'

'Promise me you won't try that again,' James said urgently, 'or I might not be able to find you.'

I sighed. 'I promise, but . . . where do you have to go?'

James didn't reply but pressed his lips briefly to mine. 'You know I have blood on my hands.'

'But you weren't guilty.'

He placed his hand against my lips. It took a minute for me to realize he was slipping through my fingers again.

'No one's perfect,' I moaned. 'Whoever's in charge here should realize that.'

James closed one eye to look at me and his lips curved upward. 'It isn't just me. Most of us who find our way to this place need some time.'

'You mean . . . that I found you again . . . just to say goodbye?' I could barely choke out the words.

He nodded sadly.

'How long do we have?'

James consulted his nonexistent watch and smiled wryly. 'I'm already late.'

He could still joke. I wanted to cling to him, beg him to take me with him, tell him that we'd both willingly be damned for eternity if it meant we could stay together, but James had a chance of redemption; I couldn't ruin that.

He held up one hand in warning. 'Don't watch me leave, Sinead. Whatever you do, don't watch . . . you couldn't stand it.'

I closed my eyes in acknowledgement of his words. He must have hesitated, because there was a shadow in front of me and his lips touched mine. Only seconds passed before the full weight of his departure hit me. I wouldn't be a coward this time. I would watch him leave to catch one final glimpse of him. My eyelids tentatively fluttered open and caught the glint of his hair, but a beam of light shone directly at me, making me fall to my knees.

'Are you all right?' Sister Catherine asked.

I reached out my hands and patted her arm as she crouched next to me. There was a pinprick hole in the centre of my vision that made the world amorphous.

'I found James but lost him again,' I said.

'His time away will be but brief, Sinead.'

'How brief?'

'That's impossible to answer. Four minutes can feel like four hundred years when you're deprived of the one you love.'

'So what becomes of me?' I demanded furiously.

Perhaps it was the sunspots in front of my eyes, but Sister Catherine appeared changed, her hair black, her lips full and her eyes now dotted with flecks of violet.

'You have a choice,' she told me. 'Go back to the life you left behind. Or stay here and wait for James.'

'But what would I do here without James?'

'As I have done,' she said. 'The job of a guardian is a tireless one, not for the faint-hearted.'

'Can I leave, or see anyone?'

'You cannot go beyond the wall encompassing the estate. The only people you will see are those close to death. It will be your job to help them, to invite them to make the right choice.'

'So that's why Patrick came here. You sent him his own personal invitation.'

'He had been close to the edge so often,' she said with sorrow. 'It was only a matter of time.'

The full enormity of what she was asking hit me. Was I ready to give up my life? Everything in this journey seemed to have led me to this point, but still I wavered. There was one thing that could make up my mind. 'James feels so far away already,' I said. 'How will I reach him?'

I could hear the gentle rustle of Sister Catherine's robes

and her voice seemed as gentle as a zephyr. 'You're halfway there, Sinead. Never forget that.'

Hearing these words made something explode inside my head. It felt as if all my past memories and the future I would never see were condensed into a single, beautiful moment. My heart was bursting with emotion, but I didn't want to go back. I took a deep breath, now certain of what I should do.

'I'll take over your duties,' I said with conviction. 'James is worth waiting for.'

Sister Catherine must have stood up, because colours were rising in front of me, the empty space in my vision getting larger. Her hand took hold of mine for just a second.

'I'm going now, Sinead.' I could tell from her voice that she was smiling.

I scrunched up my eyes, trying to focus. Sister Catherine wasn't alone. She was hand in hand with a man slightly taller than her, and the sun glistened in his hair, creating a halo of light. They were disappearing into the horizon. Then everything went black.

# Epilogue

Harry moved aside the climbers that cascaded to the ground. He stared in confusion. A network of brambles, poison ivy and bindweed had cut off the secret entrance to the Benedict estate. He couldn't fight his way through unless he wanted to be ripped to pieces. He tried to peer inside. The grounds were unkempt and overgrown, although the pathways were free from vegetation as if someone walked along them often. It was difficult to imagine what Sinead had been doing here for fourteen days. According to the villagers, Benedict House was in a terrible state of repair, virtually derelict. For years, until her recent death, old Mrs Benedict had been the only occupant.

Harry leaned against the crumbling wall, his face twisted in anguish. He still felt responsible for Sinead's disappearance. If he'd searched Patrick's flat more thoroughly things might have turned out differently. At least she'd been spared the grim discovery of her brother's body hanging from the bell tower. It was too horrific to think about. While Sinead had been staying in the converted chapel looking for Patrick, he'd been so close to her.

His phone beeped. It was a message from Sara, asking what time he'd be back. She didn't have to say what she really meant, but he knew. *It's time to come back to me. It's time to let Sinead go.*

Harry took one last look. There was something eerie about this place; the complete and utter silence was profound and unnerving. He jumped. There appeared to be a woman's face looking at him, but it was only a marble statue looking forlornly into the distance. It was weird, but he felt close to Sinead here. He picked up a dandelion clock from the ground and gently blew the soft white seeds, watching as they dispersed in the air. He hoped that Sinead had found what she was looking for;

He hoped that she found all the time in the world.

# Acknowledgements

A huge thank-you to Darley Anderson for giving me the opportunity to see my novel in print.

A massively colossal thank-you to my agent Madeleine Milburn – all-round wonderfully talented and inspirational mentor (and part-time angel) – for her constant support and for telling me it was going to be OK when I needed to hear it most.

To everyone at Quercus, oodles of gratitude for EVERY-THING, too many things to list, but a special thank-you to Sarah Lilly, an amazing editor, for her insight and guidance, not to mention patience and endurance – both needed in abundance!

To Talya Baker – fab copy editor, linguist and grammar queen.

To my foreign publishers, an insanely big thank-you – you've made the world so much smaller and friendlier.

To my mum for being so proud and to my dad, the brightest star, for still being with me.

To my sister Jan for her proofreading, pep talks and relentless optimism.

To Pete, for cooking me gorgeous meals and putting up with my writing angst (insanity)!

To Linda Harris, RGN, for all your help and for being such a lovely person.

To Karen Murray – I couldn't get by without the Brie and sympathy, and to Alex Murray a big thank-you for being my first teenage reader.

To my sons, Mike, Chris and Mark – for simply being in the world.